‖‖‖‖‖‖‖‖‖‖‖‖‖

◁ **W9-API-263**

DEATH PATROL

The NVA battalion spotted the six-man patrol. Compromised! Nothing to do but shoot and run. Quick-released rucksacks dropped from their backs. Each of the scouts emptied a magazine, full automatic. Quick-kill! Quick-kill! Then they ran.

Harry Pitts had the radio and he summoned the chopper to come back and get them. He couldn't believe what he heard. The chopper pilot refused!

The six scouts raced and ran; there was really nowhere to hide. They were outgunned and outmanned, heading into the longtime dark of the Deep Serious Something.

ACTION ADVENTURE

SILENT WARRIORS   (1675, $3.95)
by Richard P. Henrick
The Red Star, Russia's newest, most technologically advanced submarine, outclasses anything in the U.S. fleet. But when the captain opens his sealed orders 24 hours early, he's staggered to read that he's to spearhead a massive nuclear first strike against the Americans!

THE PHOENIX ODYSSEY   (1789, $3.95)
by Richard P. Henrick
All communications to the USS *Phoenix* suddenly and mysteriously vanish. Even the urgent message from the president cancelling the War Alert is not received. In six short hours the *Phoenix* will unleash its nuclear arsenal against the Russian mainland.

COUNTERFORCE   (2013, $3.95)
Richard P. Henrick
In the silent deep, the chase is on to save a world from destruction. A single Russian Sub moves on a silent and sinister course for American shores. The men aboard the U.S.S. *Triton* must search for and destroy the Soviet killer Sub as an unsuspecting world races for the apocalypse.

EAGLE DOWN   (1644, $3.75)
by William Mason
To western eyes, the Russian Bear appears to be in hibernation—but half a world away, a plot is unfolding that will unleash its awesome, deadly power. When the Russian Bear rises up, God help the Eagle.

DAGGER   (1399, $3.50)
by William Mason
The President needs his help, but the CIA wants him dead. And for Dagger—war hero, survival expert, ladies man and mercenary extraordinaire—it will be a game played for keeps.

Available wherever paperbacks are sold, or order direct from the Publisher. Send cover price plus 50¢ per copy for mailing and handling to Zebra Books, Dept. 2723, 475 Park Avenue South, New York, N.Y. 10016. Residents of New York, New Jersey and Pennsylvania must include sales tax. DO NOT SEND CASH.

A LONG TIME FROM HOME

By Michael Costello

ZEBRA BOOKS
KENSINGTON PUBLISHING CORP.

ZEBRA BOOKS

are published by

Kensington Publishing Corp.
475 Park Avenue South
New York, N.Y. 10016

Copyright © 1984 by Michael Costello

All rights reserved. No part of this book may be reproduced in any form or by any means without the prior written consent of the Publisher, excepting brief quotes used in reviews.

Third printing: May, 1989

Printed in the United States of America.

Patricia Jo Street, thank you

CHAPTER ONE

The truce was in effect.

It was a wet, new Christmas day. In the first hour of its darkness someone had whistled "Taps." Harry Pitts had heard it. But the rain slapped down so hard that the sound came apart.

Monsoon is cyclical, he had been told, spanning all time for men who dwell within it. Exploding and receding always, heavy seasons and light, long seasons and short. It has been gentle, cooling. It has been all-consuming flood, unforgiving.

It was then a thin morning mist clinging to men and machinery. White men and green machines, intruders in the Orient.

Harry Pitts swabbed his forehead with a damp green handkerchief, wiping away moisture and oil. He had been a two-digit midget for so long he had grown accustomed to it. Then he became short enough to sit and swing his legs over the edge of a dime. He was tall enough, but he was short: very little time left in-country. And if there were a man happier about the prospect of leaving, he couldn't imagine him. He prepared for his last patrol.

They all did. And they were all short. They had come to the war together and were collectively glad that their part in it was nearly finished.

They were six silent men leaning together, heads craned

down, straining forward into the waves of wind, the deafening drone and crack of helicopter blades whirling. It was a bleak time. Predawn gray. Damp. They climbed and sat silently in the Chinook, smoking cigarettes and staring at their boots. The great green bird groaned, creaking as it rose against the sky, becoming black and stiff on the horizon. It joined its circling protector: a deadly Cobra Gunship. The machines moved out over the dense dark jungle. Dark specks stuck, flying over endless primitive rot and growth.

Sgt. Harry Pitts, the Duke, was puzzled. Why a big Chinook for a six-man patrol? Forty feet of chopper with blades front and back. He let it go, being no stranger to senselessness. He was an infantryman in the United States Army, a grunt.

The Chinook shook. The crew chief shouted that LZ Zebra would be attained in five minutes. He was correct, an old hand, a pro. Elephant grass gave and bent beneath the wind-blasting blades. The doorgunners were tense scanning the terrain, but like the six men, they too were silent. They leaned and they looked. They did not shoot. LZ Zebra was cold. The chief shouted luck and the six soldiers hit the grass, their rucksacks momentarily making them clumsy. They moved quickly into the brush: a unit coordinated and smooth, a team. They were a Long-Range Reconnaissance Patrol, LRRP, Lurps; each man was a scout. The Chinook shot up high into the circle of the Cobra. Both ships climbed, diminishing to silence. The elephant grass swayed behind the six silent men.

The sun was coming up copper, the jungle dripped green. The patrol fanned out and crept, collectively catlike, toward the river it sought. The men were eyes and ears, all eyes and ears. They were wet, first beneath their packs, then beneath their arms. Then they were shocked; they came to the river too soon. The LZ was inaccurate, at least two grids wrong. First they saw the battalion: NVA regulars covering the far bank. Uniformed and armed to the teeth: The North

Vietnamese Army, no black-pajama VC here. Sunlight began to glint from the river ripples. The jungle drone of a million locusts began to rise.

"Sonuvabitch!" one scout gulped.

"Like flies on shit," a second one said.

Then they saw the patrol that saw them. Compromised! Nothing to do but shoot and run; each of them knew it and each of them did it. Quick-released rucksacks dropped from their backs. Each scout emptied a magazine, full automatic. Quick-kill! Quick-kill! They hoped. Then all of them ran. Duke had the radio; ripped it from his pack and slung it with a rig of his own design. He summoned the Chinook immediately, anxiously, on the run. He couldn't believe what he heard. He tried again, hoping. But the reply was the same. The Chinook pilot refused to return: his Cobra protection, his gunship, was gone. Run to the closest friendly unit, the pilot suggested. Sergeant Pitts had the directions.

Duke ran and ran, pleading, threatening. The enemy soldiers dogged close behind, their number increasing. The scouts took turns heaving hand grenades and emptying magazines. And all of them running, running; sweating and sprinting. Duke damned the pilot over and over. The pilot said over and out.

The patrol reached the elephant grass, the wrong LZ Zebra. The men tore into the blades and disappeared. The six scouts raced and ran; there was really nowhere to hide. They were outgunned and outmanned, heading into the longtime dark of the Deep Serious Something.

They ran until they couldn't, no telling how far. Escape and evasion seemed out of sight. They made a hasty perimeter; they had to rest. Lungs heaving, hearts pounding, the sweatwet soldiers lay grim and intensely afraid. Duke raged into the radio, tears in his eyes. Squelch and static was all that came back. He was breathing in lunges, and the smell of things moist and rotting, and the sting of things burning wedged in his nostrils. This was a spooky situation and he

9

didn't have to think to know he didn't like it. He would prefer to be involved in some less exciting game. Flat-out boredom looked dandy.

"Sonuvabitch!" one scout sobbed.

The NVA cordoned the field. The six scouts shivered and started to move. Each direction they scanned was a rising black of smoke. The smoke turned to fire and a flame wall: a far wall, Duke observed, but a wall, a trap, a noose. He spoke madly into the handset, beseeching the sky.

A voice cracked from nowhere and came across the clouds, trickling out of the radio: scratchy and mighty and sweet. It crackled, requesting grid coordinates and smoke. Duke gave approximate position, in the middle of a soot-and-fire circle with Victor Charlie outside. "That's a roger, a roj," said the voice; "Be there ASAP."

The field fast became more fire than field. Dudley Worth stood to shoot but his face exploded: the first to go. Shattered and scattered.

"Sonuvabitch," shouted the Ox.

Carl Diel bought it next. A grenade landed smack on his back. He tried to turn, started to squirm but the bomb blew him in two. Gobs of flesh flew.

Duke attached the M-20 and started pumping grenades out into the flames. He wished for rain. He spied Rat Malloy get stitched with holes up from his knee to his head, lifting and twisting him, dropping him. Duke cried at the sight of the Rat lying there bleeding and leaking his brains. He didn't notice his tears. The chopper chopping thunked overhead. "Red smoke," he yelled into the radio handset, then threw out the canister. A quick sob wracked him, surprised him.

The chopper started to descend: a Huey supplyslick, its doorgunners pouring out lead. It's raining, thought Duke, raining red tracers. The NVA shot up at the ship, green streaks from the grass. The helicopter dropped toward the uncalm eye, the murderous center of a hot lead storm.

"Sonuvabitch! Those boys have got balls!" The Ox said it

10

smiling and died with a smile on his face, shot through the heart, just one shot.

The helicopter hovered. The doorgunners' barrels were white spewing out crimson. The gunners themselves were soot-black and smoky.

Duke didn't know who was dead or who was alive. He went wild, he and Zap Rossi. They dragged the bodies limp to the ship. The doorgunners were shouting, but the scouts didn't hear.

Duke and Zap slapped the bodies onto the deck; blood and guts everywhere. It took them both to heave in the Ox. Then the top of Zap's head turned to bits and was gone. Duke mechanically snatched him up into the ship. As he did so he noticed the starboard gunner's legs, covered with shredded cloth, sopped red. But the man strafed the field, hot brass flying, bouncing. LZ Zebra was a bloodswarm of screeching confusion.

The horizon was black smoke and leaping pillars of orange flame. Bullets cut the sky. Green tracers and red sizzled on the wind, hot lines crossing, converging, the ship at once a weapon and a target, giving and receiving fiery metal projectiles. The Huey rose through it all listing, coughing, hull full of holes. Duke sat his solid self on top of five silent men, one of them and not one of them. He emptied clip after clip from his .45, the spent slugs hitting the grass near the blood and the bone and the flesh of those five men. His tears were gone, blotted into his face. He noticed his wetter leg, wet-red with his own blood. He tied it off and leaned against the bulk of the still warm Ox.

He stared vacantly for a time, then heard the shouts. The starboard gunner was babbling, loud. Duke crawled over the heap on the deck and saw the gunner's legs were riddled, shattered for sure. He shot the gunner with morphine and tied off his thighs. He looked gratefully straight at the man whose eyes were fixed on the space outside. He crawled over what had been Dudley and Zap to check the other gunner

11

who was dead, shot through the head.

"Sonuvabitch." Duke spat. "Some sonuvabitch is going to pay. For this that pilot will pay. Goddamn cruddy cocksucker." It sounded like the appropriate thing to say to himself. Then he fell silent and still, stiffening, for the rest of the ride.

The sky unloaded a slow gray rain. The machine guns hung loosely like broken bones from the sides of the ship. The barrels hissed.

The helicopter landed at Bien Hoa air base dripping and whipping blood in its wind.

Duke and the pilot, one Wally Riley, helped load the one good gunner into the ambulance. Wally rode along to talk with Duke.

But Harry Pitts spoke first. "That was so damn decent Wally Riley. I don't know what else to say. I owe you my life. There it is."

"We took a vote. A unanimous yes." Wally Riley spoke slowly. "Merry Christmas."

"You're decent men, brave and true." Pitts didn't know what else to say. He saw the blank eyes of the gunner that was still alive and knew the other gunner would be in a rubber bodybag, as would each of the five dead scouts. He told Wally about the chopper pilot who would not return. Claimed the scouts' chances were much better earlier. They must find his name, flush his butt out, and turn his ass in. He should be fed to wild dogs. Wally Riley agreed.

Harry Pitts winced, noticing now the pain in his leg. His face was streaked and charred sooty from gunpowder smoke. His uniform was torn and wet and dry, caked and cracked with sweat and mud and blood and tears. He smelled of ashes and guts and shit; he smelled of death. Medics took the one good gunner, then came for Sgt. Harry Pitts, the Duke. He told Wally Riley that he didn't feel good. Wally said he believed. Told Duke that he looked like hell: "The pits, Harry, the pits." Somehow they laughed.

12

CHAPTER TWO

Buck Sergeant Harry Pitts, the Duke, recovered with relative ease. His thigh had been torn, not badly, and no bone had been hit. But the full weight of what had occurred that morning of his last patrol was crushing him. Wally Riley was shot down days later and lost. No one seemed willing to check Pitts's story concerning the pilot who manned that Chinook. No one was interested.

Sergeant Pitts had been debriefed and debriefed. But that pilot's name remained obscure. G-2 (Intelligence) informed him that a warrant officer pilot flew the mission, but the pilot claimed no knowledge of any call concerning a compromise that day. And the Chinook didn't check out; the helicopter situation was quite unclear. G-2 simply couldn't feel right about divulging the name, considering the way Sergeant Pitts thought things happened that day. All that terrible confusion was bound to mess with a man's mind, screw up his view.

"I imagine that's the intelligent attitude," Sergeant Pitts had said. "But you boys won't mind if I consider you dumb scumbags. For the dead ones, don't you know."

The G-men didn't crack their masks. They politely excused themselves.

Harry Pitts went mad, certainly snapped; but he kept his madness welled inside. He wrapped a length of sturdy green tape around his dog tags, against the noise and the jungle.

The old tape had been removed by medical personnel. He taped the tags tightly and pressed them between thumb and fingers; he would be wearing those tags in-country a while longer.

He was released from his ward in Long Binh, scheduled to fly back to the World, away from the war. But he found the right office, talked to the right officer and extended his tour: He'd heard of a platoon he'd just love to join. The officer told him that he'd done the right thing, that the platoon he sought would be damn glad to have him. Sergeant Pitts wanted to join his new unit as soon as he might, to hell with a leave. Maybe he'd take R&R later. The officer appeared naturally fat to Pitts: a pudgy, soft pogue, a housecat; his jolly face jiggled as he hollered, "*Okay*! I'll cut orders today!" Sergeant Pitts snapped a salute, a smirk on his face. The fat officer cried, "Fuckin' crack-troop!" and returned the salute: sloppy and slow, the best he could do. He flopped down in his chair and stuck his face in a Sergeant Rock Comic Book. Sergeant Pitts laughed and marched out.

Outside was heat and dust. He walked on a newly oiled dirtroad toward the warehouse that stored his gear. The dust stuck to him suddenly, clinging to his uniform and his skin. It rose in whorls, red and yellow like the country's colors. He extended his tour not to kill more Vietnamese Communists; he never took particular pleasure from that. As often as he remembered to, he thought of them only as VC, gooks, Martians; not men. He knew that more killing would come though; it was the nature of things there at the war. Harry Pitts was there to hunt the pilot: the man who dropped him and the five other men in the grass that day. His mission expanded from the monomania of survival it had become. He took a passionate attitude. There was a scale to balance, vengeance to wreak. He believed he had a score to settle and that it must be settled in blood. How the hunt would be accomplished, he didn't know, only that it would be. All of the obstacles that the war and the Army could concoct

14

would be surmounted.

He was now a Man with a Mission: a secret soldier within the vast Army of the West. A knight dispatched by a dead legion of honor. A man with a purpose and the vision to know the destiny of that purpose. He became something stronger than he had ever known before. He accepted his quest readily and with pride. He linked himself with the violent heroes of legend, with armor and horses and swords, the swift and terrible cavalries that rode the American wilderness, and the great red chieftains who stood against them. He would act with determination and simple straightforward sense, as Maj. Robert Rogers had done. In 1759 against the French and Indians, Rogers's Rangers were the country's first Lurps. Harry Pitts was fond of Robert Rogers's journals. And the major's first standing order was "Don't forget nothin'." Sergeant Pitts wouldn't forget. He was flooded with intent; his actions and thoughts had collected a focal point. He'd finally discovered a direction that was right and honorable. His universe was dense with things to do, *the* thing to do, plans for the ruin of evil. Some ideal had been restored, some link with resolve that the war had obliterated. He had been a mud-spattered grunt in a seemingly invincible force that had been stymied. Perspective had been screwed up. The horror of means had blurred the value of ends. But now his vision surpassed previously unhinged references. It was cold and clean and clear.

His new unit, the CRIP, had been recommended by a former scout, a friend. It was described as easy duty, skating: a small unsupervised group somewhat vulnerable but the independence worth it. His six-month extension kept him in-country for more of the new year: 1968. The year was not three weeks old. He would soon witness again a Buddhist New Year brought in during Tet, a traditional time for Oriental celebration; that Buddhist New Year, the Year of the Monkey.

15

CHAPTER THREE

The CRIP was stationed at Ho Nai, a sprawling settlement of adjoining hamlets on Highway 1. Ho Nai covered a hill overlooking the provincial capital, Bien Hoa, a smudge in the distance. Thousands of Vietnamese inhabited Ho Nai, its huts and shacks, churches and temples, back alleys and old French colonial buildings teeming with humanity. Christian refugees from the North mingled with other converts around and in the churches in the southern sectors. The sickly sweet smell of Buddhist incense perfumed the heavy heat rising in the northern.

From high above in a helicopter Harry Pitts saw the place as a seething mound of maggots writhing in colorful garbage. During descent the larvae illusion transformed to ants, red and brown, scurrying soundlessly everywhere without pattern. Finally as the ship hovered and touched down, Ho Nai became Ho Nai: a rambling hodgepodge of pens and listing structures straining, bursting, spilling hordes of Vietnamese.

CRIP was an acronym for Combined Reconnaissance Intelligence Platoon: twenty men of varied enlisted rank with a vague mission. There was one lieutenant, Masters; he led the men in their mission: monitor activity in the village, aid the chiefs, work with the Popular Forces to secure the area. The CRIP was garrisoned at the village midsection in

16

an old French fort: yellow cement and stucco, cracked and walled, a square dirt courtyard in the center.

Buck Sergeant Harry Pitts, the Duke, stood on the red-tile roof of a section of the old yellow fort. The helicopter that dropped him chopped the air up and away. When the ship was high, he heard the noise of Ho Nai: a reedy raucous din, deafening compared to the bush, a racket to be dealt with.

He heaved his gear and climbed down to the dirt. He reported to Lt. Ripley Masters. Sergeant Pitts saluted and told the lieutenant that would be the last time. The lieutenant asked the sergeant his name.

"Duke," said Pitts.

"Duke? No Sergeant Pitts?"

"Shit," said Pitts. "Where do I bunk?"

Jungle Jim Grogan stomped through the dust to shake Pitts's hand. He was tall and lean like Pitts, his boots kicked up amber clouds. They were old friends. He had recommended the CRIP to Pitts. They embraced; they had been through it. They abandoned Lt. Ripley Masters in the courtyard beneath the red and yellow flag of the Republic, drooping on its crooked wooden pole.

Jungle Jim had a bunker that had been a room in the fort. Now it served as his hootch. Sandbags and cement. Small rectangular pillow of colorful rubber woven over wood. Sleeping mats of purple and green hemp rolled on the floor. A table. A stool. And military gear.

"Paradise," said Duke.

"You got it," said Jim.

Duke stowed his stuff and Jungle Jim packed a small, carved wooden pocket pipe. They smoked and shot the shit. Jungle Jim said that the only thing dumber than being in this sorryass war was dying in it. He claimed Duke must be mad.

"Why so?" asked the Duke.

"You extended your tour."

"So did you, sucker."

17

"This is true."

"What for?"

"So I wouldn't have to shine my shoes. Being in the stateside Army is dumbest of all."

"There it is."

They laughed and smoked and coughed.

Jungle Jim explained the platoon: It was manned by many strange sorts, all had come from the field and all had either extended or were on tour number two. Nightly patrols were sent to various borders of Ho Nai; they saw occasional action, usually light. There was a bridge to the north manned by the Popular Forces, the PFs, the local militia, the ruff-puffs. CRIP kept a squad there to insure that the PFs would stay. The bridge was sporadically rocketed.

Duke took this in without particular interest. He told his friend about how it was on the final patrol with the LRRP. And how he must find the Chinook pilot to set matters right. News of the five dead scouts saddened Jungle Jim immensely; he had known each one, served with them all. He agreed that this pilot should be dealt with severely; fatally. He wondered why a Chinook. "Kinda big, kinda clumsy," he observed.

"I've wondered myself," said Duke. "But a Chinook it was, most definitely so."

Jungle Jim led the Duke out of the compound across Highway 1 to a shack of a store where the men drank beer: warm 33. The tiny tin-roofed structure was clapboard and cardboard. Inside sat rickety bamboo tables, stools, and plank benches. Two American fifty-five-gallon drums supported the scrapwood bar. American concrete blocks supported the plywood floor. Scabby kids served the beer.

Duke drank and watched the smiling *papa-san* pop bottles open. They all seemed to smile, squinty and servile, perhaps conniving, it was their mask. All the bitterness and outrage and heartache men were capable of hid behind it. Harry Pitts knew it, but this was not his concern. He sipped his beer until he tasted the sour sediment that lined the bottom of the bottles. He spat on the floor disturbing red dust. "I gotta start trailing that pilot, maybe tomorrow."

"Maybe so but tonight you're on the bridge." Sergeant First Class MacFee sat down at Duke's side, sucking beer. "I'm Mac," he said between sips. "You're in my squad."

CHAPTER FOUR

He was Duke because most combat infantrymen possessed a name other than their given one. The more accurately the nickname described some discernible trait in the soldier, the more likely it was to stick. Harry Pitts earned his during frightening and uncommonly close combat. He smashed a VC's head to pieces with the wood butt of the enemy's own AK-47. He held it by the barrel and swung it batlike home to the Oriental face. One swat and the man's head broke, a unique and shocking occurrence. When it was done he turned to Dudley Worth, whose own face had so recently exploded, and said, "Home run! A goner. Kocked 'um out of the park just like old Duke Snider used to do at Ebbets Field." Harry Pitts had been a fair baseball player as a kid. He had little interest in the game, but he could hit. He modeled his swing after the veteran Brooklyn Dodger Duke Snider whom he admired for no particular reason.

Dudley Worth began calling Harry Pitts the Duke and it stuck. So sometimes he was Duke, sometimes *the* Duke, and always he was Harry Pitts. Duke the part, Harry Pitts the whole.

If anything dominated the deadpan mask that was Harry Pitts's face, it was the eyes. A bit too close together, bright green and often filled with expression; they were set deeply in the angular, zip-lipped stone face. His hair was dark and he scraped off the dark beard infrequently, often sporting a standard wino trim. He appeared a larger and truly sadder Buster Keaton.

Essentially boredom, an aimlessness, had caused him to become a soldier, to come to the war. He had always been bored. Neither various jobs of work nor on and off schooling, nor his extended hunting and fishing excursions into the mountains of New England filled that one bottomless region of him. That region which might only be filled by being somewhere else, doing something other than what he was. That space spread over him during quiet times. About the only time he wasn't indifferent was when he was with his young woman. But even that began to revolve solely around sex. So when the war presented itself, he looked to it. He lacked the creativity not to. He was a young man and the only truly difficult aspect of leaving for the war was leaving his lady. It was like tearing his heart out and stomping on it. But he did it.

James Grogan had been a telephone lineman in rural Ohio, adept at climbing. A man of large athletic proportions, a strong, graceful swimmer, he indulged in the exercise at every opportunity. Beer-barrel chest and square jaw, Jungle Jim looked like a young Johnny Weissmuller. He was Jungle Jim, J.J., Jim: James Grogan.

He considered himself a serious sort, kept a journal of his observations and experiences. He had come to the war with ideals concerning aid to an oppressed people: fighting the good fight. His ideas about men and soldiering fostered a respect for the ideas and abilities of Harry Pitts. He liked the man and admired the way he understood being in the bush, the way he handled crises and terror with an inner control.

The men were different and the same. James Grogan had liked his life in the World. Been more enthusiastic in the face of the morning than Harry Pitts. Grogan had liked his work, which he saw as more skilled than the work of most men

21

as young. Climbing the poles, dealing with power. He liked being outside and unconfined, able to move about and function, even in the sweeps of winter snow. "Think of all those dates for sweet screwing that are set up over the phone," he would say. "Electric dreams buzzing through the wires. Me and Ma Bell, we keep the boys and girls together no matter what the weather." Then he'd laugh; he was a good laugher. He'd say he might try college when he was out of the war. They were on weekend pass in Seattle, Washington. Pitts told him he had investigated higher education, found it lacking. "Of course," Pitts had added, standing at a bar across a sleet-slick street from the University of Washington, "my sketchy attendance and general bad attitude may have colored my view." Pitts had never worked a job he liked either. He figured his attitude should mellow. He was young.

Harry Pitts and Jim Grogan spent as much time in Seattle as they could manage, almost every moment permitted them away from winter Fort Lewis. Their first pass from LRRP training they took the bus to Tacoma, found the place depressing. Bleak as Fayetteville, North Carolina, worse than Columbia, South Carolina. A service town. Bars and pawn shops, tattoos, hostile attitudes. Seattle possessed all this as well, but much, much more to the good. Pitts thought it the cleanest, newest real city he'd ever seen. He and Grogan liked to ride the monorail, haunt the old World's Fair grounds. They had seen the folksinger Judy Collins there in concert, their last pass before Vietnam. Although Pitts knew he would never meet the woman, he fell in love with her. Her voice. Her golden presence. Her. And Jim Grogan felt the same. They became fans.

They liked to hang around the university district, watch the hippies. They were amazed at the number of young males who claimed to be AWOL, deserters.

Enlisted soldiers both, paratroop jump-school training before LRRP, Pitts and Grogan did not attempt to understand the deserters. Jim would say he thought them possibly chickenshits, but he wasn't sure, wasn't making any absolute judgments. Harry Pitts didn't care about them one way or another. They were just there and odd, like fags.

The Ohio Grogans had always fought their country's wars. So Jungle Jim claimed his excuse was tradition.

And Harry Pitts's people, New Englanders mostly from Maine and Vermont, had been soldiers. How far back Pitts did not know. But he knew his grandfather had made World War One. An artilleryman in France. Pitts kept the old man's field notebook which was filled with terms like base deflection, projectile, powder, fuse, barrage, method and rate of fire. The old man's unit brass was screwed through the upper right corner of the back of the book. A tarnished circular piece, the 308th Battalion, crossed cannon. And on the page marked November 11, 1918, words in the man's clear script: *Fini la guerre.* And though Pitts's father didn't tell many war stories, Pitts knew he had been wounded in World War Two, European Theater. Pitts kept an old promotion warrant presented to his father in 1942. And he saw his father's old boxed military decorations as special, fine. He liked the things.

After Harry Pitts had enlisted he kept it a secret. Eventually, he first told his father, who thought it an acceptable idea. But Harry wanted to tell his girl friend, Ann, that he'd been drafted. Easier to explain. Conscripted. Had to go, no choice. They had known each other as children, grown apart and come together again as lovers invading adulthood. He finally opted for the truth just a matter of days before induction.

"My sister Mary is coming to visit this weekend," she said to him. They were in Burlington, Vermont, where she went to college, where he'd dropped in and out of college, sometimes worked. "I'll have to spend most of my time with her. Of course you could join us." A small smile.

23

He was walking her to her dormitory. The night was cold, dry. He did not like sister Mary. He drank from a pint bottle. "Yeah. Well I'm going into the fucking Army next week." Kept walking.

She stopped. "What?"

"The Army," he said through the whiskey. "I'll be leaving for the Army."

"When?"

"Next week. Say hello to Mary."

"Don't be like this. You're not really a bastard. Why are you trying? You must have known before tonight."

"I didn't want you to worry."

"Oh God." She spoke through her coming tears, trying to hold back. "That's lame, Harry. Didn't want to worry me. I think you're confused."

"Goddamnit!" he said. Enraged at himself, not sure why. "I don't know how else to put it." He could feel the whiskey at the back of his throat.

"Oh God." Her tears came. But she said she would wait.

Then he was in the Army, training, home on leaves, training, going to the war, staying in the war. And Ann, his closest friend for years, his lover, his woman back home haunted him. It was as if he at once craved and dreaded her. Craved who she was, her self. Dreaded the commitment a man should make. Why was she such a colossal question in his life? He loved her, or thought he did. He'd never felt that demand to be close with any other human being. But he left. And left again when he stayed in the war. And still she decided to wait, to remain a part of him. And he believed her. He didn't know that he wanted the responsibility. Didn't know whether he truly wanted her to wait. Wouldn't it be selfish to expect it? Her solitude created an obligation, forged what should be a stronger bond. There stood the emotional mountain. Ignorance and indecision fed each

24

other. He found himself in a circle of confusion. The closer he came to home, the more real his confusion became. He could step out of things, or into the center for focus, clarity. But he put things off. Didn't take either step. Stayed in a blur.

When they had been in Vietnam a short time, Jim Grogan received word that his girl back home had found somebody else. A Dear John Letter. Grogan told Pitts it made him sad. "But it must make her sad too, some. I know her. She'll be a little sad, but she told me; so it's not cheating. It's probably the best move for her. I wonder who the dude is. Maybe I'll visit when I'm home. Probably not though."

The incident set Pitts's mind to thinking about how he might react under similar circumstances. He could not imagine it. He wondered about that.

Harry Pitts and Jim Grogan both had known they would go to the war. That's what infantryman were for. Called up for combat. They met at LRRP training in Fort Lewis. Both had volunteered, thinking the smaller, better trained units preferable to regular infantry line companies.

One Seattle Saturday night they walked until dawn. Touring the slick damp streets. Talking, shooting the shit. Smoking cigarettes.

"Do you think you could kill somebody?" Grogan said to Pitts that night. "I sure don't know about me."

"I guess we might find out." Pitts's voice was flat. He didn't know.

"Guess you're right."

The men were different and the same. They were parts and wholes and searchers. They were simply that rare and complex relation: friends.

CHAPTER FIVE

The platoon two-and-a-half-ton truck transported Mac's patrol to the southern span of the bridge.

The bridge was small but strategic. Jungle Jim told Duke about it, and Duke took it in, watching. It spanned a fifty-yard mangrove swamp to link sections of Highway 1. Wood carts pulled by water buffalo, and Lambrettas laden with refugees from the North creaked and sputtered south in tired, daily clumps. Some days hundreds crossed the bridge. Some days a dozen. A green creek wound through the swamp under the bridge; the creek swelled to a steady rush of river during heavy monsoon. When the waters receded, bodies and parts of bodies had to be excavated from the muck. Sweeps of green rice paddies stretched flat to the east and west. One poor hut-hamlet existed just north of the bridge, another hut-hamlet and Ho Nai and the road to Saigon stretched to the south. PFs lounged yapping and smoking in two large wooden shelters jutting at both sides of the blacktop at the center of the bridge, their weapons strewn about carelessly. Dust and shards of clay stuck everywhere.

Duke and Jungle Jim and Mac and a soldier named Jack marched slowly through the late afternoon heat to a bunker dug into the southwest bank of the built-up bridge. Mac and Jack moved across to another sandbagged bunker on the northeast bank.

The PFs laughed and lounged in their solid shelters built

comfortably above the ground with U.S. Army Engineer lumber acquired to build solid, permanent bunkers down in the ground. They wore uniforms and had weapons around, but they were farmers. Duke eyed them and thought of the local VC guerrillas. In black pajamas and rubber sandals, Charlie appeared the farmer. At night he was an expert thing of terror, a killer. These ruff-puffs on the bridge had about as much going for them as a nest of baby rats discovered by a bamboo viper.

Lt. Ripley Masters rode up in a jeep with an M-60 machine gun mounted high between the seats. His driver was an ugly foul-smelling soldier: short, stocky, purple scars on his face—the Animal. The lieutenant's German shepherd sat in the rear, when the jeep stopped the dog jumped and stood, forelegs on the M-60, hindlegs on a seat. The lieutenant talked with Mac and the PF leader; he had secured a 60-millimeter mortar for the PFs. He and Mac attempted to explain its function and operation. Duke and Jungle Jim smoked dope.

Duke looked around; he enjoyed the view: lush foliage, creeping green stream, immense sky, thunderheads and lurking monsoon. He watched Jack obey Mac.

Jack followed Mac everywhere and did all he was told. Jack was a kid, most of them were. Jack the Kid. He hailed from Georgia, same county as MacFee. Even reenlisted to extend and be with his idol Sergeant MacFee: a ruddy-faced lifer, solid and hard, wrinkled and gnarled before his time. Mac told Jack to burn brush near the bottom of the northeast bank so the field of fire, the killing zone, would be improved. Jack got a good blaze crackling, he fed it with gas from a five-gallon can. The flames licked that gas right up into the can. That can exploded and Jack became a screeching human torch. He pranced about swirling in fire: his hair all orange, he slapped at his uniform and left patches of skin that bubbled and burned. The PFs gaped down the bank yapping, not moving. Duke got there first and knocked

Jack to the dirt. Jungle Jim kicked him and rolled him. They grabbed Jack, whose flesh was mush under what uniform was left, and set him into the creek. Duke, who always carried medical gear, shot him with morphine and stared up at Mac who called the helicopter, the med-evac. Most likely they would never see the Kid again.

When the helicopter was gone Duke asked the lieutenant about a medic, a doc.

"Yeah, we've got one," Masters mumbled, "but he was sick back at the fort."

"It figures," snapped Duke.

Jungle Jim simply sighed.

The absolute blue of that Oriental sky first changed to turquoise and took streaks of amber, then turned purple, fading as the sun took burgundy, sinking behind the paddies into a swamp. The amazing changes the sun put the sky through often went unnoticed. But Harry Pitts rarely missed it. He liked colors and always noticed them.

Little fires were lit. PFs squatted and cooked in tins. Duke and Jungle Jim stretched concertina wire over the southside of the bridge. Mac and Animal, who stayed to replace Jack, did the same at the northside. Mac called in the situation report: sit-rep negative, roger and out. The four CRIP soldiers ate from cans: cold C Rations near the north bunker. Duke consumed canned white bread with globs of peanut butter. He wished he had a nice tangy onion sandwich. He washed the stuff down with warm water. No one spoke of Jack.

The sunlight was gone. Stars and moon were coming through as the dark deepened. Duke couldn't understand the PF fires. "What the hell is their problem?"

"They're gooks," said Animal. He was a New York City street savage who had been fighting all of his young life. All of it.

"The man's brilliant," said Mac.

"He speaks brilliance," said Jim. "Brilliance and truth."

Animal had squatted next to Duke and had spoken directly into his face. When he got up and moved off, Duke turned to Jungle Jim. "That Animal's breath smells like something crawled into his mouth while he was sleeping and took a shit on his tongue."

"There it is," said Jim. "Being in a bunker with the dude is like being shut in with a bear."

When it was full dark and Duke saw the stars shining from all the wrong spots, the light show began. Distant flares and rockets burst in the sky. Minigun tracers rained red in the dark from Cobras and Spooky: deadly flying machines that spit fire and death from above. Artillery thundered and thumped up a slight distant glow. The war seemed far off. Duke watched its reflections and the night for hours. He occasionally ducked into the bunker for a cigarette with Jungle Jim.

The PFs lounged, smoking and yapping, some hanging in hammocks inside the jutting wood shelters. The honcho set up the new mortar in the middle of the bridge between the two comfortable shelters. He fumbled and seemed to explain things, pushed away advice and laughed like a loon with the others. He fired an illumination round, a parachute flare. The mortar was adjusted somehow to shoot straight up: one hundred eighty degrees. The PFs danced and pranced, hooting in the artificial white light. The idiotic honcho fired a second, same as the first. On the bridge it was daylight. Duke was flabbergasted. The four CRIP soldiers slipped phantomlike into the bunkers dug into the earth.

When the light burned out, the first rocket hit. It slammed the east shelter, followed quickly by a second. The shelter exploded to splinters of wood and torn bodies flinging and flipping. The west shelter was packed with PFs, all awake now, all trying to escape. Duke heard the confusion of senseless rats deserting, too late, the trap.

29

Another rocket launched from back in the paddies slammed, landing home. Dead PFs everywhere, screaming and crying, bleeding and dying. Arms and legs, heads and hands pitching and rolling, severed and torn, slapping the dust. Then it was over except for those who didn't get totally wasted: sobs and groans, wails and whimpers.

Duke called for Spooky and lots of illume. He knew it would be too late, the VC were gone, vanished into the landscape, roaming back home. But he called for the plane just to make sure. The old C-47 flew over just before the first glistening of day and churned up some of that landscape. The flareship was armed with 20-mm Gatling Guns that shot three hundred rounds per second. It circled and shot for fifteen or twenty minutes. Then it flew away, into the morning.

The sun lit that landscape and the bridge which was paved with dead Vietnamese. A truck would come for the few that survived. The Americans removed the wire barriers at the northern end of the bridge.

The PF honcho lay wheezing, dying in the dirt. He attempted to raise what was left of himself on his one good arm. When he opened his mouth, his teeth fell out in a blob of blood.

"Fuck him," said Mac who spit in the air and kicked a dead head out of his path.

"You're a mighty hard mother there Mac." Duke walked behind him and side-stepped the head, nearly tripping over a boot full of foot.

Sergeant First Class MacFee turned and spoke to Duke. "I was in the peacetime Army for seven years. And every night for seven years I prayed for war." He spoke with an easy Southern drawl, bass and clear.

A grit, thought Duke. A shitkickin grit. He went to the southern concertina barrier and yanked it aside. An ambulance and a deuce-and-a-half rolled in to collect bodies. Wailing women followed, hobbling and quick-

30

stepping to the carnage. They sat on their haunches and wailed and wailed. Thin young boys helped load the night's work, checking pockets, stealing boots whenever they could.

The sun rose and with it the stench on the bridge. Duke lit a cigarette and turned his back to the bridge. He held himself, didn't crack his mask. It took small strength. This was not his affair. A morning rain dropped. He thought of his mission.

CHAPTER SIX

Back at the old French fort, Duke and Jungle Jim exchanged views of vengeance, revenge. Its pros and cons, reasons and justifications. Duke claimed that personal revenge was the only true form of justice. He admitted the concept would be difficult to administer. There were laws and courts and the entire labyrinth that constituted a legal system. But what of a crime that didn't fit, a crime to which no one would admit? Was it not up to the victim of that offense to seek the criminal, to make him pay? Duke was a victim, as were Dudley and Carl, Zap, Rat, and the Ox. Hell, everyone was a potential victim of a bastard like that pilot! Duke had survived and vengeance was his.

"What about these gooks?" Jungle Jim gestured out of the fort to the people of Ho Nai. "Victims for sure. This is a war. Who do they make pay? These wretched women, these crippled kids, these stupid men. When comes their judgment, their settlement?"

"Wretched and stupid is right. They will judge when they decide to go their own way."

"They're sad, my man. Sad but trying. Making the effort."

"No. They're running. They'll never make it; one day there will be nowhere to run, just more hell to pay. How can so many of their military units fall apart and run in the face of battle? It happens often and you know it. That's no goddamn effort in my book. When you will no longer fight for what is yours, you're dead and don't know it. It's only a matter of time before these gooks in the Republic lay down stone cold. It hasn't dawned on them yet to stop breathing."

"It's true. Their organization is bullshit. But they're human beings without much use for politics. They just want to be let alone to live and it can't happen. And they're sad. They've got nobody to pay back for it because they are simply part of it all. Like all of us."

"That's their blues, not mine. I'd like to not leave that pilot alone, not let that dickhead live."

"Settling old scores generally means new trouble."

"The score ain't so old, J.J. The game's just been delayed."

Jungle Jim knew a personnel officer stationed at the air base in Tan Son Nhut, a pal from back in the World. Lieutenant Rizzo should certainly be able to locate the Chinook pilot. Jim also knew of a way to travel south to Tan Son Nhut. A fellow they had scouted with now drove the edible garbage truck from north of Long Binh down to Saigon.

"Let's go for it." Duke stood, ready.

"Find the jeep," said Jim.

They did.

The Animal drove them to Camp Frazier-James just north of the huge Second Field Force complex at Long Binh. The camp derived its name from two grunts killed early in the war. Duke spat at the notion. It was a bullshit rally, somehow insulting. He figured Frazier and James would feel the same, if they could. On the way the Animal had stopped the jeep and fired the M-60 into a pack of poor mongrels sidling and sniveling about the roadside. The Animal snarled a sick sounding laugh; he blasted the mutts into mud. He was still smiling, stretching the angry scars on his face, as he drove away. Old women and kids went for the dog meat. The kids fought off the living canines while the *mama-sans* gathered the dead, beating the heat and the bugs and the dogs. Duke looked at Jungle Jim who shook his head, apparently disturbed by the situation. Duke thought the Animal's act rather dull, stupid really. But then the dude's moniker was Animal, he was just being himself.

Duke and Jungle Jim, Sergeants Pitts and Grogan, cleared their weapons (M-16s and .45s) and marched through the gate. One of the infantry battalions was on the base en masse for a stand-down. Pitts and Grogan walked through the area which looked exactly like an armed encampment of savage warriors, which is what it was. The grunts were on a five-day respite from the blood and the mud and the boredom and the terror. The men got stoned or drunk or both, each in his own way. They all ate hot food and might bathe daily: a rare privilege. The grunt brass had provided Lambretta loads of Vietnamese whores.

A wisp of a girl approached Harry Pitts offering short-time for two hundred piasters or three dolla MPC. He refused, waved her off with a wan smile and she giggled that he was a fag. She trotted off. Harry Pitts knew that she had been wrenched from her family farm like the rest of them. Either consciously or in her mother's womb. J.J. was correct, a sad situation, this: a bummer for the gooks. No joy ride for the grunts either. But he couldn't dwell on such matters. He was a Man with a Mission.

He and Jim found the Consolidated Mess Hall and Cpl. Red Green. Red was a big black outlaw from East St. Louis. He had been attached to an infantry line unit whose captain deployed two platoons so that when dark dropped they fired upon each other. They fired and fired and many were massacred. Red went wild and beat the captain severely about the face and head but he felt an odd mercy and did not kill the man. This mercy proved wise along with the fact that he possessed a Silver Star, for he was merely reduced in rank and given a job that the Brass considered humiliating: driving the edible garbage truck and responsibility for the burning of the camp's crap. "Garbage and shit," he liked to say. "Beats the bush any fuckin' day."

34

The three soldiers reminisced and talked of the five recent dead ones. Red was happy to help with a ride to Tan Son Nhut. He'd wait at the Cholon PX. If they could get there by four P.M. they'd have a ride back.

When the two-and-a-half-ton truck was stacked high with table scraps scraped from the trays of all the camp's support troops, Red drove off. Jungle Jim rode shotgun and Duke stood in the bed with Private Lake and the garbage. Private Lake's duty was to guard the garbage, to keep Vietnamese from stealing it whenever the truck stopped in populated areas. He was a bleached Aryan sort with cruel eyes.

Outside the camp they locked and loaded their weapons.

The sun blazed high, the heat hung oppressive. The land was deep green paddies, defoliated plain, and great gaping bomb craters. Huts and rubble lined the road. Bent and beaten refugees plodded past scrapwood Coke stands, their pitiful belongings across their backs. The truck drove, passing military vehicles and honking Lambrettas out of its way. The edible garbage stank in waves rising with the heat. Duke faced the hot winds and saw to the west a larger-than-life bluemetal statue: a tribute to the ARVN (Army of the Republic of Vietnam). A huge Vietnamese soldier sitting on his pack, his rifle resting across his knees. On his ass, thought Duke. It fits.

On the outskirts of Saigon, traffic thickened along with masses of people and temporary hootches. As soon as the truck stopped at an intersection, it was ambushed. A mob of women and little brown kids swarmed the bed of the truck, screaming and climbing and grabbing globs of garbage. Private Lake lambasted a few with a club he kept: a Louisville Slugger. They climbed and clung and cursed.

"Numba ten fucker."

"Goddamn shit GI."

The truck took off and Private Lake batted fingers and knocked off those that hung on. Duke lit a smoke and faced the hot wind.

On a scarred street where the truck slowed to a roll, a gang of young boys begged for cash.

"GI you gimme Pe!"

"Gimme money Joe!"

"GI, GI gimme one dolla!"

Private Lake reached in the pocket of his jungle pants shouting, "Money, number one money!"

The boys' eyes almost went round as they stretched out their arms and chased the truck. Private Lake repeated his act over and over. The boys were punching and kicking, knocking each other to the cement. The truck picked up speed and so did the boys. Private Lake laughed, claiming he had money to give. The last two boys were racing so fast after the truck and an idiotic dream, that when they crumbled to the pavement, it scraped them bloody and cracked small bones. Still they bleated and fought with themselves. Private Lake hooted and swore. Duke kicked some trash and said shit this stinks.

Cpl. Red Green stopped the truck near the air-base gate and told the scouts he would wait at the Soul City Bar until four. Get to the Cholon PX and they'd find Soul City. He drove away as Private Lake booted young boys from the heap of food.

Sergeants Pitts and Grogan bullshitted the MPs at the gate and got in. The base was big. Sandbagged bunkers between aluminum Quonset huts, brown canvas tents, fifty-five-gallon drums stuck in the ground for urinals: pisstubes reeking and swarming with flies. There were wood buildings for the Brass. Artillery and aircraft parked at random. Thick black smoke wafted from barrels of burning turds.

They found Lieutenant Rizzo at his desk sleeping in front of a fan. Grogan pounded the desk and Rizzo's head jerked up. They all laughed. Rizzo noted that Pitts sort of smelled. Grogan told him they wanted to find a pilot who had done them a good turn, they owed him something but didn't know his name, only a mission he had flown. The lieutenant wrote down the information. He could obtain the name but it would take a few days at least. Grogan thanked him. The scouts left and Lieutenant Rizzo put his head down on his desk.

They unconsciously quick-stepped through the dust and heat and bits of floating black tar. Both men felt relieved to be off the base. They left the chambers of their M-16s empty; SOP in Saigon. Their pistols, however, were locked and loaded.

They hitched a ride on a jeep. The driver was heading for the USO club to pick up a major, his boss. Jungle Jim suggested they go along and call home over the Amazing Pacific Cable. "Don't often get a chance to go to Saigon," he said, "and we've got time to kill."

Harry Pitts agreed. Voices from home; they were sounds he had not heard for a long time.

The last time Pitts heard home voices had been during his short last leave.

Eating with his parents, Pitts asked: "So what do you think about me going to this war?"

Mrs. Pitts, placing a forkful of carrots on her china plate, her early American hutch behind her, framing her. "As a mother, I must admit I'd rather see you as an accountant. But I believe I've always known that something sensible as that would be beyond you. Perhaps not beyond you, more out of the question." She smiled, a thin woman, low light playing on her graying hair. "I'd just as soon nobody went. But these are political considerations. Are you politically motivated, Harry?"

"No."

"I thought not. This war business is, of course, something for you to decide. It is not at all like the war of our time, your father's and mine. But I'd not try to stop you any more than I'd try to convince you to go. I'm afraid I wouldn't be much help in your decision."

His father, Mr. Pitts, sipping tea. "He's already decided, it seems."

"True." Mrs. Pitts ate her carrots.

"It's your own decision." Mr. Pitts again. "Of course. I went to war and I'm not sorry. But I'm also alive. So, Harry, the situation is that you must survive the experience. Then think what you will about it. This is not much of a topic for us right now, you know."

"Right." Harry Pitts ate some potatoes. "The food is delicious." It occurred to him that he had grown up and away from one war, his father's, the world's. He had grown toward and into another. He was not sure whose this one was. He was going to find out.

Pitts and Ann alternately spoke in marathons or walked in silences. Those last days together were difficult.

"It's odd Harry," she said to him. Her voice created no echo; clear, it blotted quickly into the heavy snow. "It's odd for me to think of you as a soldier in an army." Pitts could see her hot breath rise, white steam.

They walked on a level empty road. The road had been plowed. The snow piled on both sides. Ice-glazed and bare, apple trees stood crooked in a field.

"Well," Pitts said, "it's not so odd. A lot of men do it."

"Yes, Harry. But it's the young ones, like you, who go to the fighting. So it's odd for me. That question, Harry: Why?"

"There is not always an explanation for what we do."

"But Harry, we were brought up to see one. An explanation, a reason for what we do." She held her head down in the fur collar of her coat.

Pitts looked at her small boot prints. He was wearing hiking boots and jeans, a parka. He guessed he didn't look much like a soldier. Had to keep a ski cap over his military haircut, however. Cold. He watched her walk in her boots and coat. He knew what she looked like. A lean body. Brown hair she wore long. Eyes quite large and such a deep blue they sometimes appeared black. He could not see her eyes then. He thought she was beautiful. He didn't know what to say. "You have beautiful hair." He touched it. Soft.

"I was thinking of cutting it." Her face still in the collar.

"No."

"Goddamnit," she whispered. "Time is a killer. I hate it."

He could see that her body moved in a kind of tremble. He stopped walking and held her. He could feel her silent sobs. "I love you," he told her. He hoped he understood what it meant.

One of the very last things she said to him, after that awfully silent drive to the airport, was a simple request. Her face toward a wide window, jets roaring, streaming the winter sky. Her eyes closed. "Come back, Harry." Her eyes open, face to his face. "Please come home."

The jeep stopped at the USO club front door and the two soldiers thanked the driver and walked under the red, white, and blue canopy into the club. It was crowded with clean soldiers, men in business suits, and journalists in stylish bush jackets. And women. To Harry Pitts's mind, the most beautiful women in the world. Clean, healthy American nurses and delicate Orientals in bright *áo-dàis*.

He and Jungle Jim went upstairs to a roomful of telephones. Their calls would take about an hour to go through. Harry Pitts had decided to phone his lady rather than his father. His father would only tell him again to be cautious and always alert; he would remind him that he had no brothers to pass on Pitts blood. Yes, he would phone his lady. Perhaps the sound of his voice might help explain the extension she surely didn't understand.

He and Jungle Jim placed the calls and walked back downstairs to the snack bar and ordered cheeseburgers and fries and beer. They feasted in silence, with ketchup and relish.

Jungle Jim passed the rest of the time drinking with some Australian troops. He had taken an R&R in their country.

Harry Pitts took beer in the lobby and smoked cigarettes and watched women. Those western ones, those Orientals, they provoked dreams of the lines of legs, the smooth movement of thighs. The variety of jutting buttocks, the curve of hips. Unhaltered breasts that looked like breasts: hard and soft and swaying and rigid, inviting. The feline sweep of necks, the infinite myriad of lips and noses and those mysterious eyes, that hair. They were beautiful and the grinding ache got worse. What would he say to her? How to explain what he couldn't explain. It would be tremendous to hear her laugh. But she wouldn't laugh. He sat and stared and felt small and alone in a vast dark space.

Jungle Jim came for him. The time had come. He followed him upstairs, his system surging with rivers of adrenaline. He picked up the receiver and asked for his operator. His heart was bass drumbeats. What would he say? What could he say?

The operator informed him that there was no answer, no one home. The phone had been called and called. It rang and rang dozens and dozens of times. No answer. Nobody home. So sorry. Good-bye.

He hung up and went down to the lobby and smoked. He was stunned and nonplused at the same time. There were dozens of possible reasons for her not being home. He almost felt relieved. Still, he thought something was wrong. He didn't know what it was and he couldn't find out. Something must be wrong. What the hell was he doing anyhow? Trying to call the World across the Pond: the great Pacific! The World didn't want to hear from him or anybody else on this Sucker's Tour. Sure his home folks would like the sound of his voice but what would he say? "Stop crying." "I'll make it." "In my own time."

Jim came down smiling. "It was neat," he said. "My dad

40

said he was proud. There'd be wine and whiskey and thick steaks soon. And we'd talk. Shoot the shit.

"The old lady was trying but didn't make it. Started crying. I didn't mind though. Expected it, really. My sister sobbed some too. But the old man was cool. Got back on the promised booze and good talk. Knew I'd make it. It was neat. How'd yours go?"

"Nobody home." Pitts lighted another cigarette.

"Too bad. A bummer."

"Yeah."

They went to the street and flagged an open three-wheeled taxi in which the driver sat in the rear, a Pedicab. Jungle Jim told him to get them to the Cholon PX. The driver commenced pedaling, his legs noticeably hard, bulging with muscle. Like VC legs thought Duke.

"This is illegal," Jungle Jim pronounced after looking the driver up and down.

"What?"

"Americans are forbidden to use these taxis because the gook driver sits behind the passengers. He could slit throats all damn day. So let's keep an eye on each other. If you stop moving or talking too long, I'll blow this bastard's brains all over whatever's behind him."

"I'll do the same."

They each lighted cigarettes and watched. Scenes materialized and faded. Calm then clamor then silence then ragged din. Zoom and halt and rise and fall and empty and full. Death and life. No warning. Sneak attack. Quick kill. Just like that: erratic machine-gun bursts, jumpcuts in a movie.

The streets of Saigon swelled with traffic: like buboes in a plague. Japanese motorcycles, bicycles, military vehicles of varied design. On the sidewalks people moved and made noise as if they woke up on the right side of the world. Occasionally stumbling over one of the army of maimed rotting in the sun, they moved on. They might trip over the

41

truth, only to forget it and go: they had to. Harry Pitts took it all in, knowing but unmoved.

Jungle Jim wiped sweat from his brow. "A bladdy fackin' scorcher, mate," he said, imitating the Australians from the club.

"Hot enough to make your eyes melt," said Pitts.

The sun glinted off the head of a bald young Buddhist wrapped in bright orange and flanked by his peers. He drenched himself with petrol, then transformed into flames brighter than his robes. As he collapsed to a ball of burning flesh and boiling blood, his brothers made discordant music mixed with prayer and hope.

Harry Pitts's eyes stung from the smoke and the gesture. A dramatic gesture: the ultimate sacrifice, a silent scream from a soul for peace on earth. The price of peace is steep, he thought. And murky and steeped in blood. And unglorious.

"Crispy Critters," observed Jungle Jim. "You can't get away from them. It's amazing. I've been in Saigon maybe five or six times and this is the third one of these suicides I've seen."

"Kinda like Jack," said Pitts. "Burning because of the advice of some higher authority, some idol that goofed."

When they reached the Cholon PX, the driver demanded too much: an exaggerated fare. Jungle Jim threatened to blow his ass in the air and paid the fair price. The driver pedaled away bitching about Americans and the Chinese of Cholon: both foreigners he hated.

Hookers hung the barroom doors with sex for sale. Bits of their bodies flashed and moved in crude sexual simulation to American music blaring inside. Crippled children and useless soldiers crawled about begging and crying and trying to smile, their eyes so hollow a man might see all the way to their toes, if they had any.

The men found Soul City Bar and Cpl. Red Green. A whore straddled a stool at his side. She wore a green army T-shirt, red letters embroidered across her small breasts proclaimed I'M A FUCKING MACHINE.

They drank a few beers then made for Red's truck. It was empty. Private Lake had hosed it out. Vietnamese women stood in long lines holding crates and ID cards certifying that they were loyal citizens, FRIENDS of the REGIME. Harry Pitts understood the situation: These cards were obtained from their corrupt countrymen, their own fat leaders, at great cost. For the young, bribes of flesh. The old, money or a promise concerning their adolescent daughters, or sons. Their IDs okayed, they received a ration of American edible garbage scooped with spades from great mounds covered with fat flies.

At the beginning of his tour such a scene might have caused Pitts to comment, perhaps even feel sadness. Now it meant nothing; it wasn't enough. As they climbed aboard the truck, the soldiers didn't even joke about it. The situation simply did not touch them. The men were unplugged from their emotions.

Harry Pitts, aware of his own emptiness, sensed within himself a spreading numbness. He was not uncomfortable with it. He assumed the ability to plug back in, to burn again in some remote future with the charge of human electricity.

Red drove to Ho Nai without being attacked, left Duke and Jungle Jim and sped back for Camp F-J. Jim moseyed into the fort.

Harry Pitts watched the brown truck become a blur in the dusk. His eyes ached. He felt deserted, but knew in time he would not. And he felt somehow that was wrong. But time would take care of that too. He drifted without pattern around his mission. Another day down. He still had his balls, no broken bones.

CHAPTER SEVEN

Pitts and Grogan ate C Rations. The afternoon was about gone. They sat outside their hootch in the fort, Pitts chowing down on boned chicken and a can of peaches, Grogan sampling turkey loaf.

The Australians at the Saigon USO reminded Pitts of his own Rest and Relaxation leave, his R&R. I&I the grunts called it: Intoxication and Intercourse. Like Jungle Jim, Pitts had waited late into his tour in order to go to Sydney. Something about mingling with round-eyed women, being among western architecture, hearing English as the spoken language. Something like going home. He had been in the shit for ten months.

Simply boarding the commercial airliner was a lift. Smiling stewardesses. Troopers in the best mood they'd been in since coming in-country. Landing at a civilian airport wasn't bad either.

At the R&R Center everything looked splendid to Pitts, the little bits of Sydney he'd seen looked splendid, the people at the center smiled splendidly. Splendid, he repeated it to himself. Splendid. He chose a hotel in downtown Sydney. He skipped the various opportunities to sign up for planned activities.

He sat through a mandatory speech about what not to do. Don't be dumb drunk in King's Cross; the whores and pimps will screw you. King's Cross was, of course, the nighttime

44

party nexus where most of the soldiers went to get dumb drunk and screwed. And the big park in the city was off limits. This was where the hippies operated. Though Australia was a U.S. ally in Vietnam, a portion of the population, like back home, opposed the war. So stay away. The park was antiwar demonstration territory. Home of Aussie pinkos and faggots. Avoid the place.

Pitts checked into his hotel and didn't know quite what to do first. The place was splendid. Nicest room he'd occupied for a long time. Carpet, double bed, upholstered chairs, an oddly ugly and long rectangular print of some cityscape. He showered. The hot felt grand. He got into the jeans and shirt he'd borrowed from Jungle Jim. The clothes were loose. He had only military shoes. The Army had a curious regulation about those shoes. You had to wear class-A shoes to board the R&R plane. No boots. A lot of grunts in-country had only boots, generally filthy. So they had to borrow or steal shoes that rarely fit. Sad scene when a grunt was turned away from his plane for lack of proper shoes. Could be an ugly scene, too. Pitts imagined himself violently impatient if so victimized. He could hear some officer asshole telling him to find some shoes, catch the next flight, you'll only lose a day. One precious day. Pitts figured if he found himself in that predicament, he'd knock the asshole officer down, steal his shoes. Desperate times demanded desperate means.

Pitts ordered a room-service steak dinner. Just after it arrived, knocks sounded on his door. He got up from the food, which he found splendid, opened the door. Two women. Young ones. Not sure what was up, he invited them in.

"Come in," he said, wondering why.

They breezed in, giggling, all smiles, short skirts, legs. Sat in the chairs.

Pitts returned to his steak, on the edge of sexual fantasy.

"So you're a Yank are you?" Short redhead, dyed, purple lipstick.

"That's right. Maine."

"Good food?" Tall blond, accent a tad heavy, nasal, green lipstick.

"Splendid. Shall I order more?"

"No thanks." The redhead. "We've got other ideas. We like to get to know the Yanks. Intimate-like." Giggles.

The blonde giggled too, stretching her green lips, crossing her legs, kicking high. "Intimately is the word, deary. Yeah, intimate. Know what it means, Yank?"

"I have an idea. Call me Harry." He finished shoving his food in.

"So how do you like Sydney, Harry?" Giggles.

"Seems splendid. Just arrived, you know." Pitts had been dining, *dining* was the way he saw it, without his shirt. Had it hanging in the steamy bathroom, thinking some wrinkles might fade.

"You're skinny." The redhead with the purple lips. "Skinny and brown-like; you should eat more."

"Eat more!" The blonde with the green lips, kicking her legs. "What an idea. Eat more!"

Pitts thought this was splendid. "Let me get my shirt," he said, grinning. "We'll go get some drinks."

The girls giggled.

Pitts zipped into the bathroom. He was about to say: Or we might stay here, I'll order drinks. But the door slammed behind him. Something slammed against the door. Pitts was a little confused, adrenaline pumped. By the time he shoved up against the door enough to push the chair blocking it aside, he was mad. The girls were gone. They had jammed a chair between the bathroom door and the bed. The room was small.

Pitts's borrowed AWOL bag had been emptied. His money was in his jeans but they had snatched his Seiko watch. He could buy another Seiko, cheap in Vietnam, but still it hurt. Then he noticed the space on the wall where that long ugly print had hung. What sort of bullshit was this? He understood the watch, but a three-foot-long blurry print?

He felt furious. He didn't think much. He found himself in an elevator, going down. Breathing hard in a rising rage. He noticed well-dressed older passengers eyeing him. He realized he had forgotten to put on his shirt. Fuck them.

He stormed from the elevator. Raging at the desk clerk, he heard himself. Loud. Profane. A crowd gathered as he demanded, "Somebody better find my fucking watch! Goddamn cunt thieves! How can you miss the bitches strolling around with a three-foot ugly-ass picture? What kind of a shithole is this anyhow?"

The clerk said, "Sorry, mate. How about another room?"

"Another room! That's it?"

Then Pitts realized not only was he shirtless, he was barefoot. Standing there in the swank hotel lobby, the subdued atmosphere, half-naked, cursing, shouting. Showing class. "Thanks. Another room would be swell."

Then he had to walk through the wide lobby, the crowd. The marble floor felt cold under his feet. He got on the elevator alone.

From his new room, Pitts went out to a barroom. Public house. He wore his shirt and shoes, as well as his jeans. Almost everybody stood at or near the long bar. Sawdust and nutshells were scattered on the floor. Smoke hung like a sky beneath the high ceiling. A lot of noise. Pitts liked the place. He ordered beer. He looked around. Everybody in the room was male.

"Right, mate," the man next to Pitts said. "Ladies drink in the next room. The lasses and the lads. Men only in this section. You a Yank?"

"Right."

The man shook Pitts's hand. He was a heavy man wearing a brown suit. "Call me Rod. Got my boy over there, Vietnam. He'll do all right, God willing. Got a Buick though; don't know about that thing. Bloody Yank tank."

"I like Fords." Pitts was feeling better. He noticed some

47

poor looking savages at one end of the bar. These men held big mugs which they dipped into a wood barrel. Dark liquid dripped. Then they drank their mugs down. Pitts asked Rod about it.

"Slopshoot." Rod told him the barman dumped the remains of the drinks, beer, ale, whiskey, wine, all of it, into a trough behind the bar. Trough emptied into the barrel. Man down on his luck could dip a mug for a pittance. "No reason for a poor Aussie to stay sober." Rod laughed.

"Slopshoot." Pitts liked the sound of it. He watched a man whose face was twisted, a single eye in it. Only one arm looked intact and he wore a ragged trenchcoat. He used his arm to dip and drink hungrily from a slopshoot mug. Probably some sort of veteran. "Slopshoot," Pitts repeated. "Now that's a thoughtful idea." He wondered how many smartasses spat in the dregs of their drinks.

"Bloody right fine idea, mate!" Rod stood Pitts a beer. They drank.

Pitts asked: "So where are the Aborigines? Where can I see some Aborigines and boomerangs?"

"Boomerangs are sold everywhere. As for Aborigines, I ain't sure." Rod motioned to the bartender. "Mate, this here's a Yank. Wants to see some Aborigines."

"Aborigines?" The bartender shook his head. "Bloody aboes, you mean Australian niggers?"

"I guess," said Pitts, surprised, not knowing why.

Rod said: "Niggers? Why didn't you say so? I could point you to some niggers. Let them live right in town these days."

"Do yourself a favor, mate," the bartender said. "Stay away from them niggers. Bad business."

Rod and the bartender looked at each other; they laughed a loud bar-pounding laugh.

Pitts went to a movie. Saw a Hollywood production about Satan screwing some woman. An art film. The naked woman reminded Pitts of Ann.

In the morning he phoned a woman named Lottie, whose

name and number he'd gotten from Jungle Jim, along with the clothes. J.J. claimed Lottie was an exquisite specimen of the fair sex, boobs like basketballs.

"Sure," Lottie said. "Come on 'round." She gave him her address.

Pitts went out and purchased some clothes that fit, new shirt, new jeans. He hailed a taxi. Rode past the big park but he didn't see any action. The sun was up, the day clear. Pitts liked the lack of rain.

Lottie's apartment shined, a bright clean one, splendid view of the park. Lottie was older than Pitts had expected. She had two kids crawling around. Lottie was a smiler. Tall, full-breasted, those basketballs, tangled brown hair. They talked about Jungle Jim, whom she knew as Jimmy. She prepared a sumptuous lunch, some kind of spicy chicken, and they drank wine. She smoked pot. Pitts felt easy near her.

"So perhaps," Lottie said, smiling, "I'll see you tonight. You have a room?"

"Yeah. Yes. I mean I have a room, nice one."

Lottie explained, since Harry seemed a little thick, that she was a working girl, a whore. She fucked for money. Vice cops, the morals squad, arrested her now and then. Harassment. The bastards. As a rule, she didn't work days. But she said she liked Harry. And for a soldier she might break her rule, just this once.

"What about these kids?" Pitts pointed to her children.

"Not to worry, Harry. They've got the telly, and my bedroom door locks." The bright smile.

Lottie rolled with him until he was spent. Until the prospect of being unspent seemed far off. Pitts said thanks and thought he meant it. Outside the day looked even better. He wondered why Jungle Jim never mentioned that Lottie was a working girl. He would ask him. He could hear J.J. laughing.

Pitts did not return to Lottie. But he did see her again. In the neon light. Standing drunk outside the Whiskey-A-Go-Go in King's Cross, he saw her sashay his way. He hardly recognized her. She hugged him and smiled. Heavy makeup, red wig, sexy slutty wonderful short dress, net stockings, spike heels. Thanks, he told her. She winked, went into the Whiskey.

Pitts was on his way away. He had just come out of the place. He had looked in, heard the music pounding like bombs, a slim female singer with silver hair screaming like a victim. Colored lights assaulted her. You could tell the soldiers by their haircuts. The place was packed with soldiers. Pitts heard constant conversations about the bush, the war. Grunts in the war talked about the World, and here in a real part of it, a facsimile at least, they told war stories.

Pitts spent most of his R&R alone. He went to see an antiwar demonstration in the park. The scene was not peaceful. Demonstrators and police raised hell with each other. Pitts guessed it was about the same as the peace rallies at home. Ann had sent clippings.

He walked around the Sydney streets day and night, seeing movies, hitting bars. He didn't want to sleep much. Wasted time. But he really didn't do much, walking about all day, into the night. He thought he might like to come back some day, bring Ann. He found himself thinking more about her there in the city, more than he thought about her in Vietnam.

Their final days together had been filled with a frantic kind of physical love-making. As if she wanted to keep as much as she could of him there with her. The emotions and incessant closeness became strange, even for a couple so young.

At the airport that last day Ann tried not to cry and almost made it. Pitts just wanted to leave. The scene was terribly uncomfortable. He had said good-bye to his parents at their home. Her father drove to the airport. Ann standing there, Pitts holding her. He could feel her shoulders shaking. Her father handing him fifty dollars as they shook hands. What the flying fuck? Fifty bucks! Pitts kissed Ann's wet face and was gone.

Jungle Jim nudged him. "What are you thinking, man? Five hundred piasters for your thoughts."

"What?" Pitts looked at his boned chicken can.

"Where are you? You've got the thousand-yard stare."

"Sydney. I was thinking of Australia."

Jungle Jim grinned. "Bloody great, hey mate?"

"Splendid," Pitts said.

CHAPTER EIGHT

That night Lt. Ripley Masters decreed that a recon team should set up an observation post in the tree line west of the paddies, north of Ho Nai. Late afternoon rain had drenched the land. The team would move out during dusk: gray, muted dripping dusk. "Set your Seikos, suckers," said Mac. And Duke and the others wound their watches. Duke was reminded of helicopter blades as he turned the luminous hands of his watch around. Chinook blades and blood.

Muck sucked their boots; black water soaked their legs. Mosquitoes clouded about their heads. The men sloshed across the paddies, then into the swollen creek that flowed further east beneath the Ho Nai Bridge. The deep creek current steadily kept water lapping around their chests; they waded slowly, stolidly, weapons raised: Mac, Jungle Jim, and Duke. The water swirled about the Animal's neck.

A flotilla of drowned rats clung to clumps of dissipating turds. It slapped and brushed Duke, surrounding him. He cringed, cursing softly. He used his rifle butt to shove the vague carcass downstream. He pushed quickly, his lips zipped.

It was dark when the men ducked into the trees. The rain had begun again. They found a thicket of bamboo and crept into it, blending with the landscape. The rain slacked to a drizzle. They set out Claymore mines and set up a tiny perimeter; ponchos wrapped over shoulders.

Mac called in the position and the negative situation report. He sat next to the radio, drew his bayonet and stabbed it into the mud. He lined several hand grenades next to the knife and speculated: "Men," he whispered, "I got a feeling they're gonna get us tonight. Don't sell your asses short though, remember you're fuckin' Americans. After the little *banzai* bastards overrun us, save one grenade." He pointed to the frags sitting near his knife. "Pull the pin with your last bit of life and lay on the spoon. Then die if you must. When one of those slopes kicks your ass over to ransack you, the frag'll blow and you'll take one with you after you're dead."

The Animal nodded. Apparently it made sense to him. He fished for grenades.

Duke moved away. So did Jungle Jim.

The watch went well: two awake, two asleep. At 3 A.M. the rain stopped. At 3:30 Duke heard a sound of heavy movement. Walking in the brush, away from the paddies, hidden from view. He woke them all. They listened, intensely silent. The rustling would cut a path close, west of their position. As it did, Mac claimed it was Cong.

"I can smell um," he said.

The men trained their weapons.

"Waste um," he growled.

They sprayed and strafed, shattering the almost quiet, almost still like an unexpected eruption exploding the ground. Each tossed a grenade: four fast blasts. Fourth of July. Duke tripped the Claymore slashing and shredding the brush. Mac hollered quit. Silence settled, no movement at all.

Mac radioed contact had been made. Victor Charlie had fled or was lying there dead. The team stayed alert: one hundred percent.

They collected Claymores and moved out at first light. They moved to the site they had ambushed, seeking dead Cong. A dead and dismembered anteater is what they found:

53

dead, shredded and stinking. They searched some more, nothing. The similarity in stench between anteater and Cong was a matter to joke about when Mac wasn't around.

But Duke cracked it first, then and to the man. "Too bad we don't have a division of those noses, Mac. You sniff out the need to have Jack burn that field of fire?" It was cruel and Duke knew it.

MacFee didn't say a word. Harry Pitts detected hairline cracks in the man's mask, barely visible, encircling one eye as it twitched. This man's stupidity, he thought, covered great portions of the earth that the Army occupied. A dull green sheet of stubborn fabric with precious few tears.

CHAPTER NINE

The patrol marched back to the fort in the dry morning. The men were wet from fording the stream again. Duke got into a dry uniform and washed his muddy one in a tin bucket. He watched Chester, the platoon RTO, imitate Jesse James. Stupid grit, he thought. The thin Southerner picked his nose and went for his gun: a .45 in a hip holster. Duke thought he would like to use a .45 to shoot the hands of the Chinook pilot to shreds. That shitbird who flew away and left the scouts to die. Blow the man's fingers off and shove a couple up his nose; he could lend the rest to Jesse James Chester, permanently.

Inside his hootch, near the command bunker sat Lt. Ripley Masters, the Digger. The Digger had been a mortician back in the World. Now he drank root beer, discussing dissections and operations with Doc Ratchit, the medic, and Kim. Doc Ratchit was a sick man. Dysentery drove him to opium. Kim was the Vietnamese interpreter, attached to CRIP from the ARVN. Kim was not his name but easier to pronounce than Kiem Ly.

Right after the crack of the shot Duke burst in sweating, looking for Doc. Pfc. Chester, that long skinny rebel, had shot himself. Practicing a quickdraw with a .45 (a weapon equipped with three safeties), simultaneously exploring his nose, he found a profitable nostril and shot through his holster into his leg. "Dude's dumb as a post. A sap. He gets

55

none of my medical stash." Medical supplies were precious, not available to all.

Doc looked disgusted and went out with his bag. Digger didn't budge, simply sent Kim for the Animal to drive the wounded private down to Camp F-J. Duke left the Digger. He thought he'd catch Doc's act.

Doc's work was sloppy, but after the morphine took effect, Chester didn't care. Duke and Doc dumped him into the jeep. The Animal drove off, Kim manning the M-60.

Doc Ratchit complained; his bowels were churning. He went to a cruddy hole flanked by foot bricks. He squatted dropping his drawers and dumped into the Vietnamese crapper next to the command bunker. He was really sweating now, much more than Duke. His face was pasty-pale. He suggested they adjourn to Gue's: an opium den. Duke agreed, sounded intrigued. Why the hell not? It might relax him, take his mind off his mission.

It was forenoon; the heat had not zenithed yet. But they were hot strolling through the maze of passages in the marketplace. The stalls held everything from dry goods to red meat to dried squid, fruit, and vegetables. The racket of the village rose from these places: a constant cacophony that reverberated and thinned out past the edges of the open air markets. Shrill speech, ancient music, shriller still, bawling from radio speakers, fowl crowing. Duke wondered how the merchants ever got accustomed to the smell, for most of it was bad, pungent.

He followed the Doc down a narrow, littered alleyway, then up an even narrower staircase to the second story of a stucco building. They walked through an ornate entrance plagued with intricate cracks. Dragons and Buddhas and multi-armed female figures ushered them in.

Doc greeted an old woman in Vietnamese. She led them through several silklike curtains to a sweet-smelling room. Rolled sleeping mats were stacked to one side; those colorful woven, rectangular headrests piled one on another. Gue sat on a mat in the middle: a tiny, white-haired, yellow old man. Several other old men lounged in hammocks sipping rice wine. Doc introduced Duke. Gue slightly smiled and snatched up his pipe: the bowl looked like a brass and teakwood doorknob, the stem stretched long, fashioned fine from wood. Doc and Duke sat down on the floor. .

The old man worked the opium with thin metal tools, rolling and kneading it over a flame from a kerosene lamp. When it looked like thick brown tar he delicately pressed it into the hole at the center of the bowl.

Doc lay down, head on a headrest. Gue placed the bowl over the flame and directed the stem straight to him. Doc took the tip in his mouth and inhaled, a mighty suck that drained the pipe. He held in ever so slightly, then blew it out: a thick white cloud.

After a minute Doc advised Duke to take his pipe all at once. "Gue gets downright depressed if you don't. Clogs up his pipe so he has to ream it and clean it."

"How many pipes do I smoke?" Duke inquired.

"I'll prescribe five," said Doc. "Ten for myself."

When they had smoked their all, drinking shots of hot rice wine all along, they rested. Doc stretched out on a mat.

Duke opted for a hammock. He floated, drifting over a wide shimmering sea. And for a while, a gleaming time, he was making luminous love, being young back in the World. And her eyes were round and dark and deep. Then he felt drunk and slow; he slept.

In and out of his sleep swirled snatches of things that been. . . .

Slouching, drunk in the university classroom, depending on Ann for notes. The professor yakking some crap about how the world had been changed by Marx, Darwin, and

Freud. Pitts, a flash of opinion in his head, stabbed the space above him with his arm. "Interruption! Interruption! I beg to differ!" Determined to put the pompous chump in his place.

"Yes?" The professor. "Enlighten us, Mr. Pitts."

Pitts stood straight up, his mind suddenly blank. His mouth open. Absolute zero. "Ah . . . Repeat the question please."

"No question, Mr. Pitts. You may be seated."

Harry Pitts down again, next to the love of his life. A grin from her.

Harry Pitts heard his father bellowing. A strong man with a strong voice, he had worked his way up in the State Forest Service. An on-and-off drinker, a serious one; man then on a binge. Booming obscenities to the walls, this before he'd stopped boozing. Vowing to his family, his wife most directly: "Goddamn you all! Leave me be! I warn you. Goddamnit!"

The man had reeled into the house reeking of whiskey and young Harry had simply mentioned it. Mrs. Pitts added unpleasantly that she wasn't surprised, at least he didn't black out and wake up in Boston this time. She told Harry: "If you ever drink like your father I'll never speak to you again."

It didn't bother young Harry but his father took it hard.

"Goddamn you both!" Mr. Pitts grabbed a bottle of rye from the kitchen, drank from it. "I'll keep at it, goddamnit, 'til all my problems are solved!" Long pull. Sweat breaking on his face. He was a powerful man and he punched a maple cabinet to splinters, smashed the bottle on the floor.

Harry was just starting high school but he could see that his father was dangerously drunk, and unhappy with his drunkenness. His mother walked away in silence, these fits

58

the culmination of years of her husband's drinking to excess.

Harry said to his father: "You ought to shut up and go to sleep. Maybe on the couch."

His father turned on him in an ugly, stifled rage: the veins in his neck bulged, his eyes bloodshot, his fists balled. He stood there shaking, containing himself, breathing hard. "Who in hell are you to say that to me!" A snarl.

"Your son," Harry said.

His father seemed to stop breathing, moving. He began to weep silently. His body relaxed and he walked away. He slept on the couch by the fire and didn't drink anymore. He asked for help and stopped. Harry Pitts felt humbled by the man's vulnerability, his humanity.

Pitts would sometimes wonder if it might be better for him if his father started boozing again. Sober, the man involved himself rather a lot in Harry's life. Encouraging him fanatically in sports, and all those camping and fishing and hunting trips that had stopped years ago, began again. Harry, not particularly fond of fishing and hunting but liking the mountains, rolled with it. Kept them both busy.

He saw the tavern, heard the talk. Pitts drinking beer in New York with Vince, the first friend to go and return from Vietnam. Marines 1965. Asking Vince about the experience. Vince not saying much. The country was a jungle, the people small. You burned villages. You killed people. Vince looked right at Harry, admitted he'd killed other human beings. Didn't brag or apologize. Just said yeah that's what you do. Drank his beer. Harry Pitts had been impressed. He and Vince had attended school together. Vince dropped out when he was seventeen to join the marines. Pitts's impressions were neither positive nor negative, just strong.

Pitts said to him: "Well holy shit!"

And Vince came back with: "You go over there, Harry.

You'll find out about shit, and it won't be holy."

A time when death entered their lives, Pitts's and hers, Ann's. Her grandmother was dying of a cancer that ate her bones. Pitts would accompany Ann, visit the old woman in the hospital, a dark religious place. The room smelled at times of a stinging antiseptic, at times putrid. The tiny room was always dim, the dying woman doing what she could. She always spoke if she were awake. She'd smile and it looked as though the act was painful for her to accomplish. She would talk to her granddaughter, who wept openly, softly. There was no shame in this gesture. They were a close and old Italian family. Then the question. Someone in the family, generally female, always got around to it.

The old woman's frail head rose up. "So when are you two getting married? You could have a ceremony here at my bed, before I go. We'll get a priest."

Ann would smile and cry and say maybe. Deep blue eyes, immense and wet.

Pitts found the question odd. The place and time odd as well.

At the funeral more weeping. More low-lit gloom, rich shadow. Family members kissed the corpse.

Leaving the gravesite, holding Ann, he felt relieved that this passage was almost over for her. He knew she had been close to her grandmother, and she was deeply emotional. Honestly shaken. They walked away from the cemetery. Her sister Mary approached, asking: "So when are you two getting married?"

Pitts had been tired of the question for over a year. He figured the woman asked here, now, as some opposite direction to take. Away from the grave. Pitts gave the bitch that much. He said, "We'll let you know." He held Ann and they walked away. He did not feel anything like she was feeling, he knew. Mostly, he felt *for* her. He thought she was doing okay though. Grace under pressure.

He sank further into the opium sleep, into a dull state of sluggish stillness. The snatches of dream blurred.

Doc shook him awake: time to go, time to split. The Duke struggled out of the hammock and fell to the floor. His head was light. Trying to move was like walking against a fire hose flowing full-force. He didn't know where the fuck he was. The man was truly dazed. He saw Dudley and Zap running across the room, along with Ox, Rat and Carl. They chased a Chinook through a wave of silk. The Chinook spewed laughter like wind. The chase *looked* like noise, but the whole thing disappeared into the silk curtains, down the stairs, away. The silence was a roar.

Doc helped him up, draped Duke's arm around his own neck and led him to the stairs. Neither made it to the bottom standing. Duke saw the scouts and the ship floating away from the foot of the stairs. He shouted he was behind them, bringing up the rear, watching their backs. He lunged forward to join the chase, crumbling and tumbling half of the way. His momentum dragged Doc one step behind. They flopped down, sliding to a heap.

Doc got to his feet and stood Duke right up again. The journey through the marketplace was a drunken dance. Duke couldn't focus on anything, he lacked discipline. Doc was damn weak, but he had to lead. Duke saw a vat of something purple, murky and maybe alive. Intestines perhaps, the dead scouts' guts in a death throe. He puked into it, then followed his bile, joining the disemboweled warriors. Sluglike eels squirmed about him. Doc Ratchit was damn mad, downright annoyed. A bummer for sure:

61

The Duke was blowing his high.

Enraged, yapping merchants helped Doc yank him out. Doc dragged him by his boots back to the fort. Jungle Jim jumped to help. He propped Duke on the porch outside the hootch, dumped a bucket of water on his head to wash off some of the debris. Then he borrowed the lieutenant's Polaroid and snapped a picture of Sgt. Harry Pitts, the Duke.

CHAPTER TEN

Duke didn't recover until the next morning. He slept like a dead man in his own stink. He got up and put on the uniform he had washed the day before and washed his filthy one. He dripped with pain from the wine and the opium and embarrassment. Some welcome news cleared the fog from his head.

Lieutenant Rizzo came through with the Chinook pilot's name. Jungle Jim took the message over the big radio in the Command Bunker, then told it to Duke.

"The man's name is Warren Buckle, a Warrant Officer attached to a flight group stationed at Bien Hoa air base. Rizzo said the information was definitely correct, but confusing to come by. We had mentioned that the man had flown a Chinook that day. Well, an assault helicopter had been authorized for the mission. The Chinook came out of left field. The pilot claimed something about breakdowns, last-minute change, no time to explain: vague. But the air force dudes on the air strip didn't give a shit and the ship took off to Camp F-J and you guys. Anyhow, Rizzo says if he hadn't been persistent and snooped out the pilot's name in connection with the assault ship, it would be like the mission never happened. Because on paper no Chinook was flown by him that day, and neither was the assault ship for the same vague reasons given by Warren Buckle. Rizzo says he deserves a medal—maybe a Star—for detective work above and beyond."

"Tell him to put himself in for one. We can be witnesses to his merit," said Duke. "The assault ship makes more sense for that six-man patrol. I questioned the logic behind the Chinook myself. But what the fuck? I asked myself. Nothing about this war makes much sense. Especially the Army. So I let it go. I still don't get the Chinook angle, but perhaps we'll know better after discussing the matter with Mr. Buckle." Why did that cruddy cocksucker leave us? He thought, and the thought stuck. And why in a Chinook? The whys of the situation didn't interest him nearly as much as the fact that it had happened. But this obviously uncalled-for Chinook deepened things, clouded them just as they appeared to be clearing.

Jungle Jim showed him the Polaroid he had snapped of him. Said he was keeping it, a priceless addition to the journal he kept.

Duke looked at himself in the unfortunate state of yesterday. "Fuck you, too," he said.

The CRIP operated a jeep and a two-and-a-half-ton truck. The deuce-and-a-half, like the jeep, was equipped with a machine gun: a 50-caliber set on a circular mount on the bed. Lt. Ripley Masters was with the truck and the daytime patrol at the bridge. His mission was to supervise the construction of adequate bunkers for the Popular Forces.

So the jeep was free and the Animal drove Duke and Jungle Jim to Bien Hoa. He wanted to score dope and a piece of ass. Grass was available in Ho Nai but cheaper in Bien Hoa. There were no whorehouses in Ho Nai and Bien Hoa consisted almost entirely of bars and whores and soldiers.

Airborne troops operating in the area or at stand-down on the base were slowly reducing the town to shambles. Most of them had understandably bad attitudes and all of them went about armed. They had seen horrific action. There were MPs everywhere: airborne cops who brutally, if not effectively, policed their own.

Getting on the base was a bitch: a hassle with men bearing badges and guns. A hassle but finally done. At the time the air base was one of the busiest airports in the world: helicopters dotting the sky, jets roaring and streaking: taking off and landing in tandem.

They found the right outfit and Duke marched in unarmed inquiring after Warrant Officer Warren Buckle. Buckle's crew chief recognized him, took him aside.

"Whaddaya want, Sarge?" The crew chief seemed surprised.

"Whaddaya think, Chief?"

"He's around. I'm no longer with him."

"Whose side are you on, Chief? You had to hear my calls."

"I ain't saying nothin'. Those decisions are the pilot's, his option. My tour's nearly over."

"What about his?"

"Not his," said the chief. Then he walked, he split, departed.

Duke found the Pilot Quarters and Warrant Officer Warren Buckle. "Excuse me, sir." He stepped inside the Quonset hut room.

Buckle said, "What?" Not looking, reading a sex magazine.

"My name is Pitts, sir. Sgt. Harry Pitts. And that's the last of this 'sir' shit."

Buckle stood up frowning at Duke. He was a big one and hard: a heavyweight on the light end of the scale. He was totally bald, his head shone like wet leather. He covered his eyes with aviator sunglasses before Duke could scope them. He wore a massive handlebar mustache, red and waxed. He reached for a .45.

"No need, Buckle, I'm clean."

"So what's up, Pitts?" Buckle faced him, eyes hidden. He

65

was a bit bigger than Duke, heavier, and a bit older, maybe twenty-five. He had zippers on his jungle boots.

"You know what's up. Why didn't you answer my calls? Why didn't you come in and pick us up? Why did you lie to the G-2 boys? Come on, explain it, Buckle. Snap it up."

"I don't follow. You've got the wrong dude."

"You lie like hammered dogshit in dirt! Your father's rubber broke in a goat and it spit you out. I ought to rip your legs off and ram the bloody stumps up your sorry ass."

"Keep it up, Pitts, and you'll find yourself in a world of shit."

"You're in one. Just wanted you to know it. I'm around and waiting. I see you as a candidate for extra assholes."

"You lousy leg. I wish to hell they'd have waxed you too. Motherfucking grunt! Risk my ass for the likes of you? Balls! *Beaucoup* bloodsnot same-same you. Souvenir me some pussy pictures from your boob-boom girl mother. I hear flies buzz around *mama-san* Pitts's cunt." Buckle's body shook as he spoke, apparently enraged. "You have *tee-tee* brains, grunt. *Beaucoup* stupids. *Di-di* dumbass, beat it." He had picked up his .45; he pointed it. The man was flying off the handle.

Duke excused himself telling the officer he'd see him around. Buckle cursed him again and threatened his life. Called him a scumbag. Told him that if he came back, he'd better come armed. Duke marched out to the jeep. The pilot's attitude shocked him; he didn't know exactly why, it just did. Jungle Jim was likewise affected.

"The sonuvabitch is making it easy: hunting our own," said Duke.

"He must figure he's one tough dude," said Jim.

"Evidently. He looks the part, big and bald and mean looking. But he seemed stupid." The act of execution would not be difficult, Duke thought. Finding a method would be. The thing must be accomplished so that he did not appear guilty. He couldn't just walk in to the man's turf and blow him away. His mission took another dimension.

Animal started the jeep and would have left rubber on the pavement, but there wasn't any pavement; so gravel sprayed behind the spinning wheels. Duke remembered Warren Buckle's excessive use of the No-Man's Nam jargon. *Beaucoup*, *tee-tee*, same-same, souvenir me this . . . , number one, *ichi ban*, number ten, get some, *di-di*; all of that and more was a gobbledegook employed by soldiers and whores. Vietnamese, French, Japanese, English; all the languages contributed and the talk was a monument to all the soldiers and whores in the country's history. Duke didn't care for most of it. There were some good phrases, of course. Back in the World created idealized images of often bleak realities, but it meant home: so much nicer than the war. There It Is spoke of truth. Be Good meant stay alive. But much of the jargon bothered him, didn't anger him; he just found it ugly and tried not to use it. He made the habitual users for lames.

The Animal drove off base into town and parked on a dirt-rut side road. He yelled and tossed pebbles at an ancient wrinkled *mama-san* squatting, black pantleg raised and stretched, defecating in the ditch dug near the road. She squinted more lines into her face, spit black beetle-nut juice, nothing more.

Animal explained that two of them would go to the whorehouse which was a few streets east. They'd leave their 16s, take their .45s. He and Jungle Jim would go. When Jim finished he'd return to the jeep, relieving Duke. The Animal planned to score a pound of grass, an illegal transaction. If something went wrong in the house, they must sky out, beat feet for the jeep. Duke watched them walk. *Mama-san* stood up and spat beetle-nut juice in their general direction, then hobbled, bowlegged, toward a line of wretched huts.

Harry Pitts recalled trudging the Annamese Corderilla, the mountain range named for the old royalty of the race. What happened to the kings? Were they part of the corruptness destroying the South? Had they cast their lots with the severe quest of the North? Or perhaps they had been dissipated, lost in the turmoil of history, peasants now, shitting in the dirt, chewing nuts, black-toothed.

When Jungle Jim strolled back to the jeep, he directed Duke to the whorehouse. He advised that the women were rather plain and recommended a blow job.

Duke found the house and neglected Jungle Jim's advice. The women were of indeterminate ages and not particularly clean: too ugly and dim to make it as bar girls. And Duke had seen some of the poorer specimens of bar girl: He recalled the Lee sisters, Ugh and Beast. He knew Jungle Jim's relationship with the Vietnamese people was more intimate than his own, so he made no judgment. He looked at the sad whores, their crooked smiles. He abstained, deciding he might conserve what strength his own jism provided for the task he had begun to map the moment he clapped eyes on Warren Buckle.

He sat on a ragged vinyl couch sampling some of the grass Animal had purchased. He pronounced it pretty fucking good and nodded approval to Animal. The whores laughed at him calling him *diên dao*, crazy. Infants bawled, babbling kids crawled and pranced about the roach-infested floor. Two effeminate young boys smoked dope and tickled each other. Two MPs burst in, pistols drawn.

Whores squealed. The two young boys ran to the MPs who knocked them down. Animal whipped the pound of grass in the point cop's face. He and Duke dove out a window two whores held open. Animal ran north, Duke south along a dike.

He vaulted a fence and found himself surrounded by huge hogs and hogshit: the stench was awful. He pushed through the herd and crawled under the fence into an alley, his front smeared with mud and manure. He ran west now, kicking at nipping dogs. He spotted the jeep. A water-filled bomb crater obstructed his path. He ran back, then darted north and turned the next corner west. Concertina wire there, rat ruts and kid tunnels underneath. Room enough. He wormed down, snagging his bush hat and back. The hat stuck and he tore his shirt and the skin on his shoulder blade. He squirmed to his knees and saw the .45, then the MP who told him to freeze.

Duke did. He noticed that the MP was a kid: maybe eighteen. A kid, but an airborne one, a killer no doubt; training a .45 on his nose. "Can't we discuss this, man?"

The kid said: "Fuck you, leg," his face full of pimples and pus. "Hear what I say. Get up slow or I'll blow you away."

"Cute," said Duke. Another asshole calling him a "leg" to insult him. Legs (nonairborne, regular infantrymen) evidently ranked just below whale shit in this area.

"No lip," said the kid. Then Jungle Jim ripped him down from behind. Stuck an M-16 in his face.

Duke snatched the kid's .45. "Better put in for a promotion before you tell your boss you lost this, shitbird."

They abandoned the MP and bolted for the jeep. Animal had it cranked. He drove it, scorched the ruts, leaving dust to cloud and rise. "Think he spotted the unit number on the jeep?" he asked.

"If he did," said Duke, "somebody'll have to travel to Ho Nai to check. Then we'll see how those boys like being drawn down on. What a totally screwed-up situation this Vietnam is! We fuck ourselves over as bad as Charlie does." He felt a little queasy considering Warrant Officer Warren Buckle. He bummed a cigarette and smoked. He ranked Buckle with the MP who had threatened him: dogs, mongrel and rabid. But the MP was just a dumb kid. Duke refused to get fanatical. Couldn't hunt and waste a man just for being dumb. Warren Buckle however, was stupid and evil and some kind of coward: a dangerous thing best destroyed.

Jungle Jim insisted Duke move to the rear and he sat in the front seat. As they switched he mentioned that he preferred his pigshit downwind. The Animal bitched about losing his dope.

CHAPTER ELEVEN

Orders came down that night that ignited Duke's slow burn. He had been with the CRIP four lousy days, and on the fifth he found himself in the field again. He was not happy. How could he be? The field sucked. He wanted to concentrate totally on his own mission, but he was ordered to the bush and he went. He was a soldier and there was simply no way around certain orders. He could split, desert. That was an option, but he knew he wouldn't use it.

The rice paddies percolated with rain. At night the drops slapped the leaves of the trees and the brush in the bush. The men slept soaking, and skin began to rot. The rain hissed and ceased in the morning. During the day the men were drowning in a heat wave. Ripples rose from the water and the mud and the jungle floor. Sunlight stabbed through the canopy of forest. Sweat hung in heavy lumps which burst from their own weight, flowing and drenching the men.

A CRIP squad was attached to an infantry line company from Camp F-J's Light Infantry Brigade. A line company was defined by Duke as mud and misery, wet boots, bloody socks, and rotten feet. The company was operating north of Ho Nai. It was thought by the Brass that a contingent from CRIP would be an invaluable guide for the company. This was in fact absurd, for none of the CRIP soldiers had been in the area before. In the spirit of cooperation Lt. Ripley Masters, the Digger, sent Kim and Sergeant MacFee's squad. They marched with the first platoon, the company's point platoon.

The first platoon's lieutenant was a sensible sort: he did not order his men into any of the tunnels they found. He simply had them blown. It wasn't as bad as it could have been. At least the platoon leader wasn't a brown-bar boot Looey. He had lived long enough in the boonies to make his bar a silver one. Small comfort, tiny really, but better than none at all. And no comfort at all was the standard situation in Indian country.

The operation was an exaggerated sweep. Of course the standing search-and-destroy order was in effect: that was SOP. They swept and searched and destroyed for days that blurred into one sun-impacted, rain-soaked daze.

The CRIP soldiers trailed the platoon's fourth squad, last in line. They were thankful for they knew too well that many commanders might have ordered them to the point position. Sergeant MacFee humped near the lieutenant.

Duke and Jungle Jim spoke during the first days of the sweep of ways that Warren Buckle might be punished. They came to no concrete conclusion, made no feasible plan. They simply agreed that he must be punished, and this they already knew. Now after the humping and the grunting, they mainly bitched about how, when they extended, they had not planned on any more of this bullshit. Jungle Jim said that things *could* be worse, though. And Duke said yeah, they could be a lot better too.

Jungle Jim questioned Duke's reason for extending his tour in the war. "I knew those five dudes too, damn well. But in total honesty I doubt that I'd take such personal charge of hunting Buckle. I understand and approve, but don't know that I'd have done it. Why so much zeal?"

"My needs, Mr. Grogan, have nothing to do with any universal, explainable theory. They are my own and I

71

understand them. Nobody gives a final, total damn about us; whether we're dead or alive. Not Mom and Pop, not anyone who let any of us come here. Most of them don't even know it. The Army cosiders us grunts: weapons. The living and breathing part is expendable. Well, I give that last damn about myself and those dudes Buckle killed. And I'm gonna wipe that cocksucker out so my world will be a better place."

"To track and terminate one American male is one damn strange reason to stay in the war."

"I suppose you have a better one."

"Not sure actually. My journal has something to do with it. I send installments home regularly. I pack enough bullshit into it, somebody might be interested in reading it. The people intrigue me. They're getting screwed from all sides, including their own."

They looked at each other and agreed that any reason was damn strange.

Spec. Four Prick Peters had joined the CRIP only two days before going on this mission. He had come from three straight months in the field with a battalion reconnaissance platoon. He was now extremely pissed off. At times Duke thought the man unbalanced, gripped by quietly raging insanity. The sweat would bead up silver on his dark face. He would mumble and grumble incessantly, his teeth locked, full lips wet and moving: parting and puckering. He had been dealt a raw deal. His eyes flooded belligerence.

The Animal's jungle rot returned: oozing sores peeling flesh from his feet. "Freakin' Masters," he'd say. "That wimp is gonna pay."

A soldier from the platoon's fourth squad, Hawk, had struck up conversation with Duke and Jim in the first days of the sweep. The three secretly smoked dope evenings at dusk.

Hawk's nose and the angle of his eyes gave him his name. He carried a large thorn: bigger than an upholstery needle, smaller than a meat hook. He hated the bush; it was driving him mad. After he had dug his fighting hole for the night, he'd get stoned and ask the Duke to tear his right eye out while he slept. "Being half blind for life would be superior to this temporary hell," he intoned. He couldn't bring himself to do it, he'd tried. He'd be forever grateful to the Duke. "It would be an act of mercy," he implored. Duke understood, but it wasn't his game, out of his league. Jungle Jim felt the same.

Harry Pitts wondered how in the hell Hawk let himself get there. He seemed intelligent enough despite his irrational request. There were ways around the infantry. He could have signed up for a longer hitch, plenty of guys did it. There was no excuse for being a foot soldier if one was totally against it and possessed a shred of smarts. All of them bitched; but for most of them that could think, something somewhere within them went along with the idea. Then there were those like Hawk, willing to tear an eye out rather than stay. They had no business there, but they existed. Plain stupidity or simple ignorance, one of those might make for the excuse.

Mac overheard Hawk's nightly request, said he would oblige, be damn glad to do it. Hawk handed him the hook, tentatively, grimacing. Mac went right to it, slashed at the Hawk who twisted his head away. The thorn caught him on the cheekbone, ripped clear to his ear, then sank inside: the gash deep and ragged and bloody. Hawk blubbered and held his face. Mac offered to take another slice. Hawk stumbled to the medic, the thorn sticking from his ear. Duke thought Mac and Warren Buckle should meet.

The lieutenant put Hawk on a supply ship in the morning. The Hawk flew away and never returned. Duke watched the helicopter go, wishing he were on it. The field was a stinkhole full of idiots leading grunts from fuck-up to fuck-up. Flying over it, away from a line outfit, was like being snatched from

73

the jaws of a tiger. Word came that Hawk took a burst of three to stay out of the field. Reenlisted for a superior position. Three more years in Uncle Sam's green. The field was a bad awful place.

The sun rose red burning away the clouds. P-38 can openers tore into the olive drab C-Ration cans. The men ate in a hush. Bits of burning C-4 plastic explosive boiled coffee instantly. Duke felt his armpit: a foreign lump, a mushy clump, a slight sting. He knew what it was and shuddered. He stripped off his shirt and grabbed the squeeze bottle of insect repellent. He raised his left elbow past his ear and squirted the bug juice under his arm. He watched the fat, black, bloodsucking leech fall dead, down in the sludge. He smashed it underfoot, smearing his own blood on his jungle-boot sole. He shuddered again.

During breakfast the men saw the smoke swirling above the paddies. Mac volunteered his group for reconnaissance which pleased none of the CRIP soldiers.

They moved out just inside the tree line around the paddy to the edge of the hamlet. The maneuver didn't take long. NVA cadre were recruiting for the VC. Several bodies were strewn about, smoldering. Some of the huts were smoking ash heaps; two NVA soldiers ignited another. They needed the hamlet's young men. About a half dozen of them sat stoically, bound in rope they had hewn themselves. The rest had fled. The burning carcasses could have been male or female. The NVA cadre were shouting, imploring: some trash concerning hearts and minds.

The CRIP soldiers crept away. Moving back through the trees, Duke watched Kim. The interpreter was a small man, he was Vietnamese. He was a handsome man always flashing a wide ready smile. His wife was very young and beautiful.

She lived in Ho Nai with their infant daughter. Phuong was Kim's second wife. He had told Jungle Jim who informed Duke. His first wife had been hanged in flames outside Tay Ninh. She had refused the sexual advances of a village chief who was VC. He and some of his band hanged her. First the chief beat her, tearing the clothes from her body. Then he shoved a burning length of bamboo into her, ramming it up to her middle parts. They covered her with petrol, hanged her by her neck and ignited her. She died horribly. Kim was very young then and the village chief was the first VC he killed. Duke figured the chief and Warren Buckle were somehow related. Kim moved gracefully, methodically now in anticipation. He did not smile.

The patrol made it back and Mac reported to the lieutenant. The platoon moved out soon, CRIP soldiers on point. The men dispersed and the march was silent. This surprised Duke, pleasantly.

The Animal went first from the trees. He gripped a bayonet with his teeth, his purple scars glistening. He voluntarily crawled, then crouched and sprang upon the enemy sentry cutting the life from him. The Animal acted silently but the sentry shouted his last shout. The platoon charged in teams, surprise on its side, doing most of the shooting.

The NVA started to flee, firing sporadically. One cadre shot one of the bound young men in the back of the head. Kim killed him before he blasted another.

The NVA soldiers who fled into the fields were strafed, mowed down dead. Two were trapped in the village. Duke and Jungle Jim shot one in the legs. He crawled into a hut and they heard screams. Kim joined them and shouted into the hut. *"Chieu hoi."* The wounded soldier shouted back over and over: *"Chieu hoi, chieu hoi!"* The man sought to surrender, so they carefully entered the hut. The man held an ancient withered woman, pistol at her head. He demanded to be treated decently. Kim told him he had nothing to fear.

"The Americans are here," he said in English. The old woman scrambled away shrieking. The wounded man lurched forward from where he lay, his legs bleeding. Kim shot him in the face, blew out the back of his head; claimed it was obvious the fucker wanted that woman and tried to give chase. The man dropped dead. Duke admired Kim's efficiency.

Men of the platoon's third squad had wounded and captured the one remaining enemy soldier. Two men from the first squad had been hit and the lieutenant radioed for a med-evac.

Kim suggested leaving the captured cadre to the young men of the hamlet: those teenagers who had just been freed. "The hamlet would be deserted," he explained. "The VC would exact severe reprisals on anyone that stayed. The place would be torched and any living thing destroyed. The young males will eagerly deal with this man." He predicted that since their homes were useless they would likely enlist in the ARVN. The young women would take refuge in a city, most of them ultimately becoming prostitutes. The old women were close to death and this simply brought them closer. There were no old men. The children that survived would join the emaciated hordes roaming the streets of whatever city their mothers settled in. Kim spoke matter-of-factly. Duke found his speech as efficient as his actions.

The lieutenant dispatched a patrol for body count, then inspected the ruins. Flames and ashes, dead animals and charred human carcasses. A hog rutted around and in one of the fried black bodies. Children tried to chase it off; they didn't cry, they appeared dull. The scene stank, as usual. For some reason the lieutenant stared at Duke who was assisting the rifle platoon's medic, aiding an eighteen-year-old Pfc. with a sucking chest wound. Duke looked back at the lieutenant and pointed to the captured NVA man. Then he—the Duke—drew his fingers across his own throat. He told himself he shouldn't become part of this; there was

76

something else to consider, a priority he had made paramount. No need to get in deep and tight with these light infantrymen. But he was there, involved to an extent. He thought he should take a stand. He made the sign again. His fingers were sticky with the Pfc.'s blood.

When the chopper had flown, the platoon saddled up and marched into the jungle toward a battalion firebase nested in the mud of a riverbank. The captured enemy protested ferociously as the soldiers departed without him. His protests were loud but not for long. The teenage males he had come to conscript tore him to bits: his head rolled.

The rain dropped early drenching the men, cooling them. They struggled through deep green jungle. The direct rays of the sun did not strike them; muted ricocheted rays shot everywhere. The heat hovered oppressively thick above the jungle floor. The hacking and cutting of dense, monster vegetation was slow and tedious and constant. The men were beat and hot and dull and slaving away: an inexorable file, mute and sluglike. The clunking cuts and swaths of the machetes, the brush breaking, the heavy breathing: Duke heard it, they all heard it and knew anyone else in the area might hear it too. But the rain came early in the afternoon cooling the men and muffling their march.

The jungle thinned and they were able to sheath the machetes. They walked. One foot in front of the other. Brains in their boots. Again. Over and over. Always. They walked through a clearing. Crippled and rusting, in that clearing sat an old French tank: a gray relic, rain-pelted, long abandoned and useless. As he trudged past it, Duke considered the Frenchmen who might have died in it or near it. He wondered if they had known what the hell they were doing, or if they were just doing. How many helicopters and tanks and jets would his—Duke's—Army leave to rot when it finally pulled out? And what soldiers would march past them wondering just who the hell the Americans were. A dead Warren Buckle stuck in his dead Chinook would be a decent addition to the debris.

The rain stopped abruptly. A trooper from the fourth squad climbed through the gathering mist aboard the tank. He yanked at the turret cover; it creaked. Then the booby trap exploded, shearing the metal cover and the trooper's arm. From the encasing jungle rose clouds of insects; they swarmed with a great humming racket. They blotted the sky, blocking vision. They buzzed and dove and descended upon the platoon panicking the men. A black blanket of bugs, stinging and flying and dashing themselves to death against the men who retreated into the trees. The storm of bugs raged about the clearing and the tank and the trooper rolling and screaming inaudibly, his mouth jammed with bugs. The insects covered the severed arm like ants on a candy cane. Then the swarm dissipated as suddenly as it had formed. No man understood what aspect of Oriental nature he had experienced. It had simply been frightening and mysterious, the jungle.

"Grisly," Duke called it. "Goddamned grisly jungle."

"Gook bugs," added Jungle Jim.

The medic rushed to the trooper. The fourth squad leader cursed the trooper, a notorious souvenir hunter. The lieutenant called for a med-evac helicopter. The trooper stopped howling. He lay quietly in shock and morphine stupor.

Lizards hissed deep gravel rasps. Rhythmic and regular. Long sound, short. Long sound, short. The men knew them by the sound to be Fuck-You Lizards. The sound of the things rose to a din. A troop of monkeys chattered from the trees and lush underbush. They threw nuts and stones and sticks and bones from the jungle thickness. The debris fell short mostly, but random chunks landed weakly around the tank, bouncing off it, floating to the floor of the clearing.

"Spooky," said Duke, and Jungle Jim nodded agreement.

Animal said he didn't like the freaking noise. He started the shooting. Several men from the fourth squad joined in: mowing down monkeys, blasting them out of the trees, sending survivors screeching deeper into the jungle.

The march for the firebase resumed. The platoon rendezvoused with its company on a low swampbank of the Rice River. The rifle company filed along the bank. Elevation gradually rose and the earth changed from swamp to red mud. The river shimmered sometimes a shallow clear blue, often a deep brackish brown.

At the firebase, the company was assigned a section of perimeter and dug neck-deep fighting holes. A mess tent slouched near the river and as the sky streaked purple, hot chow was served. The men of the first platoon were dog-tired but each clopped across the sludge field, eager for the hot food. The CRIP soldiers joined them.

Duke and Jungle Jim, Animal and Kim, Mac and Prick Peters lounged at the water's edge gobbling chicken and vegetables. They ate like orphans. When they were full, they smoked cigarettes and stared at the river rushing soft and slow, glimmering. Mac extracted his harmonica, a Hohner, key of E, his favorite sound. He first blew "Dixie," a slow, drawn, melancholy "Dixie." Soldiers within earshot fell silent. And for a time the evening gleamed.

He made more music: haunting Southern earth songs, some familiar, some not. But the men understood each strain and whine. All the melodies merging to a single hymn for all the simple things they had once known and longed for again. If they could only know these little pleasures another time, they would savor each golden moment permitted them. At the wane of that day, with the fading sun and the river and the music and full bellies, each soldier heard in his heart a song that told him what was important and what was not.

Music moved Harry Pitts. The music moved him and he

drifted home to the mountains of Maine and the woman in college down in Vermont on the shores of Champlain. They had ceased correspondence, temporarily, Ann had said. She needed time. She didn't understand: six more months in that unhappy land. When he thought of her, which was often and confusedly, he wondered why her once-crystal image had faded, the memory of her vivid in his heart but blurred in his mind. There were many things he was no longer sure of. His time in the war had put to rest certain fears and raised new ones. After the war what would he do? How would he embark on the rest of his life? And how did she fit?

He speculated about going home. He *was* going home. Delayed for now, but he would go home. Might be in a box, but he could not imagine that. So. Back to New England? Southern Maine? Vermont? Ann liked Vermont. And what to do? Go back to college. A possibility. Go to work for the Forest Service maybe. His father could get him on easily. Hell, he'd be a *veteran*. Be a Forest Service man like his father. The idea didn't sound bad. Maybe study forestry. That would at least be a direction, which was more than he'd ever taken. All his backcountry experience, from boyhood on, might make him a natural. Give him a good excuse to dodge sport hunting and fishing too, which he never particularly enjoyed. But he couldn't picture living back there without eating game. He liked binoculars mostly, but maybe he could take a deer for winter. He would probably do it alone, however, which he would like. Who in hell would want to hunt with a Forest Service man? Fuckers must be game wardens.

Get married, go to college, get on with the Forest Service. Live a decent life. This seemed like only a dream viewed from far away. Maybe he'd skip the college part. But who knew then? Perspective might change, shift to low gear. Pitts wanted the plan to sound better than it did to him. What he wanted was a life he could enjoy, with the woman he loved. Sounded simple enough but he knew that few people achieved the dream. He wanted that good life and knew he ought to. So what was he doing on the edge of this mud field near this river half a planet from home? He told himself he knew why he was there.

I'll be all right, he said to himself. Soon as I'm finished here, I'll go on home and be all right. There were things you did because you felt you needed to do them. When I leave here I'll be able to explain things to myself. But he tried to picture himself explaining an idea he was unable to articulate to Ann. Taking a walk somewhere, perhaps canoeing. Under it all he might see shit and death, everywhere. He'd try to say I love you, hope it was enough to keep her around.

I know what I'm doing, he said to himself. "And I'll damn well get home," he said out loud.

Jungle Jim said, "What?"

Pitts didn't get a chance to answer. High hammering cracks obliterated Mac's harmonica music.

A helicopter, a gunship, chopped the dim sky spewing red death. Duke glanced at the CRIP soldiers and hugged the earth. So did the rest. His heart moved like a machine gun as he watched chowline stragglers struck down and strafed, writhing and bleeding and breaking apart. He tried to burrow into the mud. He heard cries and curses.

Duke didn't trust infantry line companies: too cumbersome, too many opportunities for blunder—petty and gross. Some large dipstick was always asking for your water, begging. The sorrier soldiers shed equipment once it got too heavy. Too many of the officers were idiot children. The Infantry Line Company, Queen of Battle: The queen all right, the one on the bottom, the one getting fucked. Stink and blood, death in the mud. That was a major factor steering him to Recon. The gunship did not make another pass. For the moment the men were stunned. The confusion was usual.

Medics tended those who were hit. The soldiers took to

their fighting holes. Machine guns and grenade launchers and rockets were trained on the sky. The colonel, the battalion chief at the radio, received answer for his outrage: a mistake, erroneous grid coordinates, wrong direction. The pilot noticed too late from the near night sky. Over and out. Static. The colonel put the word out and the men griped: grim.

A friend of one who had died—a friend, not simply a buddy—approached the CRIP soldiers. His smooth face was wisps of whiskers smeared with blood and tears. In a fit of racist fury he condemned Kim. "Why not you, you fuckin' slant?" he screamed. "Why them and not a goddamn gook? It's your stinking war!"

Kim had been in the war forever. He was indelicate. "Your chopper, your bullets," he said. "Your pilot."

Jungle Jim moved toward Kim. The men were friends. But the young soldier was overcome. He hung his head and Kim touched his shoulder. The American wiped his nose and his lips and walked away, dully.

That helpless feeling, inability to control a senseless situation, invaded the Duke and shook Harry Pitts.

Four dead men: one a lifer, a family man; three not yet twenty-one. The dust-off would come with daylight. The night hung dark and deep and heavy. Full body bags clumped, vague shapes on the landing zone. Four dead men: victims of friendly fire. Somehow it seemed sadder than killed in action.

Duke thought of Warren Buckle. It would be no surprise if Buckle had been the pilot, not likely but no surprise. That son-of-a-bitch would be surprised one day though. One day damn soon.

The morning was gray. Duke hadn't slept and felt distant and gritty, rocks in his eyes, sand on his teeth. The men walked, eyes to the dirt: bitter. A few of the more cynical soldiers, those who had seen more battle, started the jokes:

"Those boys got their last meal blown right out of their bellies. Stuff was hardly chewed."

"Just like the fuckin' Army. Indian givin' chumps! Hand out something halfway decent, say a hot meal, watch your ass. Sure as shit they gonna rip it right back."

"Damn right! And they don't care your guts is in the way. Shee-it. Sorry 'bout that."

Duke half-listened. The words might be different, but the attitude always the same. He was familiar with it.

All things were fodder for jokes, the more horrid the incident, the more brutal the humor. Tales about combat and terror and death: these were the things to laugh about. And fear. Sometimes the laughter was so hard and strained it sounded insane: cries without tears.

The CRIP soldiers bathed in the Rice River. Jungle Jim swam laps, bank to bank. The Animal tossed a granade into the water and killed fish. The fish floated to the surface and he heaved in another. The sound was muffled but Duke felt the concussion on his lower extremities. He swam away. He and Jungle Jim left the water as the Animal blew more fish. They fried what looked like big bream and tasted liked perch.

The Animal crouched barefoot on the riverbank eating fish and bitching to Duke. His feet were rotten and stinking, covered with mushy ulcers. "Gook sores," he called them. He complained that the condition had all but gone away since leaving the bush to join the CRIP. "That ghoul Masters will pay," he vowed, again.

Prick Peters added that although he hardly knew the lieutenant, he thought ill of the honky bastard for assigning him to this mission. "Me not two days in Ho Nai, out of the boonies. I tell you, my man. If I get that rot, I'm gonna skin somma him." Sun flashed off the blade of his bayonet. He was thin and deep black: caramel eyes in a face of anthracite coal.

The first platoon lieutenant informed Mac that the battalion would move to another war zone. A helicopter was due to carry the CRIP soldiers back to Camp F-J. The lieutenant left. Mac told the men and their spirits lifted.

They strapped on their gear and marched to the landing zone. They climbed aboard the chopper, the dust-off ship. The CRIP soldiers made the trip to camp, keeping the four dead grunts company.

"Sonuvabitch," said Duke, kneeling next to a bodybag.

"It's a ride," said Animal. "You rather stay?"

Duke lighted a cigarette. The helicopter took off. He saw Jungle Jim watching him. He knew his friend understood what he—Duke—was remembering. He choked the dead scouts from his mind and zeroed in on Warren Buckle. Too many obstacles were hindering the formation of a workable plan of execution. He had not been with the CRIP long, but much had happened. He had hoped for more freedom. Time was necessary. And simplification. He had the time.

As the helicopter descended he was reminded of an assault on a hot LZ: that time of terror and overcoming terror, that time of gathering strength and doing more than thinking. The approach was the worst time. Taking fire and feeling helpless. Listening to the doorgunners strafe the surface, guns smoking steel and spewing red lead. Terrific vibration shaking the machines and the sky and the men. Shouts chopped and drowned in the waves of wind. Leaping into the vortex and knowing—or hoping to return from it. A terrible time, a time God damned. A time for courage perhaps. Now he hoped that he would never do the thing again. Only be reminded of it.

And why did that cruddy cocksucker leave us? And why a Chinook?

84

CHAPTER TWELVE

The helicopter landed at Camp F-J and Sergeant MacFee's team disembarked. They decided to catch a hot meal at the Consolidated Mess and walked, bent under their rucksacks, through the midday heat.

A line of soldiers in clean uniforms and black boots stretched along the side of the mess hall. A red-faced, pogue major, starched and shined, screeched at a new replacement. He dressed the kid down for some infringement regarding the uniform of the day. He yanked the scared private out of line and railed, spitting and turning redder, puffing. The private stood at rigid attention as the fat major continued his rant, like a snotnose brat tormenting his little sister.

The men of the CRIP watched a short while, then turned, about-faced and marched away ripping the dust helmet high. Better to forgo a hot meal than risk the possibility of murder. None had to speak it, each simply retreated, conscious, like the Duke, of his dirt-streaked jungle suit, his mud-gray boots, his pack, his bandoliers of ammunition, his M-16.

Duke recalled Warren Buckle's sporty flight suit, clean and smooth and crisscrossed with zippers; his shiny zippered jungle boots.

They marched to the brigade communication complex and radioed Lt. Ripley Masters to dispatch transportation. They leaned against their rucksacks, smoking and waiting in the heat. Duke noted a truckload of burning shit spewing

85

black smoke. He wanted to muster Cpl. Red Green to perhaps catch a ride to Bien Hoa on his crapwagon. But he remembered that Mac was around and thought better of it.

Nada Garcia drove the deuce-and-a-half, the machine-gun mount bare, to pick up Mac's team. Nada Garcia was a wildman. "A wacky wetback. He swam across the border and drowned his brain," the Animal claimed.

"A Mexican maniac," said Mac.

"A twisted taco bender, a crazed caballero. High all the time." Jungle Jim said it and from what he'd observed the Duke had to agree.

"One dumb spick." The Animal again.

The truck roared up the road into Ho Nai. The scrubby little town looked good to the Duke. He would rather wade in a cesspool than hump in the bush with a line company.

The street bustled with people popping fireworks and parading around as paper dragons. They made a clanging reedy music and carried crucifixes and banners and bright red and yellow bunting. The women and girls wore their best *áo-dàis*, some colorful and filmy, others crisp white. Even the children, the unwashed beggars, seemed scrubbed clean. As the season of Tet loomed closer, holidays were numerous. This was some Caodaist holy day. The Caodai religion blended Buddhism, Confucianism, and Christianity into a multisymbolic, complex doctrine. Saint Joan and Sun Yat-sen. Caodai had also been a fierce military faction against the Japanese. The independent army had been both with and against the Viet Minh, the French; now dissipated, its remnants were absorbed in the ARVN. Pagodas and steeples: Ho Nai had both. Kim explained it and Duke decided the incongruous Christian influence must have given rise to the merger.

Celebrating bands of people clumped everywhere: standing, running, marching in files, careening in Lambrettas. Music and laughter, applause and incense.

Nada Garcia was impatient and nervous, skittery. He

leaned on the horn, his dark face sweating, his eyes surprised, like fried eggs in an oily pan. He shouted in Spanish and Mac told him to take things easy. Nada bellowed incomprehensively, drooling. He floored the gas pedal.

The truck lurched forward decking the troops in the bed. It smashed two Lambrettas and knocked seven pedestrians flat. People scattered from the street like sand in the wind. Nada laughed shaking his fist out the window. He worked the gears and raced to the fort.

Mac stepped from the cab. "Mexican Maniac," he repeated.

Prick Peters christened Nada a goofy greaser. "Surprised that fool is still alive."

Kim acted detached but now was dejected. He would return to check the damage. Duke and Jungle Jim said they'd join him. Duke called for the Doc.

Prick refused. "Ain't no brother of mine." Prick Peters was a young blood from Oakland. He joined the army to escape the poverty and violence. But his blackness ran deep and told him he would return to help eradicate the degradation so it wouldn't have to be escaped. He was away from his own poverty, but the violence had erupted around him on the other side of the planet.

"Just who in hell is your brother, Prick?" asked Duke. "Who do you go to bat for?"

"Not none of them, sucker. And maybe not you, Chuck. Why you so interested in these people here in No-Man's 'Nam?"

"You see, there are Martians among us and they've got it in for us all—black, white, red, yellow—all. Cosmic Sappers. If we don't take a common stand against them, they'll wipe us all out. We need to watch out for the people and fuck the Martians."

"Martians! Hell, I know you've wasted gooks. How so?"

"Some gooks are Martians. You can tell by the ears or

sometimes the clothes. Clothes are easier, black p.j.s, but they don't always wear them."

"Don't mess with me, Duke." Prick Peters elbowed past Kim.

Duke, Jim, and Kim drove the jeep back to the scene where a hamlet chief told Kim to fuck off. They drove to the fort, walked across the street, and ordered beers. Duke drank a barrel of the stuff.

CHAPTER THIRTEEN

Harry Pitts ambled away from the beer store to the evening quiet of the deserted market place. He opened his mail.

He had received a letter from his father who always spoke in terms of nature and seasons. The late fall mountains of Maine had been a blaze of brilliant color. But that particular fall season had been vividly amiss, the first he had not hiked, and fished through a portion of, with his sole son. The father concluded by allowing that he understood soldiering. He had done it himself. But a man must be careful, duty put in perspective. "A man's gotta do what a man's gotta do" was merely a line from a movie spoken by a shallow character inhabiting a make-believe world. Pitts's relationship with his sire had always been a reticent one. This insight was peculiar.

There had also been a disturbing word from his lady back home: his woman who had promised to wait. So many young ladies promise to be true, and Harry Pitts, like all soldiers, knew he had the one that would. Her words were painful and careful and talked of time. Time was all there was and she hated it. Time was a tearing force and a mending one. What would she do with it: this extra time, this precious time? She had already nearly drowned in the deep lonely nights of the deepest, loneliest, longest year of her life. She might comprehend; she might stick this last stretch out. If she only knew why. If he might explain, she would try ever so hard to truly understand. She would write no more unless word came her way, word she could grasp, word of light shed on this nightmare. Word of a day. Again, she hated time but knowing might heal her enough to smile.

Harry Pitts strolled past the empty stalls and stared up at the sinking sun. He blinked because her eyes were in every fading ray.

He felt like eating a ration of shit. But he walked quicker through the gathering dusk to old man Gue, to opium, to rest.

He smoked one pipe and left. He walked unswervingly to the hootch and gathered a sleeping mat and headrest. He spread them on the porch outside, propped his weapon and stretched out.

A full moon rose bathing the compound with a silver white light. The stars were a dome of silver dust. Fireworks of the war were far away. A hint of wind whined.

He floated, sliding through vanished moments. He looked into the past and his heart swelled. Then it shrank and cracked. The lady and the five dead scouts: which was pivotal, which the major factor? He shouldn't have to ask. But time and distance had done work, much work.

She was dark and wonderful, delicate and strong. She was a pool to soothe him. She was rare and she loved him. Now there was great distance between them: a lifetime apart. She was suffering; she was an ocean of tears. She had been a fresh-water spring at his center feeding and cleansing. A clear, pure stream rushing: slowly smoothing gravel to marble. She was warm and deep and part of the earth. She was all the gems sparkling. She had been the precious fire burning and molding and making a man. She needed to be with him. And he should have joined her. But he did not.

Dudley Worth was thin and blond, tattooed red and blue: Boasting death before dishonor and his respect for dear old mother. A mechanic, a racer, a lover of cars. A Brooklyn boy, auto salvage his game. Smoked dope by the ton, his eyes a bit shady. A damn good soldier, as they say. Saved Duke's ass more than one time. He had a lady back on the block and a junkyard dog. He was drafted at nineteen, went without a bitch, volunteered for Recon. Dead at twenty-two, his face bashed to bits. He was worth ten Warren Buckles.

Carl Diel was a Hoosier. Tall and rawboned, a farmer back home. He seemed slow, but that was his way. He liked to analyze first, then he might act. No time for figuring when that frag smacked his back. He tried to move fast but there just wasn't time. No time to act. Indiana might miss him. State should have kept him tilling the soil, making things grow. He understood dirt and dung in a way that most people don't. He knew them as a basic mix, a fine substance. Torn in two in Oriental grass: no way for a Hoosier farm boy to go.

Rat Malloy sported beads. Wrapped the string of colored stones twice about his neck, a peace symbol dangling. A Pennsylvania thinker from the Pocono Mountains, Rat and Duke had much in common. They both agreed the time they had spent in higher education was close to wasted. Pitts had abandoned the institution. Rat had finished though. A fucking college boy! Came to the war just to see it, get some real education. Joined the LRRP for a different view. He discovered he hated the war, but he fought to survive, to protect. And when he went home he would make moves against it, tell folks about it. First he and the Duke were to spend time in the mountains, each showing the other his own. Rat had a rat nose, his teeth stuck out. But Rat had a mind that clicked all the time. His letters were poetry, his ideas clear. Duke had wept when he saw Rat's mind go, leaking into the earth along with his brains and chunks of his skull.

The Ox was huge. A tough Tennessee grit, a man you could count on. He knew he would make it. He was Regular Army. "If one man can do it," he liked to say, "then I'll make two." He didn't know the meaning of tired or quit. A source of strength and stability, a man to smile and push on. A man of the old stout heart, deep and strong as a river. One shot took him out: An AK-47 slug slammed into that heart bursting his pump as he smiled. He could have crushed Warren Buckle.

Zap Rossi wore a long mustache, black and curly. A New York City cop who got drafted: only one he knew of. He didn't see the point. Who the hell could? He carried a picture of his wife, had seen her in Hawaii on R&R. He'd grin a good grin and tell Duke there'd be no police work back in the World for him. He was a well-trained medic and planned to take more schooling, be a Registered Nurse. He'd laugh his deep laugh. "A nurse, that's what I'll be. I'll put 'em together instead of blow 'm apart. A nurse by Christ! That's what I'll be." But he lost his head. The top of it gone, pounded to pieces while aiding the Ox whom he'd thought only wounded. Damn Warren Buckle.

Then there were the doorgunners. He didn't even know them. One man's legs shot all to hell, the other dead, shot through the head.

His lady, his lover he had known from childhood, from the beginning. There was everything and nothing to tell her. She was It, the One. When he thought of the fine things: the clear and the dear levels of living, he thought of her.

When he thought of them.

The five dead scouts, their friendships so strangely intense. Absolute trust, no man may fold. Strong and together down to the last. His memory remembered and remembered; they became more than they had been: heroes welded to his mind's eye.

And Ann, what could she say? He could feel her tears. How could he stay? Ease back home Harry Pitts. There's nothing to fear. The five scouts, so large, swollen in death. Which was pivotal, which the major factor? He shouldn't have to ask. But he did.

A weight moved over his left arm. It nuzzled, gnawing and

tugging him. It dissipated his dreams and drew him awake. He gazed at a fat rat: as big as a bulldog, damp and covering his forearm and fist. His blood just naturally froze. His heart heaved and pounded again. His eyes popped wide. He still couldn't budge: frozen with fear. Time stopped; it seemed forever, like a dentist drilling an exposed nerve for many moments. He gained a healthy respect for eternity and wrenched free, flinging the thing. He snatched his .16 and emptied it into that fat paddy rat. He shuddered as he shot. That rat came apart.

The commotion shocked the compound awake. Men grabbed guns and manned the bunkers. Men tripped and sprawled and cursed. Men hit the dirt, hugging the earth. Men leaned together, locked and loaded. The compound settled, silent and dark. A wisp of smoke from twenty ejected cartridges wafted. The rat's naked, twisted tail twitched.

Duke calmed. He felt drained and stupid: a doped-up fool, outright folly.

CHAPTER FOURTEEN

"I've got what you need." Jungle Jim sat down next to Duke. "You seem a mite jumpy this evening." Jungle Jim produced a pint bottle of Jack Daniel's Tennessee Sour Mash Whiskey.

Duke was smoking a cigarette, trying to calm down. "Where in hell did you get that?"

"Came in the mail today." He twisted off the cap, handed the bottle over. "Be my guest."

Duke took a short pull. Didn't often get treated to whiskey. And never Jack Daniel's. Burned a little. But a sweet burn. He handed the bottle back.

The night was quiet, and still very clear.

They drank for a while in silence.

The day and the night were turning into a marathon of body abuse. Duke had noticed how he had been getting fucked up regularly here lately. Matter of availability. He had owned a taste for alcohol long enough to have lived through hundreds of hangovers. But today was an Olympic effort. Bottles of beer at *papa-san's* store, opium at Gue's den, and now a bottle of whiskey with Jungle Jim. Just a pint, but that would more than do the job. Low tolerance. Duke would likely jack his tolerance back up back in the World.

"You'll die drunk." He could hear Ann's sister Mary warning him.

Sister Mary was married to a dentist, nice guy, easygoing. Harry Pitts liked to eat dinner at their place, he and Ann, because of the limitless free booze. The drinks were not exactly free, however; he had to put up with Sister Mary. Sitting there at the round maple table in the dining room the size of a barn. Mary in her black dress, sucking spaghetti. The dentist, Ethan, sipping wine. And Mary laughing occasionally. Pitts consuming copious portions of wine. Last leave before the war.

"So you're actually going to that war?" Sister Mary dabbed her lips with a red napkin.

"Apparently." Pitts sipped Bardolino.

"Apparently? What do you mean, apparently? I thought it was a conclusion." More spaghetti. "Perhaps there's hope for you yet, Harry."

"How about some bourbon?" Pitts smiled around the table.

"You want drugs?" Sister Mary seemed to be speaking to somebody in her spaghetti bowl. "Ethan's got drugs, legal ones. You could get sick, be physically unfit for combat duty. Something like that."

"Thanks, but it's too late for that sort of thing. I don't know that I could live with myself."

"Harry, believe me, it's not you I'm thinking of. It's my little sister Ann. She is obviously hooked on you, though I've never understood it. I know she would rather you be here, or anywhere other than some goddamn war in China."

"Vietnam."

"Vietnam, shee-itnam, what's the difference? It makes no sense to me. I mean, who gives a shit about those people? I should think you'd care more about Ann here. You think you'll like fucking Chinese whores over in shee-itnam?" Sister Mary stabbed a hunk of garlic bread with her fork.

Ann said, "We don't need too much more of that, Mary."

Pitts said, "You got any bourbon?"

Ethan, the dentist, sucked his teeth and motioned to the

bar behind him. Pitts hardly ever heard Ethan talk around Sister Mary.

Pitts went for the whiskey.

"That stuff will kill you," Sister Mary said. "The way you drink it."

Pitts, holding up the Jack Daniel's, said: "Anybody else?"

Ethan raised his hand.

Pitts made the drinks with ice and water.

"Harry." Sister Mary dropped a slab of pork on her plate. "Everybody gets out of this thing. I know Ethan could swing it. He's got good friends that are M.D.s. I mean why risk your ass? For Christ sake let the niggers go. Why you?"

Pitts brought Ethan a drink, carried his own to his place, sat, drank. This was the first time he'd heard Sister Mary use the term nigger.

"Well?" Sister Mary glared.

Pitts said: "I like to hang out with niggers."

Ethan laughed.

"I don't see what the fuck is so funny." Sister Mary glared at Ethan.

Ethan drank.

Ann said to her sister: "Harry is going, Mary, and he's leaving here in a few days. I don't like the idea much but he *is* going. We're simply going to have to accept the fact. It's not going to be simple, but Harry and I will handle the situation. We will have to try anyway."

"Well." Sister Mary. "Well, I think he's one dumb son of a bitch."

Pitts said: "What did you say about my momma?"

Ethan laughed.

Mary glared.

Pitts finished his drink. "Another belt, Ethan?"

Sister Mary glared.

"No thanks," Ethan said.

Pitts went for another.

"Only an idiot would go to this war." Sister Mary sliced

into her pork. "I'm telling you people, I seem to be the only voice that makes any sense on this matter. Harry gives me smartass answers when all I'm trying to do is make the twerp hear the sound of sense."

Pitts came back with his whiskey. He thought that Sister Mary was probably correct. But sense, the sound of it, the lack of it, the possession of it, had nothing to do with his going to the war.

"I'm only trying to help," Sister Mary said, chewing.

"I know," Ann said, almost a whisper.

"If you two were married, Harry would be different." Sister Mary looked at Ann. "I'm only trying to help."

Pitts said: "Maybe you should have served fish and rice, help me get accustomed to shee-itnamese food."

"Jesus," Mary said, glaring. "You're an ass."

"No." Pitts polished off his drink. "No I'm not. And my name is Harry."

"I don't have to put up with this!" Sister Mary threw her red linen napkin at Pitts. The table was too long, distance too great. Her toss landed the napkin on a candle, toppled it. She jumped up, told Ethan to fix the goddamn candle.

Pitts said: "If I can have another drink I promise to shut up." He got up and made himself another. He figured she wouldn't give him too much shit, him a soldier going off to war and all. Like it or not Sister Mary had to see it. He carried his drink back to the table.

"For a young fellow," Sister Mary said, "you drink too much."

Pitts raised his glass, smiled at Ann, took a sip. Hell, he liked to drink. He couldn't drink as much as he liked in the Army. Maybe the Army was good for something. He could not be always drunk, or in the process of achieving inebriation. That is, as long as he remained a peon, private soldier, private first class and such. Make sergeant and you could function smashed all the time. A hell of a lot of them seemed to. The trouble with drinking seemed to be the cumulative effect, the long haul. So Pitts had miles to go. His father told him that you drank to celebrate; you drank to forget bad times; and if nothing was going on you drank to start something. There was always an excuse, a reason.

"You think it's going to be like the movies?" Sister Mary arched a painted eyebrow.

"What?" Pitts was hoping she was about finished.

"This war. You think it's going to be like John Wayne kicking ass, never running out of bullets, never getting hurt?"

Pitts was amazed. What did he have to say to this crazy woman? What could she want to hear? How about: I'll kill a thousand men, bite off their tongues. I'll cut out their hearts and feed them to dogs. I'll know the taste of blood and the texture of guts. Maybe Mary wanted something like that. "The movies? I don't think it will be like the movies, no. I'll be there a year, a movie lasts about ninety minutes, two hours. You know John Wayne got killed at the end of *The Sands of Iwo Jima*, his best war flick."

"Harry!" Mary slapped the table top. "You're turning into a real jerk!"

Pitts turned to Ann. "Do you think my mother will be disappointed?"

Ann said: "I think she had clues."

"And you?"

"I've always been disappointed in you Harry. But then I've always set you rather too high in the scheme of things. It's like I'm disappointed you're not Apollo or Thor or Pecos Bill. Dr. Zhivago would be nice, too. But I know you're Harry and I'll settle for you." The smile, the eyes.

"Thank you." Pitts got up, kissed her forehead.

"What a crock of crap!" Sister Mary again.

"I think I'll have one for the road." Pitts headed for the bar.

"Drink all you want." Sister Mary rose, walked over to Pitts. "You two stay here tonight. Stay the rest of your nights. I'll call Mom, tell her Ann's staying with me." Sister

Mary kissed Harry Pitts, hugged him.

Pitts detected traces of tears around her painted eyes.

"You're foolish, Harry." Sister Mary held his shoulders. "You just don't know what you are doing. I don't really know either, but I know it is foolish, at best. But I'll shut up now. You two use the guest room." She walked away. "Come on, Ethan."

Ethan went, waved good night.

Sister Mary said: "Harry, watch the whiskey. You'll die drunk."

Jungle Jim said: "Tastes mellow, doesn't it?"

Duke Pitts swallowed some Jack Daniel's and said yes.

They talked about women. Not the broad badass snatches of tale, the obscene regularity of male bullshit. But simple stories of remembrance, of longing, of trying to know.

"We used to go on picnics," Duke said. "I liked to watch her eat. We would be in the mountains, summertime mountains. I liked the way her mouth looked. I liked to watch her smile, outside. It made me feel good. I don't know why."

"We liked to go to the beach." Jungle Jim stared into the night. "The beach was special for us. We didn't live near one. No oceans in Ohio. Really we only went twice. We'd drive all the way over to Virginia Beach. There would be a crowd of us and we'd camp. I liked seeing her body up against the ocean on the sand at sunset. Made me feel special that she was with me."

The whiskey was gone, bottle drained.

"I'm drunk," Duke Pitts announced. "On top of everything else, I'm drunk."

"I am with you, mate."

"What the hell do we do if we get hit?"

Jungle Jim said: "Die drunk."

99

CHAPTER FIFTEEN

That morning Animal sat in his green skivvies in the early yellow sun. He leaned against a pillar on the compound porch, his festering feet propped on a sandbag. Said he hoped the sun would suck the poison and dry the jungle rot. He sharpened and honed and oiled his bayonet.

In the center of the courtyard, beneath the flagpole, lay strewn the guts and bones of Lt. Ripley Masters's mangy German shepherd. The ragged hide had been hoisted half mast. Blood smeared the pole and soaked into the dirt.

Duke and the Digger, Lt. Ripley Masters, sat in the Command Bunker. Digger spoke with pride of his work in the World. Talked of cutting and sewing and embalming, of painting dead faces and adding extra hair. "Make Uncle George look like his old self, better." He described cheap funerals and resplendent affairs. "Pine boxes and mahogany caskets. Closed and open. Sometimes half open—only had to dress the upper half, tie a ribbon around Uncle George's dong." He chuckled, pleased with himself.

Duke felt like hell from the night before. He found the lecture boring. He led the Digger to the door and they ducked out of the Command Bunker. Blinded by the sun, they marched into the dog's insides, kicking bones about. Duke puked. He never could get used to being surprised by carnage at close range. Plus he was still woozy from the alcohol and opium. He cursed and side-stepped, stomping his boots.

Digger was struck dumbfounded. He swore loud and long, crying and spitting. He lowered the hide and found a foul bloodstained standard-issue sock stuffed where the dog's eye had been. A piece of a map was pinned to the sock. The map depicted a bush area north of Ho Nai, near the Rice River. Crudely scrawled in black on the map was: RIN-TIN-TIN SUCKED EGGS.

Lt. Ripley Masters's spirit broke some. He glanced at the Animal asking weakly what he was doing. Animal teased the bayonet blade over his whetstone, saying that it must be kept razor sharp. "The local VC, they're a leathery lot: tough old dogs that need to be diced well." Using a short and choppy motion, he threw the bayonet the length of the porch, into a section of the wood railing. It reverberated a hum as it sank in. Animal wiggled his toes and grinned.

The Digger dug a grave next to the flagpole and scraped the remains of his pet into it. He rolled the hide and sobbed rapidly over and over as he placed it in the hole and covered it. A mortician, a routine dealer in the death of man. The death of his dog shocked him deeply, and him alone.

Duke didn't exactly enjoy what had occurred. He rinsed the bile from his mouth with warm canteen water and thought no, it hadn't been a class act, lowbrow for sure. But it would be just to sic the Animal on that fucking cur Warren Buckle.

CHAPTER SIXTEEN

Duke's hangover was a sweaty, foul, lumpy creature that punched his brain incessantly. He didn't feel as bad as he might because he heard that a supply run was necessary, soon. A trip to Camp F-J, a chance for Bien Hoa. He and Jungle Jim walked out of the fort, across the street, to a café next to the beer store. They sat on crude wooden benches and leaned their weapons on the attached table: a picnic type. They were too large for the furniture but they managed. *Papa-san* and *mama-san* opened for business, smiling. The men drank a thick, strong coffee sweetened generously with a heavy cream like liquid cannoli. They slurped hot vegetable soup and soaked it up with fresh-baked hunks of long bread loaves speckled with bitty black bugs. Jungle Jim lighted a packed pipe and passed it. The day was getting rosy. Even Duke felt it.

After breakfast they opted for haircuts and wandered down a lane winding next to the fort. They waded through an ebb and flow of black-haired children. The houses there were patched French Colonial and basic shack.

"Get the old ears lowered." Jungle Jim grinned as they walked.

"Roger. Should feel clean for supper at Kim's." Duke looked forward to dining with Kim. There was a good chance for opportunity to visit Bien Hoa and Warren Buckle within a day or so, depending on the supply run which was overdue. He looked forward to that also. Planning was fine but getting nowhere, really. Action was necessary, further communication at least. Mission took time, he understood this and actually had nothing else pressing. And food with Kim would be refreshing.

They found a shop Jim had patronized before. Duke sat down first. Jungle Jim kept the weapons. The barber was new and glanced at them sideways, his eyes reptilian and bulging, his mouth arrogant and nasty: a frogface, a venomous toad. The parlor was clean, the linen fresh, the tools shiny.

The Toad commenced the cutting. He oiled Duke's dark hair and his angular face and his neck and his ears. The oil lay on the skin thick, sweet and slick. The Toad took his straight razor and scraped oil and hair from Duke's head. Duke sat rigid when the blade worked in his ear and slid over his forehead and nipped off brow between his eyes. He started to sweat. The Toad's constant mutterings grew louder and more pronounced. His popeyes gleamed, he chuckled and laughed. He yanked Duke's head back by the hair and flicked the razor around his neck.

Jungle Jim stood slowly raising his rifle. The Toad laughed a wild laugh and drew a trail of blood beneath Duke's tense Adam's apple. He held the blade to the neck teasing and toying and cursing in Vietnamese. He drooled.

Jungle Jim spoke and trained his M-16 on the Toad's nose. "Dung Lai, time to quit, zip," he said evenly. "Dung Lai, most ricky-tick."

The Toad tickled Duke's throat again, then quit. He folded the razor. He poked at Duke with a long sharp fingernail, he chuckled, he chided.

Duke grabbed for his gun grasping the barrel. He batted the Toad on the back of his head, then swatted the frog face and watched it crack smacking the floor. "The Duke strikes again," he said. His hand trembled some, but he shuddered it still. He felt his neck stinging, striped twice thin red.

"Our yellow brothers we're defending," said Jim.

"Gooks we're killing," said Duke. "Just who is who, anyhow? How does one know?"

"Isn't that what we—you and I—are doing here? We're checking it out, man. This is where everybody meets himself. Find out just what you are and how well you like what you meet."

They went back to the fort. Jungle Jim skipped the haircut and shaved himself with a Gillette Blue Blade in a steel safety razor.

Kim had invited them to dine at what he called home with him and his wife. So they washed well and put on clean green jackets. Duke and Jungle Jim strolled down the street through the heat toting rifles like briefcases, armed with a mere bandolier. It was an easy walk. They passed the boiling babble of the marketplace and approached Kim's hootch: his house, his apartment, his home.

Duke and Jungle Jim knocked on Kim's door. He answered. Inside the small front room they lounged comfortably drinking cold 33 Beer. The icebox was a hefty styrofoam cooler marked in American boldface: ICED HUMAN BLOOD. The furniture was bamboo and sparse. A few framed photographs, some Caodai religious symbols, a hand-painted tea set, a hand-woven fan for each man: What was there was immaculate. Sun streamed in; candles shimmered in corners.

Kim's young wife Phuong exhibited their infant daughter decked out in tiny traditional robes like a painted Oriental doll. Phuong delivered the daughter to her own old mother who tended her silently, out of sight. Phuong glided about serving tea and bowls of spicy morsels. Her áo-dài was a wisp of bright yellow and speckled alabaster. She was truly lovely: her amber skin drawn smoothly over the delicate lines of her face to her ravensilk hair drawn tightly about her skull and falling softly. Her eyes were almond encasements of deep wet emeralds. Her hands moved nimble and sure. Harry Pitts watched them; they provoked images of painted birdfeet: a nightingale perhaps. He knew much of birds from the country of his home and long ago noticed their absence from this Oriental sky. Phuong, her fragrance and her being and her home and her food, was downright good, bottomline all-fucking-right. A waterfall in the desert. The wonder of woman.

The men talked of war and of the people and the land. And of friendship. They spoke easily among themselves, their eloquence implied more than stated. Kim theorized that the Vietnamese people were extensions of their land: the mountains and valleys and deep green paddies, the rivers and jungle, the great wet swamps, the mud of the Mekong Delta. They were farmers who lived for the land that kept them alive. How could the foreign soldier understand this? Or care about it? Or even know it? The land of Vietnam had been fought for and for. It was straining, becoming haggard and torn like its people.

"A sad state," Jungle Jim consoled.

"Kind of a tragedy, a nobody-knows-why situation," said Duke.

"Correct," Kim conceded. "Absolutely correct."

Friendship was important. They decided they were doing their best: Duke, Jungle Jim, and Kim. And Duke naturally thought of the five dead scouts, and Warren Buckle, walking and breathing. It was difficult not to think of the bastard.

Kim complained of his carbine: an old M-2. He needed a 16: a black automatic to defend his home.

"Let's snag him one," Jungle Jim propsed, and cracked a 33.

"Could it actually be arranged?" Kim inquired, his eyes wide pushing to round.

"Done," said the Duke. He knew he'd be at Camp F-J and possibly Bien Hoa air base within a day or two. Both bases were overloaded with all kinds of supplies. And he genuinely liked Kim. This poor, ragged race needs more like him, he thought. Many more.

They drank and talked and felt generally fine. Duke and Jim thanked their host and departed. They strolled through late afternoon past a hamlet television set provided by the American Armed Forces–Vietnam Television Network (AFVN-TV). A crowd of youngsters milled and sat in anticipation: TV tonight! Some holiday treat, a rare delight.

First a young American wearing starched jungle fatigues faded in. He read some war news: his story was that the Americans were whipping ass. He predicted weather: more monsoon. Sounded like Walter Cronkite discussing rain. Then the crowd cheered as *Combat* started to roll. "Combat! Combat!" the kids squealed. "Vic Morrow! Vic Morrow!" They pointed to the screen and chirped in quick sharp tones.

Duke didn't understand the excitement. He gazed at Jim and they grinned. They marched for the fort leaving the audience huddled and rooting for the good guys, the heroes: World War II troops, Kilroy, the GIs.

Distant thunder boomed. Things were hushed.

CHAPTER SEVENTEEN

Mac's team manned the bridge that night. And Nada gave his money away. He had one thousand dollars, an even thousand in MPC (military pay certificates). He showed the roll to Duke and scoffed about the Chevy of his dreams. "A snazzy low-low rider, man." He tossed the notion off as disgusting materialism. He proposed that these poor villagers needed the money more than he needed a car. He made a sweeping gesture in the general direction of the hamlets of Ho Nai. Duke agreed with a shrug; he really had no opinion.

Nada Garcia's already strange brain had gotten stranger. His thin, dark face, streaked with black mustache, set itself in a perpetual frown. His black eyebrows drew down straight across his glazed eyes. He began speaking only of his woman, his hot señorita, his Latina lover back in L.A. And he spoke only to Duke who didn't know why.

Somebody was always unloading a personal burden, a bag of shit, on the Duke. Telling him something he'd rather not hear. Those intelligence jerks from G-2. Hawk's stupid eye-gouging plot. Masters running his mouth about the details and satisfactions of being a mortician. That lieutenant who silently asked Duke's opinion on the fate of that captured NVA man. And now Nada.

Dusk rolled in like a sudden sheet of dust. Everything was fuzzy, the failing sunlight muted, diffused. It was a quiet time. Men ate. The last of the vehicles creaked across the bridge. Duke went to the northern border to stretch concertina wire over the road. He smoked a cigarette and shot the breeze with the new PF honcho: a hard little man with only one hand.

Nada Garcia nodded to them as he di-di-bopped past. He went over to the usual group of children from the northern hut-hamlet. They milled about nightly until nearly full dark. Nada exposed his roll and started to peel it. He handed out money and the kids screamed. They fought and grabbed. Dust rose. The action appeared as motion filtered in dull yellow. Nada threw bills in the air; they floated and fell but never touched ground. When his roll was reduced to nothing at all, he threw up his arms shouting hallelujah. He bopped back by Duke whistling; still frowning but whistling and smiling his lips.

Duke yanked the wire to block the bridge road. The PF honcho put his only forefinger to his temple and pronounced the man diên-dao, nutty.

The night passed. The lightshow of silver stars and golden flares was usual, the watch peaceful. Sit-rep negative. A dry, quiet dark passage for which Duke felt fortunate, because his hangover hung on. He wasn't worth a shit. Payback was a motherfucker. If Warren Buckle didn't know that, Duke would be his educator.

During the dawn, the men marched back to the old French fort. Duke thought of it as that cracked bastion of glory that never was. He liked his description and told Jungle Jim he ought to write it in his journal. Jungle Jim said sure. Nada was silent; he made directly for his hootch.

The men spoke briefly of Nada's behavior, mostly they just shook their heads and chuckled unsurprised. They were dejected because he had wasted the bucks on the gooks. Should have divided it among them. "His own," said the Animal.

"We got some more Mexicans, Chicanos I don't know

about?" asked Duke.

"Americans, fucker. I meant Americans. Red, white, and bluebloods." Animal scratched his scarface.

"Maybe the man was making amends for the people he ran down the other day. Doing it American style, handing out money."

The Animal spat on the ground and walked off.

"You're coming around some." Jungle Jim clapped Harry Pitts's shoulder. He said he'd make note to jot the incident in his journal.

Duke broke down his weapon to clean and to oil. Nada sat beside him on the porch in the court. He broke down his M-16 and tossed it piecemeal over the old rail. He glanced frowning and grinning at Duke, jumped up, and scooted back to his hootch. Duke wondered why the crazy Mex messed with him. He remembered that Nada once told him that he and his brother had wallpapered the L.A. International Airport. He said it seriously, detailed the design of the finest wall covering of its kind. Duke had wondered then, also.

Nada skipped to the porch dressed to the nines. He looked flashy in his custom-tailored, Hong Kong sharkskin suit, his knit tie knotted neatly at his neck. His silk shirt was orange. He wore Beatle boots. "The war's over," he said, his smilefrown intact. "Over for this hombre. I'm heading home across the sea. L.A. and my lady, they're for me. Not this shit." Hands in pockets, Nada Garcia hat-danced away.

Duke watched him disappear through the gate, hoped he might make it. Knew he never would.

Nada Garcia reminded Pitts of training, the young soldiers who cracked, or simply split. Sometimes Pitts wondered why some of them lasted as long as they did. Or why some waited so long to make a decision.

Pitts's first days in the army were in New Jersey. The Reception Center in Fort Dix was a place of old barracks and new inductees, harassment. Young lonely dudes a day or two in the army. Swimming in new uniforms, trying to find some temporary friends, someone to talk to, bullshit with. A thin inductee wearing wire-rimmed glasses, little older than Harry Pitts, said to him: "They cut a load of hair off your head, man."

Pitts looked at him. The guy's glasses gave his eyes an intense dimension. "They took a lot of hair off everybody's head."

"Most of mine was already gone, premature baldness. Now all these suckers look like me. It's a shock for them. Tough shit, I say." The guy smiled, put out his hand. "I'm Jackson, Tom. Draftee."

Pitts shook his hand, told him his name.

"What do you think they do with all that hair?" Tom Jackson asked.

"I don't know. But this is America, there must be a market for the stuff."

"Right. They probably sell it to wig factories where it gets glued onto plastic and sold to saps who can't handle their natural skinhead look."

They shot the shit, smoked cigarettes. Talked about home, music they liked, the rotten mess hall food filled with saltpeter, the asshole sergeants.

"So," Jackson said, "have you met your woman yet, Harry?"

"I believe I have, Tom."

"So have I. We're lucky. It was a difficult thing for me to do, coming here. It was hard to leave her. She was against it."

"How about you, Tom?" Pitts asked.

"I'm here."

"I see that, Tom. But that doesn't necessarily mean you're in favor of it. Being drafted and all."

"No man." Tom Jackson turned away, clenched his long jaw. "I'm not in favor of being here one fucking iota."

"Then why?"

"Well you know they put your ass in jail for noncompliance. But still, I've been asking myself that question since I got on the bus yesterday."

"I think," Pitts said, "getting on the bus made the question meaningless. Maybe not meaningless, but too goddamn late to turn back."

A corporal, no taller than five feet two, ran into the company area. He was screeching, spraying and dripping spittle. He picked on two inductees. Made them run in front of him. Howled at them. GET YOUR PUSSY MOTHER-FUCKING CANDY ASSES OVER TO THE MOTHER-FUCKING MESS HALL!

"See that?" Tom Jackson said. "Those guys don't know what they're in for, really, or where in the hell they're going. But they jumped right up and went. They were told to go. They didn't consider their destination. They're like me. Like you, Harry. They just went."

"Possibly. But I'm here basically because I'm curious, I wanted to come. Not to this fucking reception center, this specific place. But the army. It was something to do, a place to go. I think I came for the experience, maybe to get out of myself for a while. I'm already seeing that I won't like all of it, but I didn't expect to. Hell, I may end up hating the whole damn thing. But I showed up without any real coercion."

"Bullshit!" Tom Jackson said. "You'd have been conscripted and forced. Only a matter of time."

Pitts couldn't argue. So he said: "You leave your woman to go into the military. Something you don't have a whole lot of control over. You think that means you love her any less?"

Tom Jackson said: "Damn right!"

"Then I think," Pitts said, "you might have made a mistake getting on that bus yesterday."

Tom Jackson said again: "Damn right!"

In the early morning they were standing in a cluster. New uniforms on, new duffle bags in front of them. Sergeants shouted names. When your name was called you got your duffle bag and your sorry ass on the bus for Basic Training.

"I'm not going," Tom Jackson said to Harry Pitts, his eyes wide, unblinking behind his glasses.

Pitts didn't know what to say to this guy and his view of the army. Didn't he know the army had his ass? "I don't see," he said finally, "how you're going to get around it."

"I've met my woman," Tom Jackson said, a trace of calm there. "I'm not leaving her. I know where this pigfucker army will send me if I cooperate. That's the key, Harry. They'll ship my ass to the jungle, *if I let them*. I'm not going."

A sergeant barked Pitts's name and service number. Pitts looked at Tom Jackson. Jackson's name had already been called and still he had not moved. Pitts shouldered his gear, reported, boarded the bus.

After a while Tom Jackson stood alone in the parking lot. The buses were loaded. The sergeants went for him. Called him a pussy, a commie faggot. Told him his mother ate goat turds. They rounded up some big inductees, tough guys, real men, talked them into kicking this pussy's ass. They punched Tom Jackson. Tom Jackson punched back. His glasses broke. Military police took him. Pitts, watching from the bus, thought Tom Jackson had waited a tad too long to make his decision.

A Filipino kid later reminded Pitts of Tom Jackson. Benito Tirona didn't have to go to Vietnam. Sole surviving son. Only way for a sole surviving son to go to a combat zone was to volunteer. Benito Tirona had no plans to volunteer. But he was a draftee so he was in the infantry. Stationed with a battalion in Fort Lewis. The battalion was training for Vietnam, would go over as a unit. Pitts knew Tirona slightly from pulling maneuvers with his company, practicing reconnaissance skills. Ben was a likable short beefy dude. He wasn't too worried about his future because he wasn't going to the 'Nam. Pitts's night flight to Vietnam included Ben's company. Ben's first sergeant, a veteran of World War Two's heroic Philippine Scouts, had the company in formation at the airfield. The first sergeant had ordered Ben to saddle up, go to the airfield, see his unit off. The first sergeant called Ben out in front of the assembled company, a real outfit, going to the war together, not a training company. Ben stood with the first sergeant there in the night before his company. The first sergeant ordered Ben to face the men.

The first sergeant shouted at Ben. "You a fuckin' pussy? YOU WANNA GIVE FILIPINOS A BAD FUCKIN' NAME? YOU A GODDAMN MOTHERFUCKING PUSSY COCKSUCKER OR A MAN FROM THE PHILIPPINE ISLANDS? I'M A MAN FROM THE PHILIPPINE ISLANDS. I BEEN TO WORLD WAR TWO, KOREA, AND NOW I'M GOIN' TO VIETNAM! HOW ABOUT YOU? YOU GONNA BE A CHICKEN-SHIT PUSSY WHO CAN'T LIVE WITH HIMSELF? OR YOU GONNA BE A MAN?"

The sergeant went on for a while, berating Ben. Challenging him. When Ben finally ran back to his place in the formation, signifying he was a volunteer for combat, the company cheered. The first sergeant shouted: "THERE IS A GODDAMN MAN! TRULY A FUCKIN' MAN!"

Pitts watched from the LRRP formation. Watched Ben and his company board the big airplane. He thought Ben had been a tad too hasty in making his decision.

Tom Jackson, Ben Tirona, training, and heavy decisions early and late. Reminded Duke Pitts of Nada Garcia.

Duke slammed the bolt back into his 16, oiled and clean. He passed the early morning stripping and tending more weapons: .45s, M-60s and the fifty-caliber machine gun from the truck. Jungle Jim helped and they both laughed when Doc Ratchit stumbled, stinking of vomit, into the compound. He collapsed in a hammock hanging on the porch: an opium overload.

Mac's team had been detailed to drive to Camp F-J for a ration of C's and crates of ammo. They would take the deuce-and-a-half. They would fan out and work feverishly for a short morning time, then fuck away the rest of the day:

shower, swim in the camp pool, eat at the consolidated mess, drink American beer.

Duke and Jim planned to see Cpl. Red Green to perhaps borrow a vehicle: shitwagon or edible garbage truck, whichever was free. A side trip to Bien Hoa was in order. They hoped for a chance at harassment, Warren Buckle's presence required. They discussed possibly booby-trapping his room, to frag the motherfucker. But dismissed it: They would feel terrible if the wrong man tripped it. And Duke had a little surprise for him anyhow.

Nada Garcia was AWOL. Lt. Ripley Masters announced that if anyone knew his whereabouts he should tell him that he would be reported deserted at noon the next day. "If Nada returns," he said, "things will be okay."

CHAPTER EIGHTEEN

The Animal drove the deuce-and-a-half. Duke felt excited. The men felt well and wished to hell the war would stay away this one more day. The truck rolled south on Highway 1. The sky brightened clear as new chrome. On the road there was no sign of Nada who was headed ultimately east for his home in the West.

The men cleared weapons as the truck entered the camp. Animal drove directly to Brigade Supply. Mac found a fat sergeant and began negotiating; he was a pro. Through some intricate and far-reaching bargain he would acquire more than the CRIP's standard allocation of food and explosives. These high-ranking supply sergeants were powerful men. Pogues on pedestals to be dealt with politely, if not respectfully. Mac could sometimes even be issued American beer, a delicacy due each man: due but rarely realized. It took great skill or pressure to convince one of these noncommissioned officers to part with a portion of his hoard. Mac bargained. Men stripped off their shirts and loaded supplies.

The men sweat streams and completed stacking the stuff in record time. One man had to stay as sentry with the truck and weapons; he would be relieved in two hours. Prick Peters volunteered first watch. Animal made for the swimming pool; he would guard second. Mac and the fat sergeant took off in a jeep; he stood no watch. Duke and Jim set out to find Cpl. Red Green. They wore their .45s.

They found him driving a deuce-and-a-half, Pfc. Lake riding shotgun. And he had one too: an oily mean looking pump. The truck was loaded with crap drums: fifty-five-gallon barrels cut in half, swirling a thick stink. They waved him to stop.

"Any chance we might borrow the edible garbage truck?" asked Duke as he stepped up to the door.

"This is it," said Red. "They're one in the same. One day I haul the food, the edible garbage. The next I haul crap, GI shit. We deliver it to dinks on the road to Bien Hoa. God knows what those fuckers do with it. They trade clean drums for these."

"We need to get to Bien Hoa," said Jungle Jim, smirking and holding his nose.

"No problem, we make several grips." Cpl. Red Green grinned, gesturing to the bed with his thumb. "If you don't mind riding back there."

Duke and Jungle Jim griped as they climbed aboard. The truck lurched forward and the waste, the muck in the uncovered crappers, slopped and splashed on their legs. The stench hovered and penetrated. They faced the wind; their eyes watered, noses stung.

On the fringe of Bien Hoa the truck stopped at a busy site swirling blobs of black smoke. Civilian honey-buckets unloading. Military vehicles being cleared of brimming vats and stacked with empty ones. Lines of the drums sat burning, the contents doused with gasoline. Men and women dumped others into larger tubs. This was a fertilizer reception and distributing point. A hot, putrid place of constant, monotonous activity. A place to gag. *Shit City*.

Red's truck unloaded, he drove Duke and Jim to the air-base gate. They would have to get back to the fetilizer dump on their own. He'd take them back to Camp F-J if they made it; his last trip would be late in the afternoon.

They walked through the red dust of the air base: a noisy place with jets zooming and the helicopters maneuvering;

tanks and APCs rumbling metal; jeeps and trucks; self-propelled artillery: hell on tracks.

At Buckle's flight group area, a crew chief was giving himself a trim, squinting at a wall mirror, chopping his mustache. He wanted to know what the hell two legs wanted, then smiled. Sergeants Pitts and Grogan returned the gesture. Pitts asked for Buckle's old crew chief.

"His tour's over. He's flown the big bird across the Pond, he's back in the World."

Duke had figured this but feigned disappointment. Sgt. Jim Grogan wondered if the chief were a lifer.

"Hell no!" snapped the chief. "I'm a lineman back home. It's me and Ma Bell."

Jungle Jim Grogan had been a telephone lineman himself. This was a stroke of good luck. The two men discussed the merits of the profession. How they loved the outdoors, the physical activity. They compared notes on the various skills they employed. They exchanged tragic tales of electrocutions, of falls and paralyzed partners. They relished tense conversation of dangerous situations, of storms and wind and ice. They thoroughly enjoyed the shoptalk, speaking with authority of what they knew. It was fortunate to find someone who could talk with pride of some shared knowledge, some honest work, something done well, something that one understood as part of being a man, something other than war. Most of the combat soldiers were so young that they had never experienced this kind of pride. And it occurred to Duke that many never would.

He realized the men were thoroughly absorbed. He slipped away to Warrant Officer Warren Buckle's quarters. The room was unoccupied. Duke took a packet from his pocket. He unwrapped it exposing a huge black scorpion he had hunted for this very purpose. It was dead but shocking. He placed the arachnid beneath Buckle's pillow. Next to it he placed an olive drab patch: a small banner with the embroidered black letters: LRRP.

This was hardly satisfactory. Duke had to meet the man somehow on neutral ground. Somewhere there must be a line to cross that would bait the man, draw him out. Discovering or constructing that line was the problem, the predicament. Once drawn, Duke would not hesitate to cross it. But circumstances must conspire to create the proper situation, the decisive moment. Duke would prefer that this portion of his life be over. But it could not be until Warren Buckle's life was finished. And whatever time was necessary to accomplish this, Duke would take.

He replaced the pillow, it lumped over the carcass. On his way out, he noticed Buckle's M-16 leaning in a corner. He slung it upside down. A fine, black automatic, he thought. Just the weapon for Kim. Sgt. Harry Pitts, the Duke, ducked outside to wait for the lineman, Jungle Jim Grogan.

CHAPTER NINETEEN

Duke watched the guards at the gate. He wondered if they'd challenge him about the rifle. He wondered how far he was prepared to take this weapon-stealing, this theft of government property. He could see some creep sentry giving him a hard time, taking the job seriously. Detecting a real crime there in the war zone. Hassle. Duke didn't need it.

But the guards let them go. Didn't say a word. Hardly seemed to notice them.

So Sergeants Pitts and Grogan successfully slipped off base. Jungle Jim was obviously pleased with Duke's decision to lift Warren Buckle's weapon. "The right move, my man." He touched the black barrel. "The thing to do."

Then Duke caught sight of him. His own heart tried to muscle out of his chest. Warren Buckle riding in a jeep with two overweight colonels! A baseball hat capped his crown; his aviator sunglasses were mirrors. He spoke to the fat officers, broke them up. They all heehawed, splashing American beer from their cans, the colonels' faces violent with high blood pressure.

Duke nudged Jungle Jim. "That's our man, the one that ain't fat." He indicated the passengers in the jeep approaching, heading for the air base gate, fifty meters beyond. "The one with the fat red mustache."

"I'll bet," Jungle Jim observed, "those blubber boys think he's one hell of a hardass."

Duke stepped into the path of the jeep so that it had to be swerved. Warren Buckle, sitting in the back, locked his gaze on him. He whipped around and craned his neck and gripped the back of his seat. His knuckles went white.

The face of Harry Pitts, the Duke, was two mirror images glaring from the face of Warren Buckle. The Duke's entire body took the two places. Standing arrogantly and armed, the images receded with distance, as if boring through the glass into Buckle's eyes. The jeep wrapped itself in a blanket of dust and disappeared beyond the gate.

"I believe I could strangle that boy," said Duke. "Rip his lips off and feed his face to the rats."

"I'll bet he just came from getting his ashes hauled," said Jim. "Him and those pudgy housecats."

They walked.

"If we could discover where and what he fucks, we might be in business. Then one might snoop around to find out when and how often he comes." Duke spoke rapidly, perhaps seeing a way to draw that line, to accomplish his mission.

"Exactly," said Jim. "We might enlist the aid of Kim, or better still old man Gue. It's a start."

CHAPTER TWENTY

They hitched a ride on a half-full replacement bus. A long O.D. schoolbus with bars in its windows transporting fresh, green troops. Pale, wide-eyed and silent they sat staring. Some of them smoking, all of them young. Duke eyed them with a knowledge that would come to only some of them. The jungle hadn't been at them yet. Hadn't whittled them to grunt muscle and bone. Some of them losers. Most of them without any real education, tradeless, unless you counted the Army training—most of that having to do with killing. Most without any particular understanding. Many poor. Some would find their own courage, some mutilation and death. Many were boys about to become men, to come of age within an ancient and essentially stupid framework. None of them understood yet where he had come and where he would be. From the fringes of the American Dream so many came: too many too young, the U.S. warriors, the best and only their country had.

When Duke confronted what they were—himself included—he saw a mass of meat on a Sucker's Tour. Individual ideas and ideals transformed to fodder, temporary nourishment for insatiable appetites of power and greed. They were dudes in the Wrong Place, whatever their reasons. Bodies as weapons in the Mission, the Big Picture. It was a drag. Ultimately they would be killed, wounded, or fucked over.

Duke thought it sad that there were scumbags like Warren Buckle for these soldiers to depend on.

He recalled his own arrival in-country with other trained Lurps, the five dead scouts among them. They had weathered incongruous training during a Washington State winter of snow and icy sleet. But training had been screwy from the beginning. In Basic if the company didn't scream *Blood!* or *Kill!* loud enough every time their collective right foot hit the floor, falling out for reveille, the D.I.s sent everybody back to do it until it was done right. *Blood! Kill!* He shivered in the heat remembering how they had huddled close on the cold ground seeking warmth to sleep, wrapped in mere ponchos and liners to test their endurance night after night. Jungle Jim and Red Green had been there along with Dudley Worth and Carl Diel, Rat Malloy and the Ox, Zap Rossi and more. Lying close under pines heavy with snow. Close, in each others' pockets, chest to back, ass to groin and the dudes at either end got stone cold screwed. They had arrived with a unit, then been attached in twos to experienced teams. As their own savvy grew, they naturally grouped together again if they could. The bus stopped.

He and Jim jumped from the bus and watched it truck the new troops to Camp F-J, to the Light Infantry Brigade, to units, to the war. The bus faded into the road of rippling heat. The rot around them sank in: they were in Shit City.

Cpl. Red Green's bed was being unloaded. Red and Lake, Duke and Jim stood about smoking and breathing in shallow spurts.

"I got a buddy just joined you dudes. Name's Peters, Prick they call him. How's he doin'?" Red Green asked.

"The man seems pissed off. Other than that he seems solid."

"Well, that's natural. Tell him to be good."

They were glad to board the vehicle and head upwind from the dump.

Inside Camp F-J Duke and Jim jumped from the deuce-

and-a-half waving thanks. Duke shouted to Red, "Don't touch shit, buddy. Even with gloves on."

Red Green shot him a bird.

They reached the CRIP truck in time for watch, but Mac was already waiting. He informed them that Nada Garcia had been nabbed in Saigon. MPs discovered the man slobbering and weeping, lying on a Christian grave in a yard near a French church. He held a snapshot of his girl back home, repeated her name between sobs. He mentioned Sgt. Duke Pitts, his friend in the CRIP. The police checked things out and were cutting him slack, returning him to his unit. Masters had contacted Mac and added Nada to the supply detail. Since Nada thought so much of Pitts, Mac sent him to fetch the nutty Mexican.

Duke didn't mind. "Suppose he doesn't want to come?"

"Then leave the goof to the cops."

Duke found him where he was told he would: with the MPs at chaplain's chapel. Nada's suit was filthy, his face streaked with tears and dirt, his eyes puffed and red, his nose crusted and running. Sergeant Pitts signed for him and thanked the MPs. He asked Nada if maybe he should powwow with the padre, Father Friend, a sad-eyed gray sort who looked as if he had always lived in a closet. Father Friend smiled. Nada shook his head no.

Sergeant Pitts shrugged. "Come on. We'll get a shower and clean uniforms. You look like shit and I smell like it."

Nada followed him out. Father Friend's smile drooped and fell from his face. He shut his chapel door behind them.

They got back to supply and drew new uniforms, then hit the showers. Nada seemed dazed. He rambled erratically about his L.A. woman, his sisters and brothers, his mother, his hardass old man, his neighbors: the *barrio*, Family. Tears coursed his chocolate cheeks, mixing with the shower water. He told Duke: "Man I just don't know why I came here. Me or any Chicano; me or Prick Peters; he or any black man. You know we got the shit end of things in the World. We eat our pride, our *machismo*, every day for breakfast. Then go out and bust ass for the man. My mama works like a mule and you can bet your white ass Peters's does too. And if you think whores ain't nobody's sisters, you're damn fucking wrong. We live with the rats. They send me here to help these poor bastards when my own people are poor. It ain't right, man. It just ain't right. I got a war to fight right in the U.S.A., so does Peters. I'm going and he should join me, be my *compadre*."

Duke listened and understood. "I'm no rich man's son, Garcia. Not by a long shot. Never met one here. White is not ALL RIGHT. A hell of a lot of them suck dirt all day and watch their women wither, their kids get wrong and hard."

Nada wasn't paying attention. He dressed and stared at the photograph of his girlfriend. Duke dressed and they walked outside. He asked again if Nada wanted to speak to Father Friend. Nada looked as if he might have at that moment discovered thought. He bolted shouting over his shoulder that he was headed for the chapel.

Duke watched him zip right past the chapel, charge over a dirt berm and double-time toward the outer perimeter bunkers. Nada was fortunate he chose daylight for such a maneuver, when the killer sentry dogs slept. Duke cursed and followed him.

When he finally made it to the bunker Nada had climbed, Duke yelled for the guard. The gaurd poked his head out and told him to come up with an angry twist of his neck. Inside the sandbagged fortress sat Nada Garcia, naked as his moment of birth. The guard pointed a .45 at him. Duke tried to communicate but Nada sat unmoved, blank as a board. The guard used his radio.

By the time Mac arrived with Lt. Ripley Masters, Duke had convinced Nada to dress. They put him in the jeep and drove to the supply area. Nada only spoke of his L.A. lady— only to Duke who dispatched Jungle Jim to fetch Father Friend. Nada always wore a crucifix about his neck, a tiny gold one.

Masters was frustrated, his questions unanswered. He ordered Garcia handcuffed and called the cops. It took Mac and two fat pogues to wrestle the mad Mexican and chain his wrists behind his back. They dragged him into a wood-floored tent and sat him in a chair, shackled his ankles to it.

Father Friend arrived looking like a used pair of sneakers, sole full of holes. Nada asked to be alone with him and the Duke. The others ducked out. He told the priest he could help by unbuttoning his fly and pulling out his penis: he had to piss. To Duke's amazement Father Friend obliged. Nada pissed on the floor and jerked himself, chair and all, to it. He groveled about rubbing his face in the puddle, licking and lapping like a dog. Father Friend made a rabbit mouth and went out washing his hands of the entire situation: he couldn't help here.

Masters and Mac came back with the cops. Nada glanced up and begged for his girl in L.A. Urine dripped from his face. Duke stepped aside. This was Nada's own show and it would be damn hard to play out.

The cops whipped the chair and the man upright. They unchained and rechained him, then shoved him out to their jeep. They punched him in. Nada Garcia wept wildly, screeching like a child who woke up blind for the first time. He wailed like a siren. One of the MPs slapped his mouth bloody, palmed his nose flatter.

It occured to Duke that certain types must always be attracted to police duty. They infiltrate the ranks of decent policemen and are overzealous. They extend their functions beyond reasonable limits, become arrogant, abusive. They would rise up and stomp the decent ones to rubble; they would wade joyously waist deep in the blood of babies.

Duke watched dust obliterate the jeep. Distance and heatweight dissipated Nada's cries.

Duke recalled one Private Bork who couldn't walk and chew gum at once. He was mentally deficient and always terrified of the drill instructors in basic. He was the pathetic victim of some sadistic local draft board member. He couldn't even crawl on all fours without falling. He screwed up bayonet training: missed stabbing the dummy with every thrust. He just didn't understand the spirit: *Kill! Kill!* A huge D.I. knocked him into the sandpit and threw a hand-to-hand combat dummy to him. He bellowed that Bork just didn't know how to act like a man, probably never been laid. He commanded Bork to drop his drawers and fuck the dummy, pretend it was pussy. The recruits gathered about the pit leering and laughing loudly. Bork cried and humped the dummy. His flabby white ass welted as the D.I. whipped it with his wide hand. The recruits moved away in silence. Bork vomited and the D.I. shoved his face in it. None of the recruits particularly liked Bork but each felt for him then. Feel was all they did. The D.I. was in charge.

On the rifle range Bork snapped and trained his M-14 on the tower. He fired four rounds at it. The D.I. manhandled him. Two others helped. They beat him bloody and took him away. Harry Pitts saw poor dumb Bork some weeks later in a Special Training Company area. He walked bent beneath the weight of a wall locker strapped to his back. He was moving sandbags from one end of the area to another for reasons known only to those in charge.

And then there was Spec. Four Singe who flipped out when his brain boiled. After a sweltering march which had been like hiking through a flameless forest fire, and the long battle that followed; Singe screeched and babbled. He ran about foaming at the mouth and slugged a captain in the nuts. Then he lay down shivering and shouting about God and home. He spat at anyone who came near. When he calmed and passed out, the captain had him bound. Put him on a chopper that took Duke and the recon team back to Brigade. Spec. Four Singe made little sense, babbled on and on about somewhere in Alabama. His eyes were wild. His shouts were sliced short by the chopping of the rotor blades.

MPs met the helicopter and took the Spec. Four. They took him in a jeep, tied to the floor. They took him away, down the road to Long Binh, to LBJ, the Long Binh Jail. He was unbound and thrown in the Box: a conex container buried to the rim in the ground. He was fed some C Rations and water once a day; he relieved himself in a gas can changed every other. The sun beat on the iron top of the box all day making a metal sauna, a sweat box from which there was no escape. At dusk water was poured through the grate in the top. To cool him they joked. In four inches of wet he attempted to sleep. The moisture attracted mosquitoes like rotten meat screams for buzzards. During the day his brain boiled some more. For five days he baked, then dropped, wouldn't respond. They took him to a hospital and the boil was diagnosed. He'd never be right, if he lived at all. The doctor said it.

Duke knew this had happened. He had known Spec. Four Singe slightly. His curiosity sought it. MPs and the doc told it. He knew that the Box was in store for Nada Garcia. He knew that beatings and general brutality were in the man's immediate future, his karma, his stars. He would be broken some more, then shipped to a shrink. That was the way it was. Hell, the Army could have shot him. A deserter, he was getting a break. The Army was in charge, that's all anyone could say. Yes, if it were an act, it would be damn tough to pull off. Some degrading horror awaited Nada Garcia. Duke knew this would happen. And happen it did.

CHAPTER TWENTY-ONE

In the dusty court of the old French fort, Duke recounted the demise of Nada Garcia. He spoke to Prick Peters whose black face was expressionless. Duke told of the man's obsession with his people, his outrage that exploded, his theory on the important fight on the streets of the U.S.A.

Prick Peters said evenly that the man was right on target. The real war was in fact on the streets of the World. "I'll survive to fight it," he said. "I'll make damn sure I'm armed. I'm already trained and experienced. Maybe that goofy greaser wasn't so goofy. Gonna be a damn rough road home though. But maybe he just made up his oddass mind. Impulsive he was. Crazy fuckin' impulsive." Prick Peters sat on the porch near his hootch. He commenced to check and clean his weapons. "We shall overcome," he said.

"I never could figure out what you spades were gonna overcome by sitting and laying down and letting some scumbags stomp and shit all over you. Seems like your ancestors were chumps—letting somebody tell them they could only eat, sleep, fuck, and work in special shitholes. I believe I'd be considering taking back what those chumps never should have given up."

"You got the idea, Duke. Nonviolence is bullshit. But you got to dig that it took awhile for enough of us to know that. 'Got to take things slow,' they tell us, 'Avoid bloodshed.' Only blood not shedding is honky—plenty nigger red flowing. Plus the man's got the guns. But we're getting some." He slammed the bolt into his 16, for effect. "What seems simple and obvious to you, from your white man's view, is totally opposite in black reality: the man better dig that he puts a nigger behind the trigger here in 'Nam, ain't all of us getting wasted, we're coming back to change the World." He winked and gave a short jab of a power sign.

Duke left him there, thinking that his own real war might well be on the streets of Bien Hoa and he was glad he didn't have the added burden of being black. His whiteness allowed for a clearer, nonpolitical attitude toward his mission.

He found Jungle Jim and they strolled, armed, through the somber relative cool of late afternoon, early evening. They stopped and knocked on Kim's door. He answered. Phuong was a wisp of warmth glowing for an instant in the golden interior. Then she was gone, her bright smile lingering for the briefest moment.

The three men sat and Kim poured tea. Duke and Jim smiled broadly as they handed over the M-16. Kim's shoulders straightened slightly; his chest filled a bit; his jaw set stronger. It was fine to have such friends. He would kill for them, perhaps even die. He accepted the gesture proudly and shook each man's hand firmly. Duke and Jim felt his gratitude and were moved by it.

Kim left the room and returned straight away. He placed an intricately carved teakwood box on a table. He opened it revealing nine knives. They sparkled of age and richness. They were hand-fashioned by a Montagnard shaman: a ceremonial set, mystic and secret. The shaman had been Kim's grandfather, his mother's wild sire, the leader of a learned cult within the tribe. Kim's father had been a trader from Tay Ninh who traveled north to the highlands to deal with the tribesmen. He married a shaman's daughter: a rare coupling. Kim had never mentioned his tribal heritage. He did so now only to his two American friends, his fellow warriors. They must harbor this knowledge, never divulge it.

A Montagnard mountain man, even half-bred, was an oddity, untrusted in many quarters, sought after and killed by followers of old man Ho.

He invited each man to keep the knife of his choice: all similar and different for each was handmade. He unsheathed the five-inch double edges. The daggers gleamed: all brass and teakwood, blades sharp and silver. The Americans chose and Kim explained that now three would be missing from the original ten. His father had chosen the first and pierced his forearm in the curved, prescribed manner. Then mingled his blood with that of the Montagnard. This was a male ritual. Duke was skeptical but he flowed with it. What the hell, he thought.

Kim instructed the men. Each made a slight carving cut inside his forearm. Kim pressed his limb to that of each American. They were bound now by more than honor. Bound deeply by ceremony and blood.

Harold Pitts, James Grogan, and Kiem Ly: a new band of somehow closer comrades. Duke, Jungle Jim, and Kim: each felt privileged. Each man's pride swelled, great and even. Duke liked the feeling.

They sipped short cups of rice wine and chased them with American beers from Kim's ICED HUMAN BLOOD cooler.

Duke and Jim excused themselves and left. Outside a drunken cowboy accosted them. He stood belligerently in his tailored tight uniform and cocked Australian-style bush hat. He bitched in pigeon English that he deserved a fuckin' M-16 as much as that numba ten ARVN Kim. The man looked unarmed and stank of liquor.

Jungle Jim laughed and snatched the small Vietnamese man up like a child. He tossed him skyward and caught him under the arms. Again. Calling him little John Wayne, exclaiming how quickly news spreads hereabouts. "Ain't that something, Duke?" The cowboy stabbed at the side of Jim's neck, nicking it good with a small pocketknife.

Jim cursed and threw the cowboy down, hard. Kim rushed out and cursed the cowboy viciously. He apologized for his countryman's drunken behavior.

A noticeable number of cowboys were about, gangs of them. Tight brown uniforms, arrogant attitudes, armed with guns or knives or both. They usually banded around Saigon or Bien Hoa or some other large city. Claiming allegiance to various quasi-military units, they had branched out to the countryside lately. The American scouts had reported their increasing presence days ago. There were more milling about now than then.

Kim suggested that his friends move out. They did, past another cowboy whose skintight uniform was torn. He carried a machete and he had no nose. Just a nasty gash in the middle of his face. He looked at Duke, and Duke was startled: he didn't think there were any sights left to shock him, but there were.

Jungle Jim figured that the gook bastard probably got too greedy for air. "Damn cowboys are bad medicine," he said. "Worthless. Like a Vicks Inhaler for that sunken snotnose back there."

"They're sorry," said Duke. "Can't mean anything but trouble. They're after our necks for sure." He put his fingers to his own, rubbing the thin scabs, mark of the Toad. Some Dink version of Zorro. He could see the phantom Barber slipping in and out of shops around the Republic, slicing Ts on the throats of the enemy. Zorro the Fox, Toad the Barber. The spic wore a mask to conceal his aristocratic identity. The gook needed one to hide his ugly, caved-in face, his head with a new slope to it. "We need a division of fucking A-paches to chew them up."

"There it is."

CHAPTER TWENTY-TWO

They found Doc Ratchit and called him from the crapper. He patched Jungle Jim's neck and prescribed a short smoke for the pain. And a smoke for Duke's nerves. And one for himself for sustenance.

They slipped out of the fort into the night. Lt. Ripley Masters was there in the dark.

"Where you off to?" he asked.

"The usual mission," Doc Ratchit retorted. "Reconnaissance, Digger. A recon patrol. We're off to reconnoiter some intelligence. Keeping our thumbs on the pulse of the people."

Masters touched his finger to his chin. He mumbled of course and disappeared behind the ramparts of the fort.

The patrol prowled through the deserted marketplace. Even empty it resounded. It echoed a shuffle, a dull bump against an evacuated booth.

The men found Gue's steps and climbed them. A few satiated old men sprawled about one corner of Gue's den. They paid the three soldiers slight heed. Gue's gray face brightened. He greeted them and began preparing the pipes.

When the soldiers had settled, the smoke hung sweetly about, swirling from their lungs. Doc questioned the old man about the pugnacious cowboy and his seemingly increasing brethren. Gue had knowledge of the evening's incident, as Doc knew he would.

Old Gue stroked his long wispy white beard. His face and hands moved, his lotus positioned body remained, as always, still. He had been a scholar in his day. He continued to read languages for the mental exercise of reasoning Orientally as well as Occidentally. Although he admitted that the latter was often perplexing. He spoke, in addition to his native tongue, Chinese, Indian, Japanese, Thai, French, and English. He understood Latin. He claimed that Chinese and English had certain basics in common. This was surprising, he allowed, but did not elucidate. He discoursed now in English, his voice thin. He gestured mostly to Doc but did acknowledge Jim and the Duke. "The history of my people is a struggle for freedom, independence you call it. The Chinese dominated us until your tenth century. They were driven from the Red River Delta at the glorious battle of Bach Dang. They have never ceased invasions but have never gained total control again. They are part of our struggle still. Chinese weapons and soldiers aid the North. Dynasties ruled for the next nine hundred years, the great Ly the first. These Annamese monarchies forged the Viet-namese culture, an honorable one. The noble Dai Viet warriors even succeeded in repelling the rampaging Kublai Khan in your fourteenth century. We had our gods, our heroes, our literature. The West discovered us during the fourteenth century. Influence trickled in at first. Then flooded in during the last century. The French moved in and irrevocable splits began. The Japanese came for World War II, the French again afterward. Then Dien Bien Phu. Then North and South, civil war.

"In every country there is a faction that plainly covets little or no government. In mine, as in yours, this faction is the South. And in mine, as in yours, the North will not stand for it. It is not that we hate the Communists so greatly, we simply do not want them."

Duke wondered thickly what this had to do with the

cowboys. Doc asked.

"You see," said Gue, "we are now split into so many groups that confusion reigns. These cowboys, these gangs of obscurely aligned soldiers, mercenaries; I fear they have cast their lot with Ho Chi Minh. The season of Tet draws near and with it great upheaval. Tet is a sacred time of family celebration, a time of solidarity. Family reunions are traditional. Like the Christian New Year, the Buddhist Tet is a time for sharing and caring: a time to reaffirm relationships, acknowledge friendship. A time these northern Communist generals, whose timetable has nothing to do with the religious histories of man, will see as a time for action: a time for truce-tearing. A time right for rousing the people to popular uprising. They don't understand that we do not desire them. They will come. Tet being a time for family gatherings, movements of large groups of people is possible without suspicion. These hoodlums, these cowboys ranging about are a bad omen. They may not know for whom they act. Confusion reigns. Let us have another pipe."

The old man nimbly pressed pipes and lighted them. Duke asked about the literature Gue had spoken of. This interested him; he had studied the literature of his own language briefly but feverishly. And Jungle Jim, the journal keeper, listened to remember.

"Literature is literature," said Gue obviously. "What can be said of it? At best it is invention and speaks to our spirits. It keeps stories alive. As a young man I was a writer of verse: poetry."

"Why did you stop?" This too interested Duke. For as most who study language, he had attempted to write it. He went to war and stopped.

"For me," answered Gue, "poetry had its source in deeply felt emotion. The wars wore mine away and the opium replaced them with a dull contentment. I might dabble but the wellspring of my emotions is dust. Any that I might now

134

experience would be false and such would be any verse that sprang from them. False poetry is shallow and not worth the effort."

Duke toked the long stem. Opium smoke rose. He thought he understood the old man's words. But his mind began to wander. It fastened on a sound and zoomed back to now. He heard the name Judd. He glanced at Jungle Jim who also seemed surprised.

Gue was speaking again of gangs and splits. He rambled about the black market and the American called Judd who could supply U.S. arms to anyone for a price. "Is he where you procured the rifle for Kim, young Duke?"

"No, not from him." He listened intently as the old man told of Judd, the American bandit with an Asian wife. And of a tall, hairless brute, an American officer, who was known to be his associate, his partner.

Ralph Judd had flown in-country with the same unit that brought Duke and Jim and the other trained Lurps. Judd had joined the unit only weeks before. He had done one tour in the war already. He told wild tales and claimed to have a Vietnamese wife. He spoke the language. He was tattooed. Gold teeth gleamed in his mouth. He got along well with Duke and confided in him. Said he would split at the first opportunity. He did so but got caught and put in the Box. He was released from LBJ and sent back to the field. He walked away from a firebase one night. Armed to the teeth, even took an M-60 machine gun. It was rumored he was alive in Saigon, in the jungle, in Hanoi. Now Gue placed him in Bien Hoa. And who was this hairless one? This American officer, this brute. Who was he indeed?

Gue supplied the address of the whorehouse where one might contact Judd. It was located near a cemetery big enough for a blind man to find. The soldiers paid for their pipes and excused themselves politely. Gue smiled and cautioned that Judd-*san* was no man to deal with. "Your own military offers a bounty, a reward for his capture. If this is what you seek, make Gue no part of it." He smiled again, still.

The night was thick and starry. They moved lightly back to the fort. Duke considered the evening a fine one, all in all. Full and fine. Reconnaissance accomplished. Intelligence gathered.

CHAPTER TWENTY-THREE

The patrol slipped into the old French fort and Sergeant First Class MacFee took Duke aside to brief him. Brigade Intelligence determined that enemy rocketfire and troop movement had increased markedly. Our own artillery barrages saturated the hilly scrub west of Ho Nai nightly. As in any artillery action, dud rounds landed. An abnormal number lay about this western scrub area, too close to villages thought to be friendly. It was a free-fire zone but the peasants cooperated. For their safety, some brilliant brass hat, some stupid staff officer had decreed that the dud rounds be located and destroyed, in case the rounds didn't remain duds. Brigade informed Lt. Ripley Masters that the CRIP had drawn the mission: clean up the duds to the west and south to the borders of Bien Hoa, take maybe three days, right into the Tet truce.

Mac had volunteered his squad but due to the nature of the mission—blowing up bombs—he didn't wish to force cooperation. He would check with the men.

Duke's high was blown. He didn't mind and volunteered his services, which shocked the hell out of Sergeant MacFee.

"Didn't expect such an attitude, Pitts," said Mac.

"Well, you got it. Just make sure you don't get carried away out there. I want to arrive in Bien Hoa without my ass in a sling." The chance to be in Bien Hoa in three days was too fine to skip. The line between himself and Warren Buckle seemed to become tangible. Some shape was taking dimension. Circumstances appeared to conspire. Of course, he might be blown to atoms by one of the "dud" bombs, or shot from existence by a VC sniper, or booby-trapped into a crippled life. He might fall victim to countless mishaps. But these things were part of waking with each new day, he did not count them extraordinary.

He went to the hootch and informed Jungle Jim. Then he slept soundly.

Jungle Jim agreed to the mission more to accompany Duke than to reach Bien Hoa.

In the morning the men griped naturally. The mission meant humping in the boonies blowing huge howitzer warheads. The scrub was a free-fire zone. The men knew the villages were VC, the people out there really had no choice in the matter. The brass hats thought differently. Trudging around in hostile territory blowing up bombs that hadn't exploded. Booby traps. Snipers. The entire operation was insane. Only an officer could conceive it. Only a maniac would volunteer for it.

"Well, what the fuck you goin' for?" Animal asked Prick Peters.

"I'm makin' a detailed study of lunacy and the white man's mind. I'll consider this shit field work. What's your excuse?"

"I'm a maniac, man. Didn't you know?"

Kim smiled and stroked his slung M-16. He didn't have much choice either.

The men discussed fragging. At Duke's suggestion, they rejected the idea for the present. They would judge Mac's movement in the field. If his enthusiasms became over-zealous, they might reconsider.

"How come you're so interested in that lifer's welfare?" Prick Peters asked and appeared amazed.

"Look," said Duke, "I don't think I'd piss in his asshole if the man's guts were on fire. But we've got no reason to blow him away for Chrissake!"

"Not yet."

They saddled up and climbed to the tile roof that was the LZ. The chopper and Mac were waiting. The flight was a short one.

The helicopter dropped the patrol and buzzed away. It was a fine, clear morning. The men moved out over a rocky plain: red and yellow dirt, great tufts of strawlike sawgrass, stunted trees. Craters gaped from past B-52 raids. Evidence of napalm firestorms charred random sections. Defoliation left bare tree trunks jutting from dead, gray ground. Shrubs rotted.

Mac discovered six 175-mm rounds. Six 80-pound rounds plopped down whole like they were on display. He and the Animal set the C-4 charges while the others watched for movement on the bleak terrain. Mac shouted FIRE IN THE HOLE and all of them ran for cover. The charges exploded the shells. A bit too quickly, to Duke's way of thinking. BOOOMM! A train smashing into a granite wall. Jagged hunks of shrapnel shot in every direction. The metal screeched red-hot through the sky, wailing the song of a hundred ambulances. The terror of that sound lay in its utter nondirection. Scorching shards of steel knifed through the sky; twisting, turning, circling. Angling straight up, falling. Zooming along the ground, skipping, planing up and away. Finally burying themselves, thudding into trees or earth, smoldering.

Duke hugged the ground behind a boulder. He wished he was a mole.

"This is just plain dumb," pronounced Prick Peters.

Duke agreed. So did Jungle Jim. Kim seemed to smile with all but his eyes. Animal had no opinion but admitted he'd rather skip it. Mac called them pussies. He didn't find any more rounds for a while and they rested under some boulders. In that shade the temperature was a hundred and three.

"I say we skate over this dumbass mission," Prick Peters said. "Ain't nobody fool enough to be around this desolation but us. Blowin' up bombs in a blowed up land to protect people that ain't even here. And if they was, they'd be fuckin' with us. I say we take a walk, find some high ground and wait this one out. If we keep explodin' things, pretty soon somebody'll know we're here. If they find us, they *will* fuck with us. You all know it."

Mac lit a cigarette and said: "If, if, if. If shit were ice cream everybody'd have a cold sweet asshole. We'll take to high ground for the night, but we continue our mission in the morning."

Yeah, and if there were more MacFees there'd be more American crispy critters. And anteaters would likely be extinct. Duke thought it, but didn't express it. Not that he wanted to give Mac a break, he simply had other matters on his mind and couldn't be bothered. So he didn't say anything. Maybe he should have, but he was mainly interested in what might happen in Bien Hoa.

The men consulted their maps for hills and shot an azimuth for a suitable one. They marched over the dead land through the heat to the hill. The top was littered with rubble, an abandoned enemy base camp: shelled to bits. A few broken weapons were strewn about, some webbing and shreds of uniforms and tents. No bodies: There never were in those deserted, flattened garrisons. Hundreds of empty food supply cans and torn sacks lay about in varying stages of decomposition. All of them had UNITED NATIONS or RED CROSS or AMERICAN FRIENDS or some such symbol emblazoned boldly in English.

"Charitable organizations all," said Duke. "Purposes must be served."

The fact that the labels were printed in English infuriated the men. But the fury always came out as a bad joke, a snide remark.

"How can this be?" Kim shook his head, but he was goofing. He knew. So did the others and this was ritual.

"You see, there are folks back home," Prick Peters explained with a grin, "that claim we came here just to kill babies and burn and loot. They just know we love our lot; we're killers at heart. So they feel a need to help the other side: the noble VC. Folks know Charlie kills cause he's forced to; it's not really his way. He's killin' for peace."

"And killing for peace is like fucking for virginity," Jungle Jim put in.

"An old saying, wise but true." Duke took a long draw of hot water from his canteen. He felt betrayed by the familiar language and symbols on the enemy supplies. Feelings of betrayal fired flashes of dead men and one who should be: Warren Buckle, that hairless brute.

Animal squatted over a five-gallon peanut oil can. The can had rusty stars and stripes printed behind a benevolent American Helping Hand. Animal dropped his drawers and crapped in the can. Duke sat alone for a time on a burnt-out bunker. He smoked a cigarette, staring down at the scarred land.

They set up camp beneath a stand of bamboo. Darkness dropped, a deep dense dark, few stars.

"I still favor sitting this one out." Prick Peters spoke, softly. "Blowing these bombs is more ridiculous than I expected. Like stickin' your pecker in a meat grinder and expectin' it to come out whole."

"We have a mission to accomplish, a job to do." Mac spoke cupping his cigarette. "And do it we will, you chickenshit pilgrims." He flipped his Camel butt, burning, through the air. It arched, a miniature flare, then dropped sparkling to the dirt.

"You hardass sonuvabitch!" snapped Prick. "That shit gonna get us waxed!"

Mac moved close to Prick Peters. "Thought you said nobody else was around these parts. Whatsamatta pilgrim?"

Sniper fire ripped through the bamboo. It was high but there. Recon by fire. It split bamboo again. Mac lighted another Camel, his Zippo flame licking the dark unprotected.

Enough. Duke backhanded the lighter. Prick grabbed Mac's gunhand. Duke strangled him silent. "We'll have no more of that bullshit, Sergeant MacFee. Or we'll have no more Sergeant MacFee."

"Believe it," said Prick.

The others were prone on the ground.

Sniper fire passed sporadically near through the night. Duke called in their position and they spent an otherwise silent night. Each man monitored the dark, lost in his own thoughts. Curiously Duke's were, for a while, devoid of his murderous mission. He tried to remember things he had not done in a long time: Getting laid. She had been a beautiful, so damn young, whore in the coastal city of Vung Tau. He couldn't remember her face though, only the whiter than white beach and the turquoise sea. Charlie supposedly took R&R in Vung Tau, it was a nice place. He had asked the whore if she serviced VC grunts. She laughed a big laugh and claimed she only fucked Americans and NVA officers. VC numba ten. Getting laid: it had been a long time ago. Making love had been in another world.

He tried to remember the last book he had read and flat-out couldn't. So he thought about the last movie he'd watched. He liked the movies and recalled that one vividly. Howard Hawks' *To Have and Have Not* was one of those rare instances when a film bested its novel source. He had seen it in a small theater in Seattle. Humphrey Bogart had been brilliant in crisp black and white: a loner who understood love and friendship to be a rare commodity carrying with it certain irrevocable obligations. Bogart's heroic passage from isolation to action defined the depth of kinship, the weight of friendship. After the flick Harry Pitts headed straight for a book shop and purchased the original

Hemingway version. He liked the movie better.

Food was something to remember. Real food. Sharing a holiday meal with Ann's family. A meal days in the making. The old women creating their own pasta from whatever they created pasta from. Huge bowls of gravy: genuine Italian sauce jammed with pork chops and chicken, spiced to stay with you. Drinking beer with her grizzled father. Listening to old women speaking Italian, shrieking suddenly in laughter. Sitting at that long maple table in that cavernous kitchen, always next to her. Snow blowing up a blizaard outside, whipping against the windows. The heavy beams in the kitchen ceiling, pots and pans hanging, gleaming utensils. All the rich smoking food. Garlic bread crumbs on the linen tablecloths. Red smears on white cloth napkins. Wine. Toasts. Constant conversation. Laughter and wonderful insults. Cheeses, grated, wedged, melted. Cakes. Steaming black coffee so strong it screamed. Her sitting there at his side, smiling, eating, a repertoire of gestures in her enormous eyes. Licking cannoli crumbs from her lips, slow motion soundless dream quality. The smile.

Then would come the question. Always. Sister Mary again. Not unusual. "So when are you two getting married?"

Awkward momentary silence. Pitts grinning. Ann saying someday soon, we'll let you know. Pitts didn't like the question then or the first time some asshole asked. Whose goddamn business was it anyhow? Ann never pressed him. When was unimportant to her. She assumed—knew—it would happen and was not concerned with when. Pitts didn't look beyond them being together, but the idea of marriage did not set right. He was—he would tell himself—after all, young.

Drive-in movies in the winter snow were something to remember. Probably only remember. They could steam the inside of his Ford and they steamed it regularly. Sometimes they'd drive to New York so Pitts could legally drink in bars. He always felt strange with her in topless clubs, almost embarrassed. He would realize again, he was young.

They never lived together and he sometimes wondered if they ever would. They spent time in motel rooms in the college town. She lived in a dormitory and was required to sleep there. He lived in cheap rooms where women were not allowed. She would even have to sneak into the motel. They were not children and apparently not adults either. And this, these memories, were not old.

He groped for the sound and smell and form of his round-eyed woman. The elements wouldn't converge and he thought he should try to make that call across the Pond again.

Night was almost gone. In the gray light before dawn Duke and the others heaved into their rucksacks and marched down over the scorched earth. The plan was to head for a tree line and stream located between Ho Nai and Bien Hoa, spend the night, and move out toward Bien Hoa and a chopper in the morning. Majority rule had been invoked.

They reached the trees by late afternoon. The march had been long and hot and unflagging. They collapsed in clumps to rest in the shade. Mac dispatched Duke and Jungle Jim to fill some collapsible plastic water jugs. The stream should be a couple of hundred meters south in the trees. Nobody had slept much the night before, and Prick and the Animal were already catching up.

Duke and Jim used a trail that skirted the tree line for reference. They did not walk on it. They stayed in the trees and tracked the trail to the stream, a steady, deep trickle in a wide bed. They sat down and smoked some dope from Jungle Jim's little pipe. It had been some time since they had smoked and the weed affected them righteously. They took turns carrying the heavy water. The load felt worse than it was and they hassled each other. They were stoned stupid.

The afternoon light was deep green and bright yellow in

their eyes. They were chuckling over some simplistic joke when the first burst came. Bullets blasted chunks off trees and broke branches. They hit the dirt confused and disoriented. They were dumbfounded.

"Better get the act together, man," Jungle Jim spoke it, wide-eyed. He rolled and trained his M-16.

Duke said: "God damn! The act is tighter than frog's pussy. And that's water tight." His system surged, his muscles were knots. "Something's loose, not playing right back with the boys." He answered the bullets with silence. He gestured to Jim who knew what to do: creep like a Lurp, sneak up on Charlie, or whoever.

Duke moved painfully, slowly, sweating oceans. He decided that this dope smoking was out. A man with a mission had no use for it. After a time he saw Prick Peters prone, pointing his 16 toward where the water jug lay.

Duke called to him. "Peters, my man, what in hell is happening?"

Prick Peters whipped about. "Somebody's movin' 'round out there. What the hell do you think?"

"That was me, fucker. Me and Jim."

Prick Peters shouted to cease fire. When Mac raised himself up, Jungle Jim came up near him, rifle leveled at him. Explanation was due.

"Didn't know it was you," Prick Peters explained.

"We heard movement and shot," said Animal. "Nobody knew you dudes were fucking around in the bush."

"Just where were we then?"

"Shittin' for all I know," snapped Prick. "You got to tell a man what's up if you want him to know."

"Sergeant First Class MacFee sent us on a mission for water." Jim continued to cover Mac.

"I didn't mention it." Mac claimed it slipped his mind. Who the hell did they think would be there? "Prick knows ain't nobody else around here."

Things were tense. Prick Peters warned Mac this was no way to act. Silence settled to the jungle drone of locusts. Duke broke it.

"This is it for me, motherfucker. I ought to blow you away right here. But I'll be white about it. Be lucky it's me and not Peters; he'd probably be smarter. I even get a hint you're gonna fuck up again, planned or unplanned. I'm going to kill you. Blow your guts to mush. Scramble your brains like they were bombed by planes."

"I'll remember that pilgrim." Mac pulled at his collar fingering the rank insignia. "You remember I got rank."

"You've got shit, too, lifer. They both stink."

"You punk, I ought—"

"Shove it, Mac. You're outnumbered." Duke tried to look grim. He succeeded.

Jungle Jim suggested that Mac fetch the water. The men agreed. Mac went cursing to the trail near the tree line. He stomped down it in the direction of the water. His left foot sank into it to the knee. He yanked up hard but the boot was stuck.

His shout for help brought the others. It sounded pained.

"Booby-trapped, hardass. Plunged in a *punji* pit." Prick Peters grinned.

Mac grimaced that it didn't feel like a *punji* pit. Nothing pierced the bottom of his foot. His ankle hurt like hell.

Animal dug the dirt away. It was a new design in *punji* pits. The sharp dung-dipped sticks had been arranged to point downard and into a circle. When Mac stepped in the hole, the sticks gave. They pierced the canvas sides of his jungle boots and stabbed his lower leg and ankle as he reacted and yanked his foot up. The more he yanked, the deeper the stabs.

"Ol' Uncle Sam thought he had the pits beat with our steel soles," said Jim, tapping hit boot on the ground.

"Charlie sure did get wind of it." Animal pulled the wood blades from Mac's bloody ankle.

"And Mac sure did get the shit end of the stick." Prick Peters's grin got wider. "Looks like we'll be forced to cut this mission short."

Mac cursed in pain as Duke tended to the torn ankle. Jungle Jim called for a chopper. Kim examined the pit and sticks. Duke liked the prospect of arriving in Bien Hoa—Buckle Land—one day sooner.

CHAPTER TWENTY-FOUR

The helicopter touched down at the air base at Bien Hoa. The huge sky streaked yellow and oxblood, bathing the sector in deep warm hues. It would wipe itself full dark soon. Mac was taken to a hospital. The rest of the patrol was assigned to a troop tent. They would be picked up the next day.

Duke dropped his gear and ghosted. He disappeared armed with his .45. He reached Warren Buckle's flight group and peeped into the pilot's quarters. Empty. He slipped off base unnoticed and clung to the shadows. He found the cemetery Gue had described. He couldn't make out whether the place was Buddhist or Christian, maybe Caodai. Perhaps it was nothing more than an indiscriminate dumping ground. He used it to locate the street he wanted, Hoa Binh Boulevard, in two languages it was roughly the Street of Peace. Then he found the lane that was an alley really, across from the small temple Gue had also described. The house was not near a bar, rather in the alley off the street. Few pedestrians lingered here after dark.

Duke approached the house alone. It was large and French colonial. He climbed the stairs to the big door. Rifles at his face answered his knock. He immediately mentioned Gue's name. He was admitted to the dim interior. He asked for Judd. He was taken through a narrow hall to a wide room alive with dancing shadows where he saw him. Simple as that.

Judd had moments before injected himself with a stiff dose of opium. His ice blue eyes, melted and glazed dull, resembled an animal's. He stared at Duke and drooled.

An old Vietnamese man sat on his haunches in one corner shooting up skinny wild-looking males. They stood in line and knelt at their turn. The old man nimbly refilled the hypodermic barrel with the brown drug. He neglected to clean the needle or rinse the barrel. The room was lit by kerosene lamps and candles. The light was weak yellow: jaundiced like the skin it fell upon. Small arms were visibly abundant: American as well as Chinese Communist AK-47s and grenades. The men wore military suits, but they were not uniform. Any army they might represent was not apparent.

Judd fell back against the wall and collapsed. His nose ran. His rush receded and he stopped slobbering. He shook some of the stupor from himself and whispered shit if it ain't the Duke. He said it louder and stood up. He was a tall, thin man with blond hair and a stiff mustache trimmed to a Fu Manchu. Spittle dripped from it.

Duke moved in and shook Judd's hand. He noticed an eagle in flight tattooed on his arm in the crook where it bent. Oriental designs stretched red and blue across his chest. Judd was bonier than Duke had remembered. His skin was bad, plagued with scabs and eruptions. He stank and when he smiled, rotten teeth stuck from his purple gums. There were some gold ones that looked okay. Duke wouldn't understand how a man could let himself degenerate so. He didn't condemn Judd, he simply had no respect for him, a life-support system for disease and dope.

"I'm one surprised dude. Duke, I figured your tour was up. You gone Asiatic? Gonna stay on with me and the boys?" Judd gestured at the cowboys and junkies, all armed heavily.

"Got time left in the Army. Didn't feature doing it stateside. Didn't want to shine my shoes."

"I knew you had sense, Duke. Want to get high?"

149

"Might take a toke."

"Don't have the fixin's. We're straight shooters here."

"I'll pass."

Duke answered questions about some of the LRRP soldiers Judd had known. Who had been wasted, who had survived, who had been maimed and how. He left out the details of his last patrol with them. They discussed Gue whom Judd knew only slightly. Duke attempted to steer the conversation toward mention of the big, hairless American. "I hear you're a bandit. A dealer in dope and weapons."

"And much more. The black market is mine. There's a price on my head."

"So I heard. How do you trust these Martians?" Duke glanced at the men about the room.

"They don't care much for money. Occasionally one does fuck up though." He pulled a Bowie knife from its huge leather sheath on his belt. "I gouge the little fuckers."

The size of those knives never ceased to amaze Duke. He pulled at his right earlobe. "What do you recommend? I could certainly stand to go home a wealthier man. Think you could help?"

"Does a cat cover shit? You do have sense, Mr. Duke. I recommend dope. Get it back to the World where it's worth more than gold."

"I was thinking more along the lines of some action here. I wouldn't feel comfortable carrying weight."

"Nothing to carry. Mail it. You have access to the APO. It's an efficient organization. Gets the mail right where you send it." Judd drooled again. The saliva ran down, dripping off his chin. He slurped it back into his mouth whenever the stuff appeared to bother him which was not often.

Duke looked at the man's face. It was lumpy and dull. It reminded him of an old Maine potato gone to sprouts. He asked how this mail deal might be accomplished. He expressed anxiety. Judd assured him that it could be done. He had a partner, an upstanding officer, who managed it often.

"Just wrap it up tight and tote it to the PO. The system does the rest. Of course you need a place to send it."

"Right." Duke said it flatly, uninterested in the scam, but his curiosity concerning the upstanding officer mounted. He remained controlled. "I've heard that all parcels are opened and checked."

"My man Three-Ball says that's crap. Says metal detectors get passed over packages sometimes checking for weapons and such. And that's it."

"Three-Ball?"

"My partner plays pool. His head is kinda red and slick—clean like a Three-ball."

"Well what the hell would Three-Ball do if they opened his goods in the PO to see if what he claimed he was sending was actually that?"

"Don't know brother. Ain't happened. The man's got a set of balls on him like a tiger. He's a pilot. A chopper pilot."

"I see," said the Duke. "Some of those boys are rough mothers all right. Box the weight and take it to the PO. Brass it out."

"Simple as that. What rank you got?"

"Sergeant E-5."

"Wear it. PO clerks are Pfc.s and Spec. Fours. Most of them never seen action. Nice dudes. Don't want no trouble from a badass sergeant from the bush, a fuckin' grunt. Or a badass chopper pilot. A big, skinhead warrant officer."

"You make it sound like a milk run."

"Eyes-closed simple, Duke. Nothin' to it. Do it. Cop from me." Judd scratched his face, then his groin.

"Grass?"

"Maybe. But you'd have to send a heavy load to make it worthwhile to my mind. The bigger and heavier the load, the harder the run."

"What then?"

"Ope. Opium. I can supply chunks the size of softballs.

Dense brown balls worth big bucks back in the World. You got money?"

"No, but like I said I'd rather do something right here. I can get guns."

"Better, much better. We'll trade money or dope for guns. Greenbacks or ope."

"I wouldn't know how to off the dope in the World, and how can I get a load of cash back?"

"That's up to you. But I have connections stateside that would be happy to help with the dope. I ship them stuff all the time through Three-Ball. And he's got a scam for sending cash to the U.S."

"What's the chance of my consulting this Three-Ball?"

"Slim. He's understandably shy about his identity."

"Even," asked Duke, "as one smuggler to another?"

"Then you're in?"

"I'll think on it."

"When you're in."

Duke was tempted to let Buckle's name slip. But if Three-Ball were indeed him, as it seemed, it would be rather coincidental that Duke knew his name. Perhaps too coincidental for Judd the Bandit. He would likely fear Duke was an agent of some sort. He might murder him on the spot. Duke repeated that he wanted to think on it.

Judd danced over to an elaborate stereo setup. He switched on a tape deck and amplifier. Music blared, nosebleed loud: and the Eastern world was explodin' and bodies were floatin'. And some gravel voice was singing it, and the collosal speakers pulsed with it. Judd smiled his rotten smile and guided Duke to some hammocks. He sank into one and said: "You better decide soon, dude. This town, all these towns, this whole fuckin' sorryass country is about to explode. There's gonna be an offensive sweep so massive the sky's gonna shake for months. Probably right after the Tet truce, maybe sooner. Old man Ho's boys are gonna buckle for their dust for sure."

152

The word buckle snagged Duke's brain. Ragged images of dead men reigned momentarily. Like five movies at once, they deluged. *Flash Flash Flash Flash Flash*.

"They're gonna shoot and burn and loot," Judd went on. "Rockets gonna be flying and blasting everywhere. Charlie's been smugglin' guns and ammo by the truckload and sampanload these last days before Tet. Arms business been boomin'. Been a lot of gook funerals lately and I bet every damn graveyard in every town is a VC arsenal. Coffinloads of death. Gonna be hell on earth. Smoke and fire. VC and NVA gonna swarm. Gonna try to blow it out Uncle Sam's ass. Rivers of blood. Screaming kids. Weeping women. Wailing and gnashing of teeth. Armageddon." He got carried away "Arma-fuckin'-geddon!" His voice trailed off in drooling reverie. He slipped into what Duke knew to be the thick sphere of opium dream.

Duke spent the night propped in a corner. He watched the junkies crawl about in the shadows. He did not sleep. He held his .45 on his lap. He kept his back to the wall. The cowboys blobbed in and out of the shadows like protoplasm. In varying stages of consciousness they were moaning, mumbling, hooting reptilian things with dull eyes. They picked at themselves and their fingernails were exposed cat claws. Their noses ran and they flicked chips from their scabrous selves. Their teeth had rotted to triangles: stalactites and stalagmites from which flowed much open-mouthed drooling. Occasionally they played with their numerous weapons.

One tiny cowboy whose shock of black, matted hair hung over his bony shoulders and tangled about his waist, leaned on a nearby post. His bellybutton touched his spine and Duke saw him as a filthy black ragmop. Mop seemed concerned with the open silver-dollar sore in the crook of his elbow. He regarded the mushy thing carefully and raised it to his lips, slurping the bad ooze from it. Then he slapped the floor with his face. His head bounced once and he was quite still.

Duke didn't know whether the Mop was dead or alive. And as long as the shitbird got no closer, he didn't care.

He considered his purposes and the feelings of fierce loyalty and self-righteous vengeance that sustained him. He understood that these stirrings sprang from a still well brimming with the blood of the five dead scouts. Those men had been friends like no others he had known. Stand-up dudes. Each did what he had to and more. Theirs was the unique closeness and necessary trust of a small group of combat soldiers. Each had helped to save the other, risen to the occasion, keeping the team intact. With the team intact it lived and breathed with six hearts and minds, twelve eyes and ears and twenty-four limbs. Not one slacker, no deadbeats allowed.

Harry Pitts had trained and caroused with them stateside. They knew one another as trainees, garrison troops, drinking buddies, gripers, and dreamers. Each had wanted to be part of the vast pulse of things, to live and breathe through his own time and place. In Vietnam they knew each other as warriors. All else falling away, they had wanted to survive. And in order to survive they had to protect each other. They knew they were always just one fuck-up from oblivion. Chances are in civilian life they wouldn't have met. If they had, they would not have likely taken to one another, except perhaps Pitts and Rat Malloy. This mattered little to him. He had known them and they had been betrayed. They had performed the ultimate and final mission of the Infantry. But it had been for nothing. Nothing. And they had been the decent ones: dead, bagged and tagged and stacked like sandbags. Boxed and stacked again in the bowels of an airplane. Flown and shipped and borne to some hometown hole. Covered with dirt. No one could judge the rightness or wrongness of his feelings. He knew in his heart that his friends had been shamelessly forgotten: wasted. Their memory demanded a monument. Warren Buckle's carcass

154

would be a fitting one.

He looked into his memory and focused on a boy sobbing slightly, holding back but genuinely ticked off over the body of his murdered companion: a once-fine silver husky reduced to a matted, poisoned bag of bones. The deliberate work of a hateful neighbor, a goat farmer: A rock wall, a stone fence possessed more compassion. The boy was old enough to understand that cruelty was perverse and usually went unpunished. Justice became a personal concept as he cried alone to the winter sky and buried his partner with whom he had discussed his theories on everything, his animal that had been so many things in his imagination. It was only a dog, but he was only a boy beginning to understand what he would come to know: Justice generally ran a poor second to injustice. The wrong people got burned, became rich, died young. The justice systems existed for those who never needed them, and anybody else was shit out of luck. Handle it yourself but don't get caught.

That boy crouched the following winter amid the bare birches and looked on with satisfaction as the goat man's barn lit the gray sky. The boy glowed and the Maine hillside glowed, both warmed for a time. The boy trotted homeward. The barn listed toward collapse. Animals scattered.

The stereo tape was rolling and Johnny Cash rang in his ears, fading in and away and back again, falling into a burning ring of fire and being blue in Folsom because he shot a man in Reno just to watch him die. Duke wondered if the dink savages in the room understood, if they were even digging the mere sound of it. Fuck them. Perhaps exposing this Buckle might be the prime alternative, safest move. Get involved with Judd and his scam, suck Buckle in, and expose the ratbastard. Judd wouldn't approve such a scheme. No he'd be upset, likely get burned himself and seek reprisal. Then there would be the problem of whom to expose Buckle to. The rear was rife with corruption, both slant and round-eyed: Supply thieves, buyers and sellers, moneychangers, pimps and dope dealers. Nice enough dudes but not likely to give a damn about screwing one of their own. Still it might be done with adequate proof and a communiqué to an appropriate high ranking officer. That officer would have to be chosen with care, care he didn't have the time for.

On the other hand—his right, and naturally preferred—he might simply kill Warren Buckle. This too would take careful scheming for the appropriate situation. It would take that and much more. Cold-blooded murder was an act he never had been forced to rationalize. He had killed people, but they had been the enemy, mostly unseen: greased gooks. Executing an American would be labeled murder, no way around it. He wasn't sure he was capable of that ultimate blow. Even fragging might be easier to deal with, the victim generally being a direct threat to the killer's life. It was a special kind of offing. He had not indulged, but felt that if survival depended on it, he would muster the gall. Calculated, cold-blooded murder though . . . considering the act solemnly prickled him. His mind worked on the idea. Given the right set of circumstances . . . It would be difficult to manipulate the man into a situation while stationed at Ho Nai. Murder plainly was the wrong label for it. Revenge, vengeance, rectification, balancing the scales, justice: these were by far more accurate. He began the rationalization process before the fact.

Perhaps karma would take care of things. Rat Malloy believed in karma, and often explained it to Duke. For every action there is an equal and different reaction. Yin and Yang. That reaction, positive and negative, would balance one's personal scale. Act Right and Righteousness was in your future. Choose the degradation of Calculated Wrongness and you'd better be prepared for a rain of razor blades when you're fat and happy and soaking up sun.

Duke was prepared to give karma a helping hand. The theory was a lot of crap anyhow. He planned to bring that crap down hard on Warren Buckle though. Was he himself the dupe manipulated by some all-seeing Force of Justice? Duke the karma dupe. Murder couldn't be tolerated by such a force. How would his own act be reacted to? How would he be paid? How would his own karma be settled after balancing Buckle's scale? How would the five dead scouts know? They would approve though. But what about Rat Malloy? Yeah, a lot of crap.

CHAPTER TWENTY-FIVE

Duke woke Judd at the first hint of light during the false dawn.

He rolled out of his hammock. "Still with us, Mr. Duke?" he asked squatting and stroking his Fu Manchu.

"Roger that, and I've decided to make the deal. Now when do I meet with your man Three-Ball for a briefing?"

Judd sat in his hammock. "Man, you coming on strong for this early in the day."

"You said time was tight."

"Right, just bring us a sample—case of 16s or 79s. Then we'll deliver some bread and Three-Ball will fill you in on how much you can make. Nothin' to it."

"How the hell can I get greenbacks out of country? I could carry some, but I plan on a wad, a roll."

"No sweat," Judd stood up, wobbly. "Three-Ball got that situation in hand, too. He'll show you how to buy U.S. money orders from a postal clerk who's cool. Done all the time, man. Just send the money orders to the World."

"How about tomorrow. Say I come at noon with the goods." Duke wasn't sure what he'd have to do to procure a case of weapons and return by that time. But he must do it, he told himself. Damn straight.

"Noon is O.K. Three-Ball will be waiting." Judd began to prepare his wake-up fix. "We'll give you time on either side, no tellin' what sort of shit a man's liable to run into out there.

We're safe as turds in a sewer here though. Charlie gave me the word, straight from the horse's ass."

"Sounds like horseshit to me. You sure he'll show?" asked Duke.

"Damn straight," said Judd. He shot himself up with a small morning dose, talking all the while. This shot was not to get high but to get straight. "When money's to be made, that boy don't fuck around. One time this last Christmas we had a deal for pallets of beer down in Cholon and he used a chopper to transport the stuff. He's slick. Had a mission to fly that day and somehow got hold of a bigass Chinook instead of his usual Huey. He flew his mission, and flew to Cholon." He lit a cigarette, scratched himself and continued. "And if that ain't balls enough, catch this: After he dropped the patrol, which was his official mission, they called him back. Seems they ran into some shit. Well Three-Ball gave them some crap about having no protection and left the dudes." Judd shook his head and chuckled. "There was money to be made. And when that's the case, Three-Ball don't fuck around. He's one hard muthafucker."

"Yes," said Duke. "One hard mother, a regular desperado." He was about as steady as nitroglycerin, but he maintained. "Well I guess I don't have to worry about Three-Ball. This is a strange life you lead, man."

"Life is a shit sandwich and every day's another bite. I say to hell with the shit and everything else. Stay high and watch your ass."

"See you tomorrow." Duke left, his system surging, rivers of adrenaline. He hit the streets of Bien Hoa with both feet, solid and alone. He made his way toward the air base.

There had been no mention of the consequences of Duke trying to pull a fast one, say a ripoff or a bust. It was understood that if this were the case Duke would be summarily executed. This was going to be a delicate situation, one which required strength and timing. Although Judd had never mentioned the name Pitts, there was no guarantee he wouldn't do so to Buckle. Perhaps he had forgotten, but this could not be counted on. The fact was that Duke might walk into an ambush at that noon meeting. At any rate as soon as Buckle laid eyes on him, his identity would be exposed and the old jig would be up. Somehow he would be ready for it. At least he didn't have to worry about getting any money or guns now. And perhaps he would be enough of a surprise to Buckle to be able to take advantage of the initial chaos. The line had been drawn and perhaps circumstances might conspire for luck, Duke's side of it.

And that cruddy cocksucker left for money, and pallets of beer to be transported by Chinook.

CHAPTER TWENTY-SIX

Duke made mental notes of the terrain: big iron fence around whorehouse, two-story buildings on either side of alley, alley opens on street bordering cemetery.

He moved down the streets of Bien Hoa. People were clustered about in noisy groups preparing for holiday parades. Many men were carting incense and flowerpots in the cemetery he strode past. He thought he only noticed this because of Judd's wild predictions. Although this was none of his concern, he quickened his pace and moved onto the air base.

The corrugated metal Quonset huts of Warren Buckle's flight group beaded and dripped dew in the pink hints of coming heat. He moved to investigate the pilot's quarters on the chance that his quarry might be asleep and stabable, waiting to be sliced dead. He touched his sheathed bayonet and peeked through the screen window to an empty hootch. Soldiers and fliers were coming out of adjacent huts and Duke moved on. The murder question didn't mean much anymore.

In the near distance an airborne unit stood at attention while a bugler blew Taps over the boots of fallen comrades. Duke stopped and listened and watched. He knew this to be a futile, but somehow deep and important ritual. And on that final, mournful note, the rifle salute began and he walked away. Taps was one of those sounds that at once attracted and repelled him.

He arrived at the brown canvas tent where the CRIP soldiers had slept at the same time Mac did. Mac limped. His boot had been cut away to accommodate the dressing for his ankle.

"I thought we'd luck out and be deprived of your company awhile," said Duke.

"Sorry 'bout that," snapped Mac. "It'll take more than some shitty sticks to put me out of action, pilgrim." He flopped down and leaned on his rucksack and lit a Camel. "Truck'll be here soon, don't get lost." He said it to the group. "Where's Kim?"

"He split last night," Jungle Jim answered. "Said he got word some bad shit may come down and wanted to check on his family."

"Hell," said Mac, "this is Charlie's truce. Things'll be jake until just afterward." He played his harmonica and the men agreed that there was at least one halfway decent aspect to Mac's presence.

They waited for the CRIP truck, drinking American beer that the Animal and Prick had liberated during the night. It was warm but tasty.

Duke filled Jungle Jim in on what had gone down during the night with Judd. And Jungle Jim was both shocked and outraged.

"The bastard wasn't even afraid, he just had something better to do!" he said, shaking his head.

"He'll have something better to do tomorrow, too: a chance to do the world a favor and die." Duke drank down some beer and cited the necessity of a tight plan of attack.

"Back at the fort draw a map of the terrain," suggested Jungle Jim, "and we'll work one out."

The deuce-and-a-half rumbled by and circled back, Eddie Quick at the wheel and Ronald Cedar at the fifty. They were a solid salt-and-pepper team that had been together forever. Quick was a little New Jersey mick just naturally known as

Fast Eddie. Cedar was a 230-pound black Texan, a machinegunner—the Tree; his shadow would block the sun for ten Texas counties. He razzed Mac about his wound: "Step in some shit, Cracker?"

Everybody laughed but Mac. He climbed, without help, into the cab. The other soldiers climbed aboard the bed. Animal brought the beer. The truck rattled off the base to Highway 1 and north.

A tremendous explosion, followed by tremors of concussion and a glow, erupted to the south.

"Sounds like sappers and an ammo dump, down in Long Binh," said Duke.

Multiple distant explosions occurred in the direction of the air base they had departed. The truck climbed the hill toward Ho Nai and the explosions continued until the sound was constant, rolling thunder. The smudge that was Bien Hoa in the distance was a smoky one.

"Jesus! You suppose there was any truth in what Judd told me?" Duke felt himself getting pissed off.

"Kim had a bad feeling about the truce, himself. And obviously there's some truth to Judd's tale," said Jim.

"Yeah, but things are happening too early. Can't count on diddly-crap around here! Nothing runs right."

Fast Eddie Quick floored the gas pedal and the truck screeched through Ho Nai. People in holiday garb had ceased activity and were gazing in silent apprehension in the direction of burning Bien Hoa. Rain began to drop, a warm sprinkle.

The truck skidded through the gate of the old French fort, to a halt. The soldiers abandoned it.

But Lt. Ripley Masters came out of the command bunker shouting and jumping like a monkey that could speak. "Gotta move fast! Shit's hit the fucking fan at the bridge! Our patrol and the PFs, they need help. Get your asses back on the truck. Load up ammo and Laaws."

Nobody moved much, just looked at him.

163

"Goddamn you!" he shrieked and stomped both feet. "Those men are *ours*. Americans. They need help!"

Jungle Jim moved first. He got on the truck and looked at Duke. "Load some bullets and get aboard."

Duke frowned. "I got a thing to do."

"Damn right," Jungle Jim spoke evenly, "down at the bridge."

Duke was about to point out that he didn't really know those dudes at the bridge, when he thought better of it. He saw the face of Wally Riley and the blood of his doorgunners. And a savage wave of nausea shook him. "Roger," he said. He threw his 16 aboard and went for a case of ammunition.

Animal brought Laaw rockets. Prick Peters and the Tree stacked 50-caliber ammo. Fast Eddie fired up the truck. Masters ordered Mac to stay at the fort. Mac cursed and started ordering other CRIP soldiers about the fortifications.

A 122-mm rocket exploded somewhere in the southern sector of the village. The people in the marketplace and those standing in the streets in front of the fort broke into near panic. Gathering themselves, they made for village and family bunkers. Women wept silently and infants openly. Children laughed at the holiday commotion.

The truck was loaded and Masters assured the men that he would continue to request air support. "Everybody, everywhere wants it though. Charlie is raising pure hell."

The truck pulled through the gates which closed behind it. People in the streets scattered like gaggles of fowl. *Papa-san* from the beer store looked directly at the men in the truck. Duke couldn't determine whether the man was beseeching them or cursing them. The rain dropped harder and cooler, a stinging monsoon.

CHAPTER TWENTY-SEVEN

Duke lit a cigarette, cupping it against the wet, and listened and watched. They all strapped on extra bandoleers of bullets. As the truck drew nearer to the bridge, the staccato sound of automatic weapon fire and the whoosh and blast of rocket fire became clearer. The sky darkened rapidly, clouds swirling like gray gobs of smoke. The men were grim. The rain became colder. Thunder boomed and lightning carved the sky.

"Angels are beerdrunk again," Prick Peters said, "a million of them, pissing down a storm."

"And farting thunder," the Animal added.

The Tree switched on his tape player and Jimi Hendrix asked leeringly, "Are you experienced? Have you ever been experienced?" And his guitar thumped and whined and screamed.

The men looked puzzled at the Tree. "What the hell?" he asked and took off his shades. He took one of the warm beers from his pocket and popped it. "Beer, music, and a place to go!"

They all laughed. Duke looked at Jungle Jim and said again, "Man, I figured I was through with this bullshit."

"You could have been," was all Jungle Jim said.

Tree got into a flak jacket. The truck rammed the concertina wire, dragging it onto the bridge. The men shot and jumped from the truck and Hendrix died out.

More rockets pounded as they unloaded the ammo. Then more automatic weapon fire spilled in. Duke screamed that nobody but themselves was shooting back. "They *all* out of ammo?"

Animal and Prick found the CRIP day patrol, dead. Two with their throats slit open, a third shot in the back of the head, four and five pocked with shrapnel at the 50-caliber machine gun.

"Three of those boys got it from behind," said Prick. "Where are the muthafuckin' ruff-puffs?"

The PFs were gone, the single-handed honcho lay dead on the bridge. But the rest had disappeared. Sunk into their own landscape.

"Half those muthafuckers are VC, the rest ain't fit to wipe my ass on," Prick raged. "You still think they your brothers?" He glared at Jungle Jim and the Duke. "Musta been some Martians you didn't identify."

Duke let it go. The man had a point. "Load those bodies and put the ammo back on," he shouted. "Let's get the hell outa here!"

The men moved in crouched positions and shot out at the swamps. They loaded the dead soldiers, and Duke flashed on the last time he'd done it: not long ago enough and just as bad.

The monsoon was driving now, raining in full bone-soaking cold. The clouds swooped darker and gave the enemy gunners difficult targets on the bridge. But when the truck was ready, the driver was dead. Fast Eddie Quick had been shot in the ear and slumped over the wheel.

Ronald Cedar, the Tree, went wild and fired the truck's 50 in every direction. He was trying hard but his mask cracked and he cried as he shot.

Duke shoved Fast Eddie's body aside and started the truck. He backed it off the bridge and saw the VC swarm over the opposite bank. He backed off the road to turn, but the vehicle slid in the mud. The tires spun out great roostertails of muck, and sank. A B-40 rocket broadsided the deuce-and-a-half, knocking it on its side.

Duke climbed over Fast Eddie, out the passenger window, and jumped behind the roof. He moved to the bed. Dead soldiers and live soldiers had been flung in the mud. He shouted for Jungle Jim.

Jim crawled to him and yelled for Animal and Prick. They made their way over.

"Get as much ammo as you can carry and let's get the fuck out." Duke pointed to the boxes strewn about the truck and the bodies and the mud.

Animal popped open a Laaw rocket and fired into the VC. No detectable change, it must have killed dozens but the charge remained thick and steady. He looked at Duke who said, "I say again, let's split, vamoose."

Ronald Cedar, the Tree, managed to wrench the 50 from its mount and set it on the cab. He dragged cases of rounds near, then ripped them open. He began pouring lead into the advancing horde.

"Let's *didi mau*, Tree," Duke clapped his shoulder and shouted.

The Tree looked at him with an expression as wooden and immovable as his name. "Leave me be, Chuck." He moved his peach-pit eyes toward the cab and Fast Eddie. "We'll watch your backs," he said.

"He's dead, Tree."

"No he ain't." He looked away, evidently not wishing to discuss the matter.

Prick Peters scrambled over and held his brother by the man's giant shoulders. He looked at those eyes and the Tree told him to go. He did, and the rest followed.

Tree blasted long bursts; his machine gun chugged. He took the first slug in one of those shoulders. But it seemed only to make him madder and he stood and shot and stopped more bullets. Then a B-40 round slammed the truck and blew it up.

Duke and the men turned to see their rearguard, Ronald Cedar, the Tree, explode along with the deuce-and-a-half and Fast Eddie Quick. Fire crackled in the rain. Duke decided that if there were a place for the spirits of friends to reside, two more just moved in.

He and the soldiers turned and moved out.

CHAPTER TWENTY-EIGHT

The men ran straight down Highway 1. They carried only weapons, many bandoleers of ammunition and canteens, no rucksacks. They wore their bandoleers crisscrossed: Pancho Villa style. They were able to run quite fast. The human wave of Vietcong sweeping behind them served to spur them on past normal limits of endurance. They ran through the ragged hut-hamlet between the bomb-blasted bridge and Ho Nai. Nothing appeared in the hamlet but huts and rain.

Once in Ho Nai Duke suggested that Jungle Jim should find a more circuitous route. "Let's get off the main drag."

The VC paused in the hut-hamlet to torch it. The rain caused the activity to take considerable time. The CRIP soldiers were able to slow to double time. They settled into a rhythm and marched into Ho Nai. They had begun to think about the situation and pushed steadily on, their burning breathing audible in the rain, along with thuds of boots, the rattle and clink of bandoliers laden with full magazines, slapping scabbards. The sound and rhythm of it was like the clatter of medieval soldiers, knights to Duke: the sound of armor and weaponry and quest.

Jungle Jim took the lead and charged west into the village back alleys and lanes. The men followed. They trotted through the deserted section to a village chief's house. The man, who was headless, and his family were dead in their beds, all knifed, even the tiniest child. There was a blanket of

169

blood on the floor.

Duke checked the back yard. All the chief's hogs had been slaughtered. Rain pelted the chief's head along with the body of the disemboweled sow in which it was wedged. Flies in its eyes even in the storm.

"Sonuvabitch," said Duke. He pulled at his ear and turned quickly away.

"Damnit," said Jim, "I knew all these people." He got out of there.

Animal and Prick had climbed to the roof. The house was one of those solid, two-story models, the radio hidden on top.

"Radio's zapped," called Animal, "but get up here and look at this."

Duke and Jungle Jim climbed and looked to the smoldering hut-hamlet. Some VC were moving along the eastern border of the village proper setting fires and murdering families in communal bunkers. But the bulk of the horde was striking out east into the countryside.

"They're heading for Camp F-J's blind side," said Animal. "And the radio don't work. Maybe we could get back to the fort in time to warn them."

But a sound of great commotion came from the direction of the old French fort. A sound and fury of rockets and automatic weapons. Smoke bloomed from that section of the village, the middle.

"I imagine another human wave force is rolling through the central and southern sections," the Duke theorized. "Maybe to take the highway and attack F-J from that side."

"How do you think the fort is holding up?" Prick Peters asked.

"Let's find out." Duke climbed down, the others following. "Don't know how many gooks those fuckers left to deal with this area. Best peel your eyes."

They moved cautiously toward the old French fort through sheets of rain. Water eddied at their ankles.

The further south they traveled, the more apparent the evidence of shelling and human wave attacks. Buildings and houses became progressively more ravaged until the middle section of the village, which was nearly flattened. Bodies appeared with greater frequency. In the middle sector, family bunkers had been razed and the occupants burned and bludgeoned to heaps, dead or dying in the rain. Young girls curled fetuslike, naked on the ground. They seemed to be sobbing but it was hard to tell for some had brains leaking from their young skulls. The blood that oozed from their groins and mixed with the rain was obvious and easy to see.

"Damn, they look young," said Duke.

"Old as they're going to get," said Jungle Jim. He attempted to cover the first of these raped children. But there was neither time nor material to deal with even a fraction of them.

Duke kept telling himself not to notice much of this. It was not his concern. He must maintain his strength and move on. But even one murdered child is a tragic sight and he was not beyond comprehending tragedy.

The four men crept through the ruins of the beer store and lay flat behind the torn fifty-five-gallon drums, some concrete blocks and tin rubble. Across the highway the old French fort had been stormed and the gates destroyed. There was movement within, caused by a few vague shapes in the mist and rain.

Duke saw that one of the bodies lying in the street was that of the old *papa-san*, the beer store proprietor. He had been mutilated and his daughter lay dead beneath him. She was clothed and had a hole in her forehead. What was left of the old man's face was still set in that impenetrable mask. Duke wondered who'd shot the hole in the young girl's head. He knew that Jungle Jim had known *papa-san* and his family, probably quite well. He saw his friend seeing the dead father and child. He wished he might console this decent man, but he could not.

Harry Pitts was alert to the idea that James Grogan harbored a solid respect for the struggles of oppressed people, individuals in need of help. The man saw their plight as part of his own. He knew that every man ought to feel so, but he wasn't simple enough to expect it.

Harry Pitts's problem was that he didn't know who in the hell was whom. Which were the products of the oppressed and which the oppressor? He knew the VC to be scum, but he didn't know who they were. And those PFs on the bridge. How could they not die in an attempt to prevent such a massacre of their own. He didn't know who to take a stand for so he took a stand for himself. And that meant settling his own struggle with the man responsible for the condition of those five dead scouts. He had to have something. In the midst of the turmoil around him, his own mission ranked just beneath the immediate one of survival. Actually the survival imperative was a part of the larger Mission, the Quest.

Duke took his miniature seven-power binoculars from his jacket pocket. He pressed his eyes to the lens and scanned the fort: some enemy soldiers were tying something to the flagpole. Duke focused and that something looked about the shape of Lt. Ripley Masters. One of the VC lowered the flag of the Republic and draped it over the lieutenant's head.

"I see three gooks fucking with Masters," said Duke. "Can't tell if he's dead or alive. Can't really tell if it's him, they covered him. It doesn't look good. Don't see any more gooks." He folded the binoculars and replaced them in his thigh, flap pocket.

"Let's go clean 'em up," said Animal.

"Roger," said Duke. "J.J., cover our asses if we need it. Keep those bastards in your sights till we make the wall."

The three men moved across Highway 1. The slapping rain muffled their movement and they attained the wall of the fort. Duke peered around the gate opening and noticed Mac's body, riddled and face down in the mud, looking unnaturally flat. There was a fourth VC bending over him. Animal aimed his 16. Duke stopped him before he shot, whispering that Mac was so full of holes that he was gone for sure. "Let's go for the three first," he said.

The fourth VC had flipped Mac's body face up. A grenade with a cut fuse exploded almost immediately, blowing the VC's throat away along with great hunks of his jaw. Sergeant First Class MacFee hadn't forgotten who he was. He took one of the gook bastards with him after he was gone.

During the moments that followed, the three enemy soldiers were stunned and they never recovered. Each of the CRIP soldiers cut one down dead with short bursts of fire.

Jungle Jim joined the group and they surveyed the courtyard. The CRIP soldiers who had manned the garrison were piled like the corpses they were. They tangled gruesomely like a clump of plague victims awaiting the pits. The monsoon beat down washing and filling their collective, violated form.

"Sonuvabitch," said Duke.

"Think there might be snipers about?" Prick Peters put in.

Then the flag-draped form of Lt. Ripley Masters moved and moaned. He sat bound to the flagpole, leaning, hanging.

"Guess we're gonna have to find out." Jungle Jim spoke it and spat. "You lads be sure to watch my back." He crouched and zipped straight across the yard to the pole.

Duke didn't consider this a particularly wise move. But somebody had to do it and he was happy old J.J. was along. He watched the windows and walls as if through a microscope.

Jungle Jim walked back to the men slowly, as if dazed. He held the red and yellow flag tightly, partially bunched. His face was ashen and rain-streaked, he threw the flag down and puked in it. "Oh, this fucking war gets old." He nearly wept it. "I don't know what to do with him." He shook violently.

The Animal scrambled toward the lieutenant but turned and scrambled back. He had made it halfway. "I ain't doing it," was what he said.

Prick Peters claimed he knew what the situation was from where he stood. He'd seen it before. "Only one thing to do for the dude," he said it flatly. "Just gotta decide who can do it."

Duke was slightly confused and pissed off that he would have to get involved. He considered Ripley Masters your basic lieutenant: an idiot. He went to see what kind of trouble this idiot had gotten into.

Lt. Ripley Masters's eyes were gone, or most of them. His ears had been removed, along with his hands and feet: bloody holes and stumps. Then the ultimate VC terror inflicted upon his enemy: Masters's groin had been mutilated and his penis crammed into his bloody black mouth, recently.

It was horrible and Duke recoiled from it. But Masters seemed somehow to be alive, breathing and rasping at any rate. And Duke understood this to be wrong. He drew his .45 and killed what remained of Lt. Ripley Masters, the Digger.

The men looked at and away from him when he returned. "If the situation were reversed," he said, "I'd want it that way for myself." He said it truly and the men knew it.

Then Duke sat down on the sodden ground and removed his bush hat. He drooped his head and stared at the puddles. He let the monsoon slap the back of his neck and tried to think of his own mission, and not to let his mask crack. He was not entirely successful and waves of confusion engulfed him. He was nearly overwhelmed when Jungle Jim knelt and touched the back of his neck. And Harry Pitts reached back and held his friend's hand. Then he turned and looked at the man. Jungle Jim helped him to his feet and they embraced. Harry Pitts held tightly and slipped back into the Duke's protection. His strength returned and he looked at Jim to tell how close to the brink he had come.

Jungle Jim said, "It was the right move. Somebody had to do it, and I'm glad you were here."

CHAPTER TWENTY-NINE

The main attack was beyond the village now, moving methodically south and east toward Camp Frazier-James. The CRIP soldiers dragged their dead into one of the larger rooms bordering the courtyard of the old French fort. They lined the corpses on the floor and covered them with ponchos and poncho liners.

Prick Peters squatted over the lumpy bunch and whistled a few bars of Taps. He was a good whistler. The dirge invaded Duke's senses and he heard it and the rain outside. That simple sound had imprinted his mind, becoming one of those tunes that drift in and out of memory. He would catch himself whistling; then, the melody becoming clearer, memory would strike. As it struck now. He went out into the rain and the sound ceased.

Jungle Jim approached and said: "Seeing that village chief and his family and then old *papa-san* over there," he gestured to the shell-shattered beer store, "got me wondering about Kim and his. You still got that dagger he gave you?"

Duke reached around to the small of his back where the knife was sheathed. "Yeah," he said, "I guess we'd better find out, and then decide where in hell we're going."

"Where we're going," Jungle Jim laughed. "That's a fine one. About as good as where we're at. Or where we came from. Or what in the fuck we are doing here." He shook his head, folding the wet flag he had taken from Masters's head, placing it in his pocket.

Jungle Jim's remark was unsettling to Duke. He figured that Jim had always had some plan for his actions. Unlike himself who hadn't lately believed in much of anything he did on a daily basis. For Jim there had always seemed some pattern and satisfaction in being where he was. As for himself, he was where he was, doing what he did, simply to get by—get over as Prick might say. He had his mission. There just seemed to be a lot of shit to get through, or over. The war was slowing him down, dragging on him. It occurred to him that even so, he probably had a more definite goal, a more concrete thing to accomplish than did the U.S. Army. He had never really given a damn about the war and had often speculated that the army felt the same. He had come to it—the war—to do it, to feel it. And that was more than most.

He considered the Vietnamese and their reasons for living in all this hell. The southern ones in the Republic were doomed as far as he could tell. They were poorly organized, their leaders corrupt. The only thing they possibly had in their favor was U.S. cash and guns. The northern ones, on the other hand, had organization and mission: belief. Plus some Russian guns and cash. And some Chinese stuff, too. But it was the organization and *mission* of *liberation*—the belief—that was the edge. They left themselves no alternative to victory, no North and South.

And, as always, he wondered where the American soldier stood in the struggle. Jungle Jim had always appeared to understand that they were fighting the good fight, aiding the worthy side; fuck communism and all. Now he might be thrown askew, not quite sure. Duke wasn't sure he liked the idea. But he surely understood. Who could want to be aligned with these marauding Mongol-assholes, these vandals that had spread this fire and death? And who would want to be allied with the chickenshit dinks on the bridge who abandoned their own?

176

Perhaps Warren Buckle and Judd and other such scumbags perceived the role best and to hell with everybody else. And how many other such scumbags were there? Corruption and complicity doubtless ran deep and dark and was many pronged. There was just too much American energy generating in South Vietnam for the war to be as muddled as it seemed to be. All of the activity and hardware had to be producing something for someone.

But there was Kiem Ly and Phuong. They were dues-paying members of the human race and deserved a break. And they lived on the way to Bien Hoa.

Jungle Jim had moved onto the porch and was smoking a cigarette from a dry pack Animal had produced. He called to Duke, praising the taste of the tobacco. He joined them. The four soldiers smoked and Prick mentioned that Doc Ratchit's body was missing. The Animal added that the radio inside the command bunker had been destroyed and he didn't notice the jeep about either.

"Charlie likely drove that jeep south," said Duke. "But we might check over at Gue's place for Doc. Find him or not, we should head south and check for Kim, then move westerly for Bien Hoa and the air base."

"Why not hole up right here?" said Prick. "Man the fort."

Duke pulled a plastic pack from his pocket and extracted a map from it. He spoke as he unfolded it. "No matter how many gooks try to overrun Camp F-J, they'll only succeed to a degree. Then they're gonna either get killed or driven off. Those that split will come right back through here and there's not but four of us and no radio. I'm not going to be here." He spread the map on the slate floor. "We can make for this high ground at the southern tip of Ho Nai." He indicated the areas on the map as he spoke. "See what things look like from there. My guess is that the attack on Bien Hoa will concentrate on the air base rather than the city. We could move across country and slip into the city and take our chances on getting to the base."

"We just came through some of that area yesterday," Prick pointed out, not sounding at all impressed with the plan. "And I'll bet that old base camp ain't deserted no more."

"True," said Duke, "but knowing the terrain, even slightly, should work in our favor. Besides, I ain't giving any orders, men. I'm simply telling you what I think *we should* do and what *I am going* to do." He folded the map, slid it back into the plastic, and pocketed it.

Jungle Jim said he was with him. There was really no question there. Animal asked Prick if he had a better idea. When the man didn't answer, he shrugged and joined the other two. Prick Peters grumbled something about not staying anywhere in this godforsaken country alone.

The four men slung their extra bandoleers, picked up their weapons and plunged into the stinging rain.

The marketplace was a deserted ash heap. Black-haired children and parts of people lay strewn about it. A portion of the top floor of Gue's house had been disintegrated. Animal and Prick secured the area. Duke and Jim climbed the stairs.

The rain poured in through the blasted roof. There was nobody in the place but Doc Ratchit. He was lying on a hemp mat in an undisturbed corner, his head on a bright plastic pillow. Duke and Jungle Jim knelt next to him and saw that he wasn't marked. Jim felt for his pulse and put his ear to his chest. "The son-of-a-bitch is breathing!" he said.

They shook him violently and dragged him into the rain. He was soaked quickly and began to come around. He opened his eyes, rolled to his side and began to vomit. "I gotta get off this shit," he said, groggily. "I had the worst goddamn dreams I ever had. Scary hallucinations more like it."

Then he looked around and threw a look of total confusion to the two men standing over him. They took him downstairs and into the ground floor of Gue's house. Animal offered cigarettes from his plastic pack. They all smoked and

Jungle Jim explained the situation to Doc Ratchit. The Doc didn't say anything. He smoked and stared.

"You should thank that habit of yours." Prick Peters blew smoke at Doc. "Without it, you'd be one dead doper."

Doc still possessed his .45 and medic bag. But he explained that Gue's people operated a pharmacy in this section of the house. Small glass vials filled with a clear liquid should be searched out. These would be ampules of Maxitone, a strong French amphetamine sold over the counter in most Vietnamese pharmacies of any size. And all of them that house opium dens upstairs. "Speed, lads. Speed. A solid, smooth upper to keep everybody alert on the trip to Bien Hoa. I don't know about you dudes, but I won't make it on my own steam. The stuff'll give us extra range."

The men fanned out and searched the rubble and cabinets and counters.

Duke hoped they would be successful. Because suddenly he felt terribly tired. He had not slept the night before at Judd's. And he hadn't had much the previous night in the bush. Speed sounded great.

It was Doc who discovered the drugs. He snapped the small end of one ampule and dropped the clear liquid into his mouth. He screwed up his face at the bitter taste. "Jugs of life," he said, holding one up. "Look like tiny, old-fashioned milk bottles."

"Kind with the cream on top," the Animal pointed out, smiling.

Doc laid the stash on a counter top. He placed one of his canteens next to it and began snapping glass and dumping Maxitone into his water. "This is good stuff. Half a jug is good for all day. But considering the nature of our business, I recommend more."

The others emptied one ampule into themselves and a half dozen into their canteens. They wrapped what remained into handkerchiefs and stuffed them into pockets. Then they got the hell out of there.

CHAPTER THIRTY

The men knelt and squatted, a loose huddle beneath a tin canopy. They looked out at the jumbled junk of the marketplace, the rain. Doc Ratchit was holding them up. He stepped behind the canopied wreck of a market stall to relieve himself. Said his guts were goo.

"This dump stinks," Animal spat. "Musta sold fish or shit here."

"Could be Doc," Prick Peters suggested.

"Could be."

Rain slapped and splattered, drumming the tin canopy.

"When I get back to the World I'll have it knocked." Animal shifted on his haunches.

"How you figure that?" Prick Peters sounded unconvinced.

"Car wash," Animal said, a grin. "I'm gonna open me a car wash. I been sendin' back allotments to my bank. I'm gonna call it the Best Car Wash in the World. Sounds freakin' great, don't it? I worked in a car wash back home in Bed-Sty. Owner liked me and showed me all about them. I'm gonna be Mr. American, a freakin' hot-shit capitalist."

Prick Peters said: "Do dudes really, I mean actually, own cars in Bedford-Stuyvesant? I thought it was some kind of lost ghetto."

"Lotsa freakin' cars in Bed-Sty. Shit, Prick, spades got some of the biggest ones. Be my best freakin' customers.

Ain't there no cars in California ghettos?"

"Sure. Some of the dudes I know got nicer rides than they got places to live."

"There it is, then. You got the picture. You should open a car wash. Fuck workin' for Mister Charlie."

"Don't worry about that," Prick Peters said. "I won't be working for no Mister Charlie. I'm going back to kick ass and take names. I'll be mayor of Oakland one damn day. You watch me. I got the gift. I'll end up a lawyer and a mayor and who knows what else."

"How about you there, Jungle James?" Animal looked out at the marketplace as he spoke. "Got any cars in the Ohio sticks? Probably just squareass pickup trucks. You could start a specialty business. The Best Pickup Truck Wash in the World. Do freakin' tractors on the side."

Jungle Jim smiled for an instant. "I mostly just want to get back and look around. See some things. I've only got vague kinds of plans, general ideas. I'd like to look around some and then probably settle down. I'd just like to live, you know. I think I'd like to have some kids, some sons."

"That sounds righteous enough," Prick Peters said. "All we gotta do is get our asses out of this large sling they're in."

"Where the fuck you from, Duke?" Animal, turning his head.

"Maine."

"Got any cars in Maine?"

"A few."

"Well?" Animal grinned, stretched the scars on his face. "You could call it The Best Car Wash in Maine, 'cause I'll already have The Best Car Wash in the World."

"Hell." Duke pulled at his ear. "If I knew what the fuck I wanted I wouldn't be here. I'd be happy somewhere else. You see me laughing, happylike? See me jumping for joy? If I had any sense I'd already be gone."

They laughed lowly. Right on! God's own truth. There it is.

But Duke refused. "I'm not kidding. No chuckles for this hombre. Happy and me are on different planes; I live here. Doesn't it make your hearts bleed?"

"Bullshit is your true buddy, Duke." Prick Peters, a rare grin. "So we don't know what just exactly it is on the other side of it all you might mean." Still the grin.

"Dreams and delusions." Doc Ratchit came back. "Half-baked plans, my men. The stuff of lunacy. Of course, I do it myself. I might become a veterinarian. The animals have it over us, a better class of life form in some ways. They don't do much of this organized slaughter of their own." Doc waved his arm out at everything. "Or I might be an anesthesiologist. Put pain far, far away. Either way I plan to be around loads of drugs."

"I think we better split." Duke stood up. "I'm feeling kind of fast."

Jungle Jim stood. "You feeling better, Doc?"

"I'm cleaned out. Fresh. I'm lightning ready to strike out." He took a deep breath.

Prick Peters said: "What would we do without bullshit?"

Animal said: "I wasn't bullshittin'. I'm opening The Best Freakin' Car Wash in the World."

They moved out into the rain, spaced, looking, weapons ready.

CHAPTER THIRTY-ONE

The five men hadn't eaten all day and the drug took effect quickly. Their eyes peeled the storm. The moved through the dead village cautiously and approached a burnt-out temple, where the hamlet TV set had been and now sat smashed on the ground.

The broken tube set Duke to thinking of old shoot-outs he had watched on one. Then movement jolted him. An enemy soldier stepped from the temple out to the smoke and rain; he staggered, wounded. He and Duke stared at one another, momentarily stunned, animation suspended.

Animal moved first and blew the man down, packed his chest with lead. Duke thought the gook looked familiar, like the cowboy who had stabbed Jungle Jim. And Jim spat at the body in agreement.

Harry Pitts remembered cowboys and Indians and boys arguing: No fair! Not me! I'm not dead! But the game was gone, lost in its illusion. There were no rules to argue over. This was rigid, undisputable reality. Do or die. Do and die.

The men moved on to Kim's hootch. Duke's strength was with him, curbing his fear; he was thankful. Kim's door was splinters. He and Jungle Jim went through it.

The place was a smoldering shambles. Kim had been blown against the far wall. He sat against it filled with shrapnel and death, his black automatic cradled at the ready. Phuong was in what was left of the next room crouched in a corner, caked with ashes. She was humming softly, cradling her child. There was no sign of the old woman.

Jungle Jim approached his dead blood brother and laid

him down. Kim's eyes were wide and Jim reached down to shut them, only one would close. Duke knew some of what his friend felt because he felt some of it too.

He moved into the next room and his strength held but it was difficult. The tiny thing in Phuong's arms was a bloody Oriental doll without a head. She gave it up easily though, and Duke took her out to the rain.

Jungle Jim knelt awhile longer next to Kiem Ly: the Montagnard mountain man, a brave, but dead soldier of his country; a man killed defending his home. Jim took the folded flag from his pocket: the red and yellow banner of the Republic that had been mockingly draped over Ripley Masters's violated face. He unfurled it, placing it over Kim's body. Then he left the house.

"Not much consolation for all his years in the war," Duke spoke it sadly and Jungle Jim didn't speak at all. He tossed Kim's M-16 to Doc.

The other men were edgy at the sight of the woman.

Phuong began to hum again. And Harry Pitts thought of his lonely lady, perhaps aching but waiting safely in the hills of Vermont. He held tightly to Phuong, who rubbed her forehead on his ribs like a lost child, like a kitten. He touched the dagger that pressed the small of his back. He looked at her eyes. They were great green holes. He hoped he saw trust and, perhaps, a flicker of hope. But he knew better. They were great green holes that hardly moved. His mask nearly cracked, but again it held. For the women, he told himself. For this broken one here and the one at home. But he knew it was for himself as well.

Prick Peters asked if Duke intended to bring the woman, but it was Jungle Jim who answered. "We're bringing the woman and I don't want to hear any flak about it." He spoke in a controlled, even manner. "Like the man said, nobody's ordering anybody to go with us."

"She'll never make it," said Doc.

"Then we'll carry her." Jungle Jim gestured to Duke and they walked south for the Ho Nai hill, the three of them.

CHAPTER THIRTY-TWO

Memory invaded at the oddest moments. Sometimes Harry Pitts would be gone from the war. Unarrived. Back in the World before he thought of it as the World. These snatches from another time flashed and faded in moments. But within the moments he might see an entire old scene, hear complete conversations, or cling unclearly to impressions, fragments.

Now, climbing the southern hill of Ho Nai, he was climbing a tree in Vermont. He had dropped out of college again. Lack of money, and interest. The sign on the truck read Bud's Tree Service. Bud, who looked about forty years of solid muscle, said to Harry Pitts: "Can you climb a tree?"

"Yeah, of course. What do you think?"

Bud's face and arms looked like tanned alligator hides. Like he had spent his whole life outside. Bud pointed to an oak that looked about two hundred feet tall, a thick one. First branches looked about forty or fifty feet up. And further on up, the oak forked and grew as two trees. Bud threw a baseball that was on the end of a rope around the first big limb. The ball whizzed around, wrapping the rope. "Climb." Bud pointed to the oak.

Pitts went right to it. He felt strong enough. Old high school athlete, he had climbed ropes in P.E. Arm over arm. He moved up pretty well, steadily. About eight or ten feet from the branch, his arms gave out. Nothing left. He slid down much faster than he had climbed up. The rope burned his hands, ripped his palms. He landed on his ass, looking dumb, feeling about the same.

"Thought you said you could climb a tree." Bud stuck a pipe in his teeth, lit the tobacco.

"Thought I could." Harry Pitts stood up. His hands were on fire. "Guess it's been awhile."

"You take the rope," Bud said, "use it to pull yourself while you use your legs around the tree. Won't fall on your ass thataway. Try again?"

Harry Pitts needed the job. He tried to forget the fire in his hands. He climbed up the tree, used the rope and his arms and his legs. Only a little tough. He took directions from Bud and snapped a rope into the clamp on the safety harness he had tied around his waist and ass. Up to the topmost branch that would support his weight. Tie the rope off. If he fell, this rope should save him; he would be tied to the tree by his harness.

"Don't worry none," Bud shouted. "Those clamps and ropes are guaranteed. They break we can get our money back."

"Thanks, I was wondering." Harry Pitts took in the view. Summertime and everything was green. The sky a clear light blue. He could see mountains.

Bud had him swinging and climbing, hauling up tools. Pitts felt pretty good. The tree had another side to it. Three-quarters up the trunk it split into what amounted to two trees. Bud said: "Harry, you swing over to the other section. Whenever you got parallel parts you got to trim both. One climber to a tree."

Harry Pitts swung, a little short. He went again, grabbed a branch. Pulled himself toward the other trunk. The branch broke. He swung back, then again. His safety harness, tied too loose, slipped over his waist, off his ass, caught at his ankles. He swung to and fro. Seemed like slow tortuous arcs to Harry Pitts. Upside down swinging, seeing the ground move. Swaying, reaching up, grabbing for his rope, feeling the blood pound in his ears, adrenaline pumping, swinging, dangling, not hearing a thing but his heart thunking. I might die today. Head broken open like a melon, neck snapped. Maybe I'll get lucky, just be paralyzed. I might die here today.

One time while fording a deep stream in the jungles of War Zone D, Pitts was in a canoe on Lake Champlain, looking across toward the New York shore. Seeing Ann in the bow was fine. Her hair hardly moved in the soft bright light. The day was warm; the water easy, calm, sun popping off the surface.

Not looking back at him, she said: "Harry, what would you do in case of fallout?"

Earlier in the day they had watched a film depicting the gruesome results of nuclear warfare. The end of it all in heat flashes, heat waves and blast waves, firestorms, megatons of death.

Pitts said: "I don't know that I'd do anything."

"But I'd want you to, Harry. I'd want you to reinsert and shorten your stroke."

A stop in an EM Club at Camp F-J became a fight outside a bar in South Carolina. The EM Club was jammed with multicolored grunts in the rear for a stand-down. Music blared, beer went down. Black and white and red and brown drunken grunts.

The bar was in Columbia, South Carolina, outside Fort Jackson. A college bar near the University of South Carolina. There was Pitts, Jefferson, and Kiloq from the fort. The other young people in the place looked like college students, clean-cut ones. The rock 'n' roll music sounded pretty fair and the girls looked pretty. But the girls didn't talk to Pitts, Jefferson, and Kiloq.

After a while some of the boys spoke up though; first one guy in a loud checkered shirt, to Pitts: "How in holy hell do you do it?"

"How's that?"

"Drink with a nigger."

Jefferson was black, from Newark, New Jersey. He said: "Eat shit cracker, bark at the moon."

The checkered shirt: "That kinda talk get you hanged, boy."

Jefferson stood up. He was about five seven, hundred thirty pounds. About eighteen other college boys gathered, surrounding the table. Pitts felt embarrassed. "Let's split," he said.

Kiloq, from Louisiana, a man of monstrous proportions, an oil rig worker since he could walk, said: "I'll kick the shit out of the toughest fucker here. I lose, we leave. I win, we stay and no more bullshit. I like to fight." When he smiled he took out his upper teeth.

The college crowd pulled back to powwow. Pitts said, "Why don't we just split?"

Even Jefferson was for it. "There's too many, man. They all jump us, we up shit's creek."

Kiloq shoved his teeth into the pocket of his jeans. "How many of those boys you think ever had his eye gouged out? Or his nose broke or his balls kicked back into his belly? They're punks. Some are big punks, but still punks. I know these boys, grew up around them. Cajuns ain't always considered white where I come from. I'm Cajun and these is dumb white boys. I'll fuck up their biggest football player so bad they'll all feel it. Then we'll leave."

It was a deal. Everybody went outside. Pitts didn't like it, but he went. Kiloq and the football player, who turned out to be bigger than Kiloq, moved behind the bar. Kiloq stared at him. The football player moved and Kiloq decked him. The football player started to get up, Kiloq punched him. The football player stayed down.

"Two punches!" Pitts said to the checkered shirt. "Amazing. Either amazing or the football hero is wise, staying down. Being a college man and all."

Checkered shirt broke his beer bottle on the bar's exterior block wall. He held what was left by the neck and rammed it into the side of Pitts's head, trying to cram it into Pitts's left ear. Screaming something about niggerlovers. Pitts was shocked but moving, bleeding, too. Pitts had been a high school wrestler. He head-locked the guy, whipped him down, landed on top. He was glad because he hadn't always landed on top in high school. He had knocked the bottle neck away, thought he heard the glass breaking completely. He was glad for that, too.

"Listen," Pitts said, close to the guy's head. "We can roll around some, get up and be done. Don't have to hurt ourselves anymore. Okay?"

Checkered shirt shouted that this niggerlover was also a chickenshit. He bit Pitts's arm. Pitts got up and stomped him. When he heard the siren, he ran away.

In the morning at the motel, Jefferson said: "Let's go to another of those college bars tonight. I like those white girls. I like to drink in those joints. Which one you wanna hit?" Jefferson smiled. He looked fine, said he felt fine.

Kiloq's right hand was sunk in a sinkful of ice. He held it up. Swollen, crooked fingers, knuckles in the wrong places.

Pitts took the washcloth from the side of his head, his ear. Blood, scabs, a tight sharp soreness. He felt the bite bruise when he moved his arm.

"Which one of them college bars you wanna hit tonight?" Jefferson said. A big smile.

Outside Saigon, watching ARVN troops stepping out a close order drill, Pitts saw scenes from his own training. Heard the mad marching songs. Saw the old fantasies.

A column of troopers hitting doubletime in the dust.

> I wanna be an airborne ranger.
> I wanna live a life of danger.
> Am I right or wrong?
>   You're right!
> Am I goin' strong?
>   You're right!
> Sound off!

A dawn beginning. Forced march. Full combat gear. Red sun rising in a cold fog.

> Viet Nam!
> Viet Nam!
> I wanna go to Viet Nam.
> Am I right or wrong?
>   You're right!
> I wanna kill ol' Charlie Cong.
> Am I right or wrong?
>   You're right!
> Viet Nam!
> Viet Nam!

Running in the snow. Combat boots, utility trousers, T-shirts.

> I don't know but I've been told
> Eskimo pussy is mighty cold.

Marching up a red clay hill in the heat.

> I don't want to sit and cry.
> I don't want to wonder why.
> I just want to fight and die.
> Am I right or wrong?
>   You're right!

And if I die in a combat zone
Box me up and ship me home.
Sound off!

Companies of infantry marching in columns. Full combat dress. Rifles slung. Flags waving. The base buildings receding, the forest ahead, the sky steel.

And in her hair
She wore a yellow ribbon.
She wore it in the springtime
In the merry month of May.
And if you ask her
Why the hell she wore it:
She wore it for her soldier
Who was far far away.

She wore a yellow ribbon. Pitts would see cavalry riding out from Fort Apache, desert dust rising on the silver screen. Bugles would sound. And Ann would wear a yellow ribbon in her long brown hair.

Fantasy was a way to see.

And now again, climbing the southern hill of Ho Nai in the rain, Pitts was falling from an oak tree in Vermont. Dangling, swinging, the rope around his ankles and tied to the tree, slipping, grabbing, reaching up, catching the rope. I might die here today. Pulling himself up, holding the rope tight and close, climbing, grabbing hold of a sturdy limb. Refitting his safety seat. Climbing down, a sloppy rappel to the ground. I might have died here today.

"You want the job?" Bud, looking steadily at him.

"Yeah, of course. What do you think?" He smoked a cigarette. Back up the tree with some new respect. I might die here today.

CHAPTER THIRTY-THREE

Night crawled over the landscape as the two men and one woman crested the hill. The crumbling walls of a Caodai church blocked their silhouettes.

The amphetamine roared through Duke's blood. He craved tobacco, nicotine; but he had none. He got out his map and compass. "Near as I can tell, the country is dikes and paddies and then open scrub for about five clicks southwest," he said. "Then there's a hamlet and some jungle around that old VC base camp. We can skirt the camp and keep to a southwest azimuth. We should hit the northeast corner of Bien Hoa. Terrain and Charlie will determine when. If we make it at all it'll be tomorrow. If we have to travel through much bush in daylight, we're dead."

"Phuong is another factor," said Jim.

"True." Duke saw her sitting, her hands clasped about her ankles in the dying light. "Feed her some of that speedy water and she shouldn't hold us back as much as she might."

Night had wrapped itself about everything when the other three men topped the hill and were nearly shot by the first two.

"Decided to join us?" Jungle Jim lowered his M-16.

"We figured we'd all have a better chance sticking together," said Doc.

Duke said he didn't see the logic behind the theory, but welcomed them. "Got a smoke, Animal?"

The five men cupped their cigarettes—the last of them—enjoying the tobacco and its warmth. They leaned against the protection of the falling wall. Duke again outlined their approximate route. "The dark and rain," he said, "will help and hinder us. We won't be easily detected but we won't see too well either." They all heard several thunderous explosions to the north. "Let's go."

They doused the cigarettes and took swigs from their canteens. Jungle Jim poured some drugged water into Phuong and told her to stay close behind him. She stood up and followed his directions, appearing to understand, in a blank, listless manner. The five men and one woman descended the hill into the inky black and dripping night.

"This rain will rot your balls off," Prick Peters whispered, and it dropped down harder.

Duke led them through it. They marched on flat land now and the rain pelted from all sides. He liked the rain. And now when the monsoon was storming, roaring; he wanted to be like it: powerful and inexorable, stronger than strong because strength had no meaning against it. To be an all-consuming force and in control, free to direct. This was the measure of power he desired, that his spirit craved.

The water had first swirled at their ankles. Now it was lapping their waists. The paddies had overflown the dikes and the water flowed toward what had been, yesterday, that stream in its wide bed. Duke made for what might be a tree line, perhaps indicating higher ground. Tiny Phuong had faltered several times and Jungle Jim had to fireman-carry her.

They reached the trees and the water receded to their thighs. But the direction was wrong and would take them far off their general azimuth. They halted the march to consider things.

Jungle Jim unloaded Phuong and sat her against a tree trunk. She drew her knees to her collarbone; the dark wet flowed about them and her shoulders. She didn't hum.

The men crouched in a group.

"Compass says we gotta go back through that water," Duke advised. "No telling how deep it'll get."

"Hell, I believe I could swim to Bien Hoa." Animal swigged from his canteen.

"I know what you mean." Jungle Jim drank from his. "But we can't get carried away with this stuff. Don't want to get wired and foolhardy."

Prick Peters was for pushing on and he asked Doc what he thought. The Doc claimed that with his special water he was ready for anything.

As the men talked, Duke watched Phuong. She looked directly at him and slid ever so slowly down the tree trunk into the monsoon she had lived with all her days. She did not rise out of it. Duke wasn't sure if he should stop her or not. But he didn't. He decided she was aware of the consequences of her action. It was one of those terrible decisions that might nag him (Harry Pitts) forever. What should I have done? I know what I did, and seen in a certain light, that was for the best. But what should I have done?

Jungle Jim stood up and mimicked, pounding his inflated chest like Tarzan, like Johnny Weissmuller. He took several steps backward and tripped over Phuong's body. He splashed in the water next to it. He yanked it up and tried to revive her, mouth to mouth. The others gathered around and stopped him, it was useless, she was dead. Jungle Jim held her to his breast, and no one could tell the tears from monsoon.

Duke had to slosh over and console the man. It was simple, just place his hand on his shoulder and look him in the eye. He put his hand on the man but when he looked at him he didn't do it directly. It was night and Jim couldn't tell, but he turned loose of her and Duke sank her body.

He speculated on its dead journey. Rising with the water and propelled by the draining of the swollen stream. Surfacing and flowing with it, downstream to its mouth emptying into the river beneath the Ho Nai Bridge. The river swollen too, with monsoon and, at the bridge, with bodies. Phuong's joining those that would surface. The banks would be littered with rubble and Tet holiday decorations. And Christians and Buddhists and Communists would float and bloat together, faceless and with no country. An enormous rotting flotilla bobbing in the New Year of the Monkey, the Year of Our Lord One Thousand Nine Hundred Sixty-Eight.

CHAPTER THIRTY-FOUR

Duke checked his Seiko just before leaving the tree line. It was midnight. They had walked a long time, and stayed in the trees too long. They were in waist-deep water, again heading southwest. Twelve hours, he thought. He'd like to be at Judd's dope den in twelve hours.

The roar of rain continued and water rose over their stomachs, lapping at their chests. They sloshed through the flooding for over an hour. Movement was slow and difficult but the men were drugged with perseverance and strength. They were collectively happy to feel the water recede though. Now the land elevation rose and the vegetation became large and lush, jungleish and darker. All but Doc knew approximately where they were: the base of the hill that housed that deserted enemy base camp. They had been there not two days before. Doc had never been there, only been told of it. They all theorized that the camp was no longer deserted.

Duke was first to know the theory was correct. He halted the men and they watched beams of light bump through the jungle down the hill. Noise from a large unit of men came from behind the light beams through the rain.

"What's that?" Doc asked.

Duke answered: "Charlie looking for something to kill. Got predawn attack at the air base on the mind, for sure."

The men fell silent and became shadows. They watched as

the arrogantly noisy human-mechanical death machine cracked and crashed through the night. The men spent some time breathing, but not all.

When the unit had gone a sufficient distance, Duke took his canteen from its canvas cover and drank from it. He whispered: "Let's follow the dickheads. They're making enough racket to cover us, and they're going our way. We can break off from them when they make for the base."

Animal swigged from his canteen. "Yeah, and if there are any stragglers we could waste the freakin' pigs."

"That's a fine idea," said Jungle Jim. "The best I've heard in a while." He clapped Animal's shoulder. This was the first thing he'd said since leaving the tree line for the deep water.

Duke walked and the others fell in behind him. One hundred twenty-two-mm rockets began launching from the top of the hill, knifing through the night toward Bien Hoa.

The men tracked the enemy unit as it marched between the hill and the hamlet to the south. They had to hold up to allow several of the enemy grunts to slip into the hamlet. The grunts had separated themselves from their unit, waited, and sneaked into the tiny hamlet.

"What the fuck?" asked Animal.

"Don't know," said Duke, "but we better find out. We definitely don't want those slopes behind us, sneaking around."

"How many you reckon?" asked Jungle Jim. "I saw three."

"So did I."

"Right on."

"That's a freakin' Rog."

"Affirmative."

The grunts crept after the grunts, through the unmanned perimeter of the hamlet. They approached a thatched hootch lit brightly inside. Prick and Doc hunkered down in the mud and scanned the area, watching. Duke, Jungle Jim, and Animal crept through the slapping rain to the hole in the hootch wall that was a window. Inside one of the VC grunts was visible. He was butt-naked and grunting all right. He was wrapped up with an equally bare woman, humping and grunting.

"Charlie's gettin' some ass," said Animal. "Think her snatch is slanted?"

Another VC moved up into sight from the near corner. He undressed and jumped into the saddle his partner had just vacated. Quick fuck. Short-time Charlie. He went to work.

Duke found himself thinking of his girl friend, his woman at home. Christ! he thought, they're gang banging some farm girl or she's whoring it out and I'm thinking of hometown pussy! Dis-fucking-respectable, you jerk. Still, he thought of her.

Animal had drawn his bayonet. He whipped it mightly with that choppy throw of his. It sank into the VC's lower back on an upstroke. The man went down immediately, limp. The other VC had only his black shirt on, and reached for his AK-47. Jungle Jim had rounded the hut and was inside, swooping like a buzzard. He bashed the man across the head from behind. The man twisted and collapsed and Jungle Jim rammed his M-16 barrel into the man's mouth and squeezed off one round. It didn't make much sound.

Duke ran smack into the third VC, heading for the door to the hootch. The VC fell back to the mud and Duke went to one knee. He tried to steady himself with his M-16, but it slid away. He found the Montagnard dagger in his right hand and he plunged it into the VC's midsection as the man rose up, AK-47 dangling on its sling around his neck. Duke yanked the blade out and buried it to the hilt in the man's neck. Bones broke and cartilage cracked and a lot of blood burst out. Duke sensed all this as if it happened slowly, one crunch and spurt at a time. But it was over quickly and the man's body fell free from the dagger blade into the mud. Duke had never done that before and having the fact of death in his ears and on his face and hands and arms, and at his feet, wasn't pleasant. The magnitude of his own violence astounded him. He tasted the bile at the back of his throat, but he didn't vomit which surprised him. But he did turn away from the body immediately.

Jungle Jim said that he was getting almost as good as Duke, swinging and batting dinks down. He pulled the body of the VC who had died in the saddle out of it and flopped it to the grass floor.

"If you gotta get knifed in the back," Animal said, ducking in, "can't think of better freaking circumstances." He grinned and yanked his bayonet from the man's back. He ran his fingers along the flat of the blade, then dabbed the ends on the tip of his tongue. "Anybody got any vodka?" he asked, chuckling with himself.

Duke didn't think it was so funny, but he didn't find it as offensive as he thought perhaps he should. He walked over to Jungle Jim and the woman. Jim covered her with a wet, soiled sheet of thin cloth and Duke said softly, "Love is a bedful of sweat." The woman was a girl and her face was red lumps and one closed eye. It was already becoming one purple bruise. She got up and scurried out in the direction of another hootch, a dark one.

"People in this village are gonna get fucked for this," said Jungle Jim.

"Shit they were already getting fucked." Duke walked outside. "Let's beat feet."

He noticed the dagger again and washed it in a puddle. He sheathed it at the small of his back and still couldn't remember drawing it. He figured no one could say when the blade had first tasted blood. That it thirsted for more was beyond simple notion in his mind.

CHAPTER THIRTY-FIVE

The five men found the big band of noise and enemy soldiers easily. They followed the party twisting around and through the nighttime jungle for over two hours, until Duke reckoned by compass it was time to head south, to the border of Bien Hoa. The jungle had thinned to clumps of trees and bushes, stands of bamboo, and pools of muck in an elephant-grass savannah. And the dark wasn't as black.

But before they could break way they very nearly walked into a mortar team left behind by the main force. Two VC were setting a mortar to begin shelling the nearest section of Bien Hoa. They were busy and didn't notice the CRIP soldiers who dropped back to a bamboo thicket.

Jungle Jim thought they should kill the alien-Martian bastards, and he said so. Animal volunteered to get one. Jungle Jim wanted the other. Nobody argued. The two men crept off armed with bayonets and .45s and hate.

There was silence and rain. Then a muffled scuffling sound. Then Jim called the others. Life had been cut out of the mortarmen, and Animal lopped off an ear and pocketed it. "This little turd won't hear so well in slant-eyed hell," he said, wiping blood from his bayonet. Nobody else said anything about it.

"Let's mortar the main group!" It was Prick's idea and the others readily agreed.

Duke wasn't all for it though. He wanted to get his ass to

town. He pointed out that an enemy patrol would be dispatched to check things out. But then he realized this would only make everybody want to move faster toward the town, away from here. So he didn't argue when the men said, collectively, that they didn't give a damn, that they'd waste the slope scumbags if any caught up.

They guestimated range and aimed the mortar. There were a dozen rounds. They all took long pulls from their canteens before firing. Duke drank deeply and added to his already screaming buzz. The rounds were fired in rapid succession. Duke took the lead and they ran like boys from the bogeyman, filled with dread and joy, heading south. After the rounds exploded, Jungle Jim commented that those were the sweetest-sounding mortars he had heard.

CHAPTER THIRTY-SIX

False dawn grayed the soggy landscape. The rain had abated to a thick mist hanging and clinging to everything. Fog rolled over the scrubby plain and the five men filed through it approaching the outer limits, the perimeter of northeastern Bien Hoa.

Duke was exhausted but he didn't know it. The speed sustained him, propelled him. Hallucinations hung the fog with ghosts: apparitions of bloodless flesh. Dull lime things hiking a translucent terrain littered with torn flesh and broken bone. His eyes were wide and darting but the first dead soldier he had ever encountered bloated green at his feet like a lumpy duffle bag. He averted his eyes as he had done then when he and it were there in the mud, it growing in death. His murdered comrades paraded aimlessly, their violated forms smoking silver in the white mist. Dudley Worth reached for hunks of his head, a futile gesture to become undead. Deep pools of eyes and ears and brains bubbled. Lips stretched emitting empty cries. Nothing moved without being pain.

He brassed it out, summoned his own spirit, thin as it was, to banish those raging things that had been human. He would have to deal with them another time, alone. After he dealt with Warren Buckle.

Rockets and mortars pounded the area directly west and farther on, with more ferocity, the air base. American artillery was thumping somewhere. The men approached rolls of conertina wire gleaming, stretched, on the outer perimeter. Dawn was breaking pink. The sun felt wonderful on their sodden muddy selves.

They stopped, took a break, and breathed in that sun.

A claymore mine that was not exactly in the correct position to obliterate them all, exploded. About one third of the three hundred steel pellets projected from it buried themselves in Doc Ratchit, killing him.

The others hit the dirt just as rifle fire shot in their general direction. Prick Peters hollered for someone to toss him a fragmentation grenade. "I seen um," he said. "Gimme a frag; I was a goddamn quarterback."

Animal was nearest and tossed him two. There was a lot of yelling and Vietnamese yapping coming from the direction of the now-ceased rifle fire. When Prick gave the signal, the CRIP soldiers hosed bullets that way. He rose to one knee and rifled two quick bullet passes: BOOM! BOOM!

Animal crawled to the wire and stood up shooting. He quit the shooting and called back, saying the dudes were dead. "Nice goin', Prick. TD and extra point."

Jungle Jim reported that Doc was dead. Duke didn't know what to feel but anger. The man had been so recently so lucky: in the right place at the right time. And now . . . well, there it is.

Animal yelled that the ambush had been sprung by PFs. "These freakin' jerks look like PFs," he said.

Duke walked over. "Look like dead gooks to me."

Jungle Jim came up. "Those were supposed to be on our side."

Duke spoke walking away: "This war, this entire scene is jammed full of fuck-ups, wall to sorry fucking wall. Let's get Doc and get moving."

The four men carried Doc's body feet first, by the legs and arms, over a trail to a hut which was empty. They had first fired on the place to reconnoiter it. They laid Doc out as best they could on the dirt floor, and divvied up his ammunition and medical supplies.

They took slugs from his canteen until it was empty.

Duke used rocks to pound Doc's M-16 to useless pieces: the weapon that had belonged to Kim, and Warren Buckle before him. Duke was on the outskirts of the man's turf now, closing in, tightening the line.

CHAPTER THIRTY-SEVEN

The four men trooped over trails to back alleys, to lanes and streets; heading west toward the center of Bien Hoa and the air base beyond. The sun was the color of cardboard, failing to burn off the thick mist and fog that was monsoon in respite. They moved closer to the western explosions. More people became visible, mostly old ones carrying dead ones.

Duke constantly checked the ground, knowing this was not so necessary in the town. Considering the situation though, not a bad idea. He imagined himself out for a stroll in the park, back in the World: checking for trip wires, punji pits, mines.

In the distance plumes of dense smoke rose and the staccato sound of automatic weapon fire punctuated any slices of silence. Duke led the men in the direction of his rendezvous with Ralph Judd and Warren Buckle. There were shattered signs of shelling about, but any street fighting was apparently closer to the air base. He used the cemetery for direction. Much of it had erupted, shrines strewn about in fragments; the fog was ghosts. But the place was recognizable and it guided him to the Street of Peace.

When he came to the mouth of the alley that led to the whorehouse that was Judd's headquarters, he stopped. The others stood on the street, gazing at the sound and smoke beyond. Duke peered down the alley to the house: It was two storys, solid French colonial and still standing, shrouded in the fog. The entrance and second-story balconies were sandbagged—he hadn't noticed that before. The old ten-foot, spear-topped iron fence he had. A couple of cowboys lounged outside. They were armed.

Duke faced the others. "This is where we part company for now. I've got heavy business in that house there." He pointed into the alley.

Jungle Jim understood and nodded that he was ready. Prick and the Animal looked perplexed. "Explain," said Prick.

Duke sat down and put his back to the wet wall next to the alley. He took a hit from his canteen and laid the situation out: the history and what he intended to do now. He took another full swig and it fueled his fantasy of Man and Mission further into reality.

"Don't sound like none of my affair," Prick Peters said, his eyes bulging red roadmaps.

Duke said it was his decision, no orders could be issued either way.

Animal wiped his ugly face with his big paw. "Sounds more like my kinda action than fightin' those gooks to protect a freakin' airport. I'm with you." He grinned and drank from his canteen.

Prick Peters shrugged and gulped from his. "Let's go clean um up."

The speed was working mightily on all of them. They were crazed and not totally unaware of it.

Duke outlined a plan.

"These dudes aren't really expecting an attack: they're black market gunrunners dealing with Charlie. So they're leery but I doubt they're expecting much unless it's from stray mortars and such. We've got the buildings on either side of the alley to work with. If we can't get into them to move through, we can use the roofs."

"Roofs are the best idea," said Animal. "I used to do this

206

kind of fightin' back home in Bed-Sty. Roofs are best for surprise and vantage. But gettin' off them can be a bitch."

Jungle Jim added: "And you can bet your ass those boys have a machine gun, M-60 most likely."

"But if we could get on their roof . . ." Animal was thinking out loud.

Duke pointed out that it would likely be manned.

"So we waste them," said Animal, surprised. "That's the idea of this party, ain't it?"

"Well, actually we just want one dude: Buckle. And with the war going the way it is, he may not be there." Duke wished he had a cigarette.

Prick Peters smiled. "Well, then you just gonna have to stroll up to the front door and find out, ain't you?"

"Yeah," said Animal. "We'll take the roof. Don't none of us mind wasting gooks." He grinned and his scars looked obscene. He nudged Jungle Jim. "Not them kind anyhow, right J.J.?"

Jungle Jim advised that Animal's instincts were working.

"I can't go knock on that door," Duke said. "He might be in there and as soon as he sees me, he'll know the score and start shooting. He's probably not there yet—it's just ten— odds are he'll show though. He'll pull out of wherever he is first chance he gets and head to that house. This is Charlie's turf, supposed to be relatively free from his mortars and such. Charlie told them so and I believe they're dumb enough to believe it. Besides Buckle isn't in this show to defend a U.S. Airbase or provide air support for grunts. Strikes me as the type dude who likes to be where the action ain't."

Prick Peters said: "That don't sound so stupid to me."

Duke conceded. "Plus the man thinks I may show with a case of 16s or 79s for him to sell to Charlie. I've been told that when there's money to be made he doesn't fuck around, he shows. I'm for taking the roof and checking things from there."

Jungle Jim pointed out that the maneuver might be wasteful if Buckle were not in the house yet, which seemed likely.

"I'm not taking that chance," said Duke. "Now if one of you boys wants to, be my guest. But if he's figured me out, he'll waste anybody I send around."

Nobody volunteered.

"Now," Duke continued, "there are houses on both sides of the alley, all big two-story Frog structures, about five or ten feet apart. There are three on the west side of the alley, just north of the whorehouse, the objective. Each of you look. It's the one on the far side with the iron fence around it."

One at a time, the men scoped the alley and the objective. Each noted the sandbag fortifications. The fog continued to roll and whirl. The thick morning mist took on weight and drizzled.

When they had finished their reconnaissance, Duke spoke. "We need to get to the roof of the building next to it and balls our way across to that rear section of roof. That of course will depend on what things look like on the top."

"Let's check those first three hootches for people," said Jungle Jim. "They're probably empty, but we ought to check. Especially the one we're gonna climb on."

Duke allowed that was a wise idea. They would attempt entry through the rear doors of the first two buildings simultaneously and ferret out any potential problem. Then all should meet at the house next to the objective. He raised his canteen and toasted success.

"Here's to death and destruction." The Animal said it and poured the drugged water into himself. "Theirs, not ours," he added.

The men slipped around the mouth of the alley, past the building into the next alley which was narrower. They went to the rear entries of the two buildings, Prick and Animal the first, Duke and Jungle Jim the second. The drizzle's hiss and the rolling fog helped cloak their movements. Each building was entered without resistance and each was empty as a dead man's stare.

They regrouped and broke into the building next to the objective. It too was vacant. They climbed to the second story. The most desirable route to the roof was available: up through a crawlspace in a hall to the rafters of the flat roof. Then out the trap door and onto the roof proper. It was flat tile surrounded by a crenelated brick pattern.

"Looks like a castle tower top," observed Jungle Jim.

They crouched and waddled to one of the notches. Duke could make out smudged figures, some fifty feet away, reclining on sandbags at a bunker; a guardpost near the center of the adjacent roof which began less than six feet away. Prick Peters advised that there was no way he would jump across. He ducked back down through the trap doorway. He was about to pop back up, dragging a door he'd torn from its hinges—to walk across, when Duke whisper-shouted to stay inside. A full, high-pitched buzz descended with the weather. A giant bee in the rain.

The other troops turned to stone and clung to the notched wall like bricks. They watched an LOH helicopter, a Loach, land on the whorehouse roof. Duke attached his binoculars to his eyes. The figures that had been reclining simply moved to a corner, evidently expecting the chopper. Warren Buckle climbed out of the tiny machine and quickly disappeared through the roof. The guards scrunched next to the chopper against the constant drizzle. The fog folded over things.

CHAPTER THIRTY-EIGHT

Duke closed his mouth around his heart. He removed his binoculars from his face and twisted about, sitting against the brick wall. When the adrenaline rush receded, mixing with the amphetamine that charged his blood, he spoke: "That's the man. He has arrived. I wonder what poor bastards were counting on that Loach." Visions of rage filled his head and the space around him.

Prick Peters crawled onto the roof and dragged the heavy wood door after him. It was ten feet of heavy hand-carved mahogany. His idea was to span the roofs with it. Jungle Jim contended that the method would be too noisy. Duke concurred. "Like farting in church."

Then the whine and thump and boom of incoming mortars commanded their attention like laughter at a funeral. The rounds walked in. Exploding rocket-feet tearing up streets, great pounding boots bashing things, beating off shards of their hot metal soles and kicking them about. Explosions erupted throughout the area. Golden globes of flame ballooned and fizzled in the drizzle-impacted mist.

Careening on the speed, none of the men felt compelled to scramble to the ground and become a mole. A round landed on the whorehouse roof, tearing a portion from it. Another followed and when the smoke thinned, the Loach was only a memory. What sentinels had not been hit, deserted the post.

The roof was sooty chunks of junk.

Prick Peters slammed the big door into adjacent notches, forming a bridge to the objective. "Kinda nice the way Charlie treats his partners." He tested the door's strength, it held.

Duke moved toward it with Jungle Jim and Animal behind. "No telling whose shells those are," he shouted, raising himself to the door. "Doesn't make much difference, the way I see it."

"There it is," said Jungle Jim.

"God's own damn truth," the Animal added, nodding his head.

Duke crawled over the door-bridge and hopped to the deserted roof. The others followed rapidly. Two guards were dead among the sandbags and hunks of helicopter. There was no machine gun at the post.

Animal pointed at the dead with his rifle and winked. "Now some of these slants are downright considerate."

"True." Prick Peters spoke, tight-lipped. "But most of them go right on livin'."

And those were the last words he ever spoke. It wasn't even one of those slants that went right on living, it was Warren Buckle who shot him down. He poked his three-ball head up to check his chopper and saw Harry Pitts, the Duke. He ducked down and left his gun hand—filled with .45—pointing in Pitts's direction. He emptied it into Prick Peters who wasn't particularly near the Duke.

Duke and Jungle Jim watched the whole affair, Duke yelling warning all of the thirty seconds it lasted. Then he scrambled over and hosed fire into the trap doorway. Jim ran over and dropped his last two grenades. They feinted away for the blast.

Following the detonations, Duke crept down ladderlike steps that creaked loudly enough to be frightening, alarming at the least. He stepped onto the top floor of the whorehouse and was thankful for the relative silence. The section he stood in was deserted. Walls had collapsed and much of the ceiling and roof in the remaining sections along with the balconies were destroyed.

The Animal checked Prick and, seeing death, stripped the body of its ammunition. He joined Jungle Jim and they descended into the objective. "Prick's dead meat," he said, informing Duke.

"Figured as much," he said, realizing he never knew the man by any name other than "Prick" Peters. And also that the black people back in the World had lost a warrior, a man who might have helped the cause. Oddly, Nada Garcia came to mind, or rather his spiel about how a black man's fight was on the streets of the U.S.A. Prick Peters had come to a war about as far away from Oakland as he could get. Now he was a dead man above a street in Bien Hoa, South Vietnam. Murdered by a white man, monsoon for a shroud. "See who wasted him." It was a bitter statement rather than a question.

Yes, they had seen.

CHAPTER THIRTY-NINE

A wicked barrage of mortar rounds lambasted the alley. The front entrance to the whorehouse was a gash that could easily accommodate a tank. Random fires crackled in the haze of smoke and fog and wet.

From the charred upper floor Duke watched cowboys, whole and maimed, abandon the place. They moved as if by magic, slowly floating on the fog and dispersing into the mist. Animal winged a grenade into a group of wounded stragglers, dispersing them, too, into the mist.

From the bottom floor rose the resonant strains of Johnny Cash's strong voice. It was savagely loud and singing, "I shot a man in Reno, just to watch him die." He hadn't seen the sunshine since he didn't know when and he flippantly raged about life in a dungeon.

Jungle Jim and the Animal frowned surprise. Duke didn't. "That's crazy Judd," he said. "He's a music fan. The man's a junkie with shit for brains."

Duke cautiously moved down the staircase, sticking to the walls like paint. The interior was foggy planes of dull light. The music blared and bounced off the walls and faded out into the monsoon. He motioned to the others to follow. They fanned out and crouched into the wide room where Duke had spent the night. Several dead women hung in hammocks. Duke couldn't detect dead cowboys, but the floor was a carpet of the thickest mist, the bottom of the general

213

denseness of fog. He hoped he wouldn't trip over one.

The song ended and began again, a tape loop; automatic reverse. The huge speakers loomed into view as dull black monoliths pulsating the "Folsom Prison Blues," "I shot a man in Reno just to watch him die." Out of the blur and out of the music zoomed a screeching Ralph Judd. He was upon them immediately, as if he instantaneously took form from the fog, compressed his dispersed particles and attacked. His legs hidden in the murk, his tattooed torso glistening and scabbed, he catapulted from behind a speaker. His eyes dull and transfixed on something unknowable, his bad skin stretched gray and damp around the blond mustache, his mouth open and emitting howls, his right arm cocked and loaded with Bowie knife, he whipped it forward burying it in the Animal's neck.

Animal didn't make a sound. He had been too close to the speaker and at the wrong angle. Judd nailed him from a blind spot. He crumpled beneath the second blow from the knife which tore his chest. Judd snorted and sprang up from the Animal and into a burst of about forty rounds from the 16s of Duke and Jungle Jim. The bullets forced a foolish death dance—driving Judd twisting and jerking backward—before dropping him against one of those immense speakers. The speaker flopped down and Judd hung face up on it. His gold teeth gleamed dully in his dead mouth. "And I shot a man in Reno just to watch him die." The refrain trembled through the junkie's carcass.

Jungle Jim lifted the Animal's upper body from the mist and leaned him against one of the fat posts that held the ceiling up. The man was a bloody mess. Jim pressurized the neck wound with his hand which became a solid glove of blood. Duke rushed over with compresses and battle dressing. He shot Animal with morphine, rammed the Syrette into his thigh. Animal's purple scars were slick and twitching. "Speed kills," he said, and died. All the fight went out of him. Death took him by surprise. There was no other way.

Duke didn't really know what to think of Animal. He rarely respected the man, but he felt a loss at his death and figured he owed it to him and Prick to accomplish the mission they had joined. And it was possible that the Animal had saved Duke's ass back in Ho Nai when that wounded cowboy had stumbled into his path. He was sorry that the ugly bastard was dead. But he knew about sorry: Pile sorrow and shit in the balance and check which one registers.

The Reno song stopped and started again, ear-busting loud. Jungle Jim shot the sophisticated stereo equipment to junk. Tape reels rolled out, ribbons of recorded sound that sailed upward with chunks of amplifiers and recorders and gauges. Connective wires and jacks and popping tubes tangled with them in a series of arcs and offshoots that scattered and dissipated suddenly; falling, hissing, in the mist.

CHAPTER FORTY

Duke saw it as a joke: a far reaching, immensely tragic comedy with himself the buffoon at its center. Those five scouts were laughing their dead balls off at the futility of his gesture, because they were dead and truly nothing could alter that fact. Death itself was the final joke after a series of bad jokes. Doc and Prick and the Animal hooted at their own tragic error in judgment. And what about Phuong? She had seen the idiocy of everything and decided to no longer participate. Death was no problem for the dead. It was those left alive, with some relationship to the deceased, that caused the ruckus.

He existed in a world that was terribly wrong, a region of fire and mutilation. A world in which people were whole one minute and blown apart the next. A world where children were raped and murdered. A world to which suicide was preferable. A place where tattooed, gold-toothed men danced dead in the fog to electronically amplified music. He had dropped into the mouth of fury and there was no justice in it. The land was rotten and corruption the sun, and there was no changing it. Roll with it and be good, try to survive. Dead voices boomed that he should have stayed home, that they all should have stayed. Nothing was a mystery, and all is simply bullshit, a lie.

But Duke had created his own reality, and within it there were rights and wrongs. He could see that it might appear foolish on some cosmic level, but that was all right. The cosmos was beyond his horizon. He would persist in his endeavor to deal with the here and the now, a comical little chump dressed up like a soldier pursuing his mission of vengeance, of justice. A joke, a goof on the gods of chaos. Let them laugh. A joke has to have some timing and a sense of place, a peculiar logic and motivating force. He was at once the motivation, the logic, and the dupe because it was his joke, he created it. All of the senseless eruptions of this and that about him gave testimony to the larger reality which was the laughter he heard. Yes, let them bloody well laugh, but I'll finish this thing and everybody knows who laughs best.

And how long would it be before this game he played enveloped him? He considered this notion, but it mattered little because the game had to be played out. How long before there was no more Harry Pitts, only the Duke?

He and Jungle Jim used the Animal's ammo to spray the large clouded room with bullets. They blasted everywhere. The drug charged through Duke's blood like locomotives tracking full tilt, out of control. His eyes were green headlamps, whistles blared in his ears. Emotion fused, and spilled within him.

The end of this game was at hand, but the thing that would enable its conclusion was apparently not in the room. Bullets cut the fog and found all the walls but not Warren Buckle. Duke was enraged and screamed the man's name. Jungle Jim told him to shut up. He did.

Duke perceived the change that had taken place in his friend. The man had narrowed his scope, entered his— Duke's—reality more completely, joined in the joke. Duke knew Jungle Jim to be a better man than himself, a less selfish one at any rate. But he was happy for this slight regression, however temporary it might be. The man's capacity for violence was great and well directed.

"It's possible he escaped," said Jungle Jim, backing

against a chipped, damp wall.

"My guess is he's going to try to wipe me out. You too, buddy."

"You're goddamn right. You dogpiss grunt." Warren Buckle yelled it from an unshattered portion of the second story. He stood above them, his slick head glistening against the monsoon sky. He started shooting after he yelled and had no target but the mist.

Duke and Jungle Jim scurried to the bottom of the stairwell. Sections of the upper floor were visible through holes torn from it. But there was no sign of Warren Buckle.

"I imagine he knows where we are," Jungle Jim pointed out, quietly.

"True, but see how stupid this hardass is. He could have cut us down but no, he needed to tell us about it. The man's got a hell of an attitude. Thinks a lot of himself, thinks he's a tough guy. What a fucking idiot. He probably has to shave that noggin just to get a hat on it. Calls himself Three-Ball, shit! Eight-Ball's more like it." Duke watched as he spoke, the stairs, the holes, the fog.

But it was what he heard that grabbed his memory: creaking wood, those loud frightening alarms from the ladder that served as stairway to the roof.

CHAPTER FORTY-ONE

Warren Buckle: Three-Ball, warrant officer in the U.S. Army, helicopter pilot, murderous money leech from the bowels of subterranean America, hairless brute, badass bandit of Bien Hoa; he raged over the remains of his Loach. A jumble of obscenities emanated from him. Spittle foamed at his mouth corners and dribbled.

Duke heard the curses as he topped the staircase to the second floor. He motioned for Jungle Jim to follow up, and made for the ladder steps. He had recalled that Warren Buckle hadn't been afforded adequate opportunity to be totally sure about the fate of his chopper. He had been busy filling Prick Peters with .45 slugs.

Now Duke watched the space at the top of the steps, a dripping square of gray sky. A decision had to be made: mount the steps or wait. He was inclined toward movement, along with the speed in his blood. He darted up and those steps seemed to scream after him. He popped through to the roof. He caught a glimpse of Warren Buckle kicking helicopter debris about, swearing.

It was only a glimpse because at that same instant Buckle noticed the movement and Duke. He dove and scrambled behind solid sandbags and dead guards. Duke followed him with M-16 bullets and one 5.56 NATO round smashed the man's left ankle.

Duke had rolled onto the roof behind the trap door and

the remnants of sandbags that had once surrounded it. He heard Buckle curse in obvious pain and figured he'd hit the son-of-a-bitch. He also had noted that the pilot—now without vehicle—was armed with only a .45 pistol. There was no getting at him though. Buckle had an advantage in occupying the better position: a section of the open sandbagged fortification that had been the guardpost was intact.

Duke was clipping another magazine into his weapon when Jungle Jim emerged. Buckle opened fire and .45 slugs knocked Jim back through the doorway. Duke automatically emptied the magazine into the sandbagged wall and inserted another. His entire self thumped like a heart. "Jim?" he yelled. "J.J. my man!" And he made one of those deals with a god or a devil whose existence was only acknowledged during certain horrendous situations. "Let him be able to answer and I'll do anything." He said it to himself, offering whatever his immortal soul was, gladly. The eternity of minutes became a reality.

He remembered a scene from a war movie that had impressed him as a boy. In smoky black and white it rolled over and over behind his eyes: a GI bent over his wounded buddy demanding response. "If you die, I'll kill you!" the GI shouted. And he cursed and cried.

Then Jungle Jim cursed and it was the sweetest sound Harry Pitts had heard since Wally Riley's voice cracked the clouds. "The cocksucker shot my shoulder!" he yelled. "A shoulder wound, just like the movies!" Jungle Jim made a sound something like a hollow laugh and shouted up for morphine. "It hurts, damn it! It's startin' to hurt a lot."

Duke fired a short burst at the sandbags and fished for his medical stash which was more plentiful than usual, due to Doc's death. He flipped morphine Syrettes down through the doorway.

Jungle Jim shouted thanks. He had applied battle dressing to his left shoulder wound and stemmed the tide of blood. He

220

administered the morphine and sat back against the ladder steps he had tumbled down after the fire had fried his shoulder. Two .45 bullets had torn through but the paths were wide and throbbing and packed with bone fragments. He relaxed as much as possible, waiting for the drug to take effect. Monsoon dripped from Duke and the door, trickled down the stairwell onto Jim's neck, into his uniform. He couldn't get wetter.

CHAPTER FORTY-TWO

Duke lay, belly down, in the rain, scanning the sandbag wall through the fog that alternated from wisps of wet mist to old pea soup. The wall was not fifty feet away and he wished he had saved a grenade. The shelling had swept beyond the immediate sector but there was no telling when the pattern might switch back. He was not particularly comfortable on the roof. He decided to talk to this skinhead lame he was going to kill. "This is it, Buckle," he shouted. "End of the game."

"Maybe for you, Pitts. You meddling punk!" Buckle snapped the reply and Duke was surprised at the bitterness in his voice.

Duke continued: "The way I see right and wrong, you're wrong Buckle. And you guessed it; I'm here to make you dead wrong."

"Right and wrong are just other words for smart and stupid. The way I see it, you're the stupid. Just as stupid as any idiot who jumps out of a chopper into the godforsaken jungle looking for the shit. You step in some, then ask somebody to come get your ass out. You figure he'll be as goddamn dumb as you, and get downright nasty when he ain't. Grunts are stupid people with insipid ideas. I don't risk my ass for them." Buckle's voice had a sour sound and it cut easily through the drizzle.

It was a perspective, a view. Duke gave him that. He could

understand Buckle's rationale, see through his eyes, feel with his nerves; he did possess imagination. He supposed most people could come up with some peculiar slant in defense of themselves. But the perspective was wrong, out of whack, drawn without scale. The man's perceptions were as one-sided as a fucking contest between a bull and a eunuch. Duke thought he should enjoy blowing this lunatic's theory full of holes. He remembered a hard stripe corporal from AIT who had tortured him during a war game. The corporal had not understood the nature of the game; he was overzealous. The corporal had first frightened Private Pitts with a live snake, then walloped him in the stomach while his hands were bound behind him, then forced water up his nose, in his mouth, down his throat. The corporal acted in the name of interrogation. Corporal Pitts encountered that corporal months later on another base, during LRRP training. That corporal was Sunday-drunk in a deserted company area. Pitts struck him unfairly from behind, and brutally. That corporal admitted, through his stupor and pain, that he remembered. Pitts knew the man might have some explanation, perhaps call the incident a lesson for the real game of war. But Pitts offered no chance for it; he pommeled that corporal to unconsciousness. Afterward he felt both satisfied and empty, but mostly satisfied. Well, at least he was listening now, he thought. Call it maturity.

Buckle was shouting again: "Whatsamatta Pitts? Mr. Right got nothing to say? You've been a dunce. Realize it. It's too late for those other dunces you dragged into this, but not us. Life is action, boy. Your kind, my kind, any kind. And fuck anyone who doesn't hustle for number one. They always scratch, always rack the balls. They're losers. They're dead and don't know it. And revenge is sentiment, boy. Simple sentimental slop. Let's you and I salvage something from all this crap. A few more shots anyway."

Now old Three-Ball's perspective became an excuse. Duke knew excuses to be like assholes, everybody having one, each full of shit. Buckle sounded as if he had all the answers, everything figured out. Duke wished that all the assholes who thought they knew it all would shut up and listen to those, like himself, who did. After all this was his reality, his joke. Too bad Buckle didn't get it. Things would be so much easier.

"You know, Pitts," Buckle went on, "most people are like grunts. They spend all their time bitching about yesterday and worrying about tomorrow. Now I like to take advantage of the present whenever possible. Thing to do now is consolidate the game plan and get our asses out of the area." His voice grew erratic and louder and more distant.

Now he was making a pitch. And Duke understood that the man must indeed consider him quite a dullard, a dipstick, to be even speaking such nonsense. He possessed more than enough ammunition to simply drill the sandbag wall and watch it collapse like what it was: sand. But for some obscure reason that he could not isolate, he pretended interest in his enemy's palaver. He allowed the game to go on. "Our balls may be in a vise here. What do you propose? I might be interested," he lied.

"That's a sensible attitude. With Charlie running around like hogs in slop trying to waste us, it's just wrong, plain stupid, for us to be out to destroy ourselves. I know this town and together we've got a fair chance of escape to the air base." Warren Buckle's breathing rasped, audibly heavier and the erratic shouting over greater distance became obvious to Duke.

Duke raised his hand, then followed it with the rest of himself to a crouch. He scrambled to the sandbagged guardpost wall, rifle at the ready. "How shall we get together?" he shouted.

"Name it." The reply came from beyond the other side of the wall.

Duke stood slowly raising his rifle. Buckle was dragging his leg, making for the doorbridge to the adjacent roof. He turned the instant Duke's silhouette appeared above the sandbags. He opened fire first and Duke squeezed his trigger as he dropped himself back behind the bags. Duke's right hand had been grazed by one of Buckle's bullets. It burned. A .45 is a fat slug and it blew the knuckles and little finger, along with some palm and heel, from his hand.

But Buckle was screaming bloody murder after catching three more rounds in his bad leg. *"You sniveling scum. Motherfucking leg. I hope you're dead. Die, you turd, die!* His voice was agony and rage. He bellowed incomprehensibly, a lot.

Duke applied a compress to his hand and shot morphine into it. The act was a tad clumsy, using his left hand; but he acted quickly to intercept possible shock. He found what was left of his finger, wrapped it in a wet handkerchief and put it into his baggy thigh pocket. He didn't know exactly why but it seemed preferable to leaving it. He took a drink from the bitter water in his canteen and listened to Warren Buckle. He could lay his M-16 barrel on top of the wall and spray in the man's general direction for a few magazines and put an end to it. But again he prolonged the game. He replaced the canteen and turned to the wall and edged along its gritty surface, now and in memory knowing that this was what part of him was about: creeping and physical, mentally alert, rushing to a single purpose. The thin rain was almost cold on his back as he peeked around the side of the wall. Buckle had tied something around his upper thigh and was struggling to raise himself to the notched wall which bordered the roof and held the door.

Duke thought of how really cold it would be in the winter mountains of his home. His father would be hunting on cross-country skis with a bone bow. His father took his outdoor life seriously and had painstakingly imparted the details of it to young Harry. From the beginning the boy absorbed the lore. Up to his butt in an icy stream or stalking animals up and and down the sides of mountains, there was little else to do. But he did it without fascination; he never understood the mystique. His father had taught him respect for the animals they killed, only for food. It should be understood that all life is one and the kill is part of the hunter, enabling survival. Harry Pitts had understood this for it was nothing if not truth. But he had seen the utter disrespect, the easy, irrevocable violence men did to one another, to themselves. He believed he could respect a cannibal more than most generals. He knew he harbored a vast amount of respect for a deer, a rabbit. Much more by far than most men he knew, than himself.

And now there was Warren Buckle in his sights, dragging himself, grunting, onto the door Prick Peters had used to span the buildings, the door that had led to Prick's death. His motion was a lame crawl that, along with the snorting and unconscious drooling, gave him the appearance of having regressed some small span to his bestial ancestry. Duke ranked Buckle below it all, something rabid, best destroyed. He might offer him the same lack of respect Prick Peters had been afforded. He squeezed off a single round which rammed the man's ass.

Warren Buckle shot straight up on his solid leg. He hung there for several moments bending his good knee and clopping his bad foot like a skittish, wrong-headed horse. A bewildered and temporary refugee from the glue factory where scores of superior breeds had been slaughtered. Then he crumbled to his knee. He knelt on the door facing Duke. Duke advanced.

Buckle was unsteady but still appeared fierce. In the mist his head shone like steel, a bare wet helmet. His eyes were shadows above the flattening slant of his nose, his mouth set in angry perspective. He growled and pointed his pistol, and Duke shot him again, somewhere in the midsection. Buckle sank and sat stupidly on the door and bled.

"You make a bundle on that beer you hauled in that Chinook?" Duke asked it sardonically. "Have a merry

226

fucking Christmas? Run your mouth now, hardass. Hustle now, asshole."

But Warren Buckle could only curse. And he did so until blood coughed from his mouth. He raised his .45 and pulled the trigger, unsuccessfully. Empty. The pistol's slide action open and still. He looked at it with utter surprise. He glared at Duke and ejected the clip, fishing his pockets for another. He appeared unalterably drunk.

Duke's own cruelty began to sicken him. His bones burned. He wanted the pleasure he thought due him; it woud not show itself. Instead a picture of what he was doing formed in his drugged brain and it was an image of one nauseating mutant, dark and smelling of things long buried, hacking at another. And neither made a human sound. Duke filled Warren Buckle with the rest of the magazine, wiping him out as well as the hallucination. The body toppled off the door and fell to the iron fence below, impaling itself.

CHAPTER FORTY-THREE

Duke was wired, his brain popping, eyes lit with speed. He had to get out of there, off the roof and away. The crunching sounds of bombardment were distant but noticeable enough. He took his wet self to Prick Peters's body and dragged it through the wet grit. Jungle Jim had come up halfway through the trap-door space when Duke got the body to it. They didn't talk. They struggled with the dead soldier until all of them were down on the ground floor in the foggy greatroom. Duke trussed Jungle Jim's bad arm tightly across his chest with Animal's rifle sling. Jim didn't feel any pain; he was too wired.

They dragged their bodies out of the whorehouse to a crevice below what had been the entrance. Four silent soldiers: two of them breathing in and breathing out, two with nothing ticking but their watches. The area was partially protected with sandbags. The two men laid out the Animal and Prick.

"Let's make for the air base," said Duke, moving toward the iron gate. He saw Warren Buckle's body hanging on the fence like a trashfish speared through the gill. The metal fencepost had snagged it up through the neck and jaw and pierced through the open mouth. The rain had begun to rinse it slick, that wide-eyed steel skull on a spear. Buckle's death mask was one of contortion and gore and scattered teeth. It brought an old theory to Duke's mind: one has nothing to do with the face he is born with, but the one he dies with is earned. One of those theories that is only applicable on occasion. This was a sterling occasion.

All Duke felt was satisfaction. It was a nice change from when the man had been alive. A man who allowed himself to become crud. There was no more place for him; the joke was over, punch line delivered—nobody gets out alive but you're deader than I. His function had been eliminated. A tough guy, a belligerent dope with some piratelike picture of himself. A sorry thing that begged with every breath to have its ass separated from its place in the sun.

Jungle Jim nudged Duke softly with his shot shoulder. "That sonuvabitch didn't go down easy," he said, moving his eyes to Duke's right hand.

Duke glanced down at his torn hand, wondering what it looked like. "A point, Mr. Grogan. Moot, but a point."

"Was it worth it?"

"Yes." What else could he say? "Yes," he repeated. But he had already begun to wonder. "Let's *di-di*."

They walked away. Not ten paces later they received fire from the mouth of the alley. They ducked into the space between the whorehouse and its neighboring building. A terrific explosion from a Laaw rocket blasted the gate behind them. From the alley mouth came sarcastic shouts. "*Chieu hoi*, muthafuckas. Give it up gooks. We won't kill your dink asses!" Then came laughter and another volley.

"They're Americans!" said Duke. "Our own goddamned troops! The dumb grunts." He roared for them to cease fire. "We're Americans, *fuckin' A-mericans*," he boomed. "Christian Sons of Freedom just like you. YOU SHITBIRDS!"

The fire ceased. Duke peeked around the building at a dozen M-16 muzzles up the alley. Someone shouted for them to step into sight. "This shit really spooks me," said Duke, stepping into the alley, Jungle Jim following.

The muzzles lowered and airborne troopers sauntered into the alley saying "sorry 'bout that." A big lieutenant came close and asked, "What the fuck are you dudes doing in Indian territory? Can't tell who in the fuck is who. We're blowin' this burg up, flat-out liberatin' it from Victor Charlie. He's everywhere, even got Saigon. We may have to destroy the fuckin' place to get it back."

Duke explained that they were what remained of their unit and how they had marched—escaped and evaded—all night from Ho Nai, lost Doc on the perimeter, and closed with Victor Charlie here in the alley. The lieutenant dispatched a patrol to the whorehouse. A medic checked Jungle Jim. Prick Peters and Animal were brought from the crevice. A chopper was called for. The patrol reported Judd's body and the Loach wreckage on the roof. Buckle's carcass was taken down and laid next to Prick and the Animal. This infuriated Duke but there wasn't much he could do.

The lieutenant wanted to know about the Caucasian inside, whose body had been dragged out.

"Don't know," said Duke. "But the asshole was fighting on Charlie's team. Killed one of us." He indicated Animal. "Stabbed him."

The lieutenant inspected Buckle, noting the pilot rank and outfit. That, along with the helicopter hunks, formed a theory for him. "This pilot come in to help you?"

Duke's face set at its deadest, he spoke with no more expression than a cat. "Don't know, but maybe; yeah sure. That's probably what he was up to. Got shot down though. Never had a chance."

"Must have been a hell of a guy, a real hardass. Regular fuckin' hero."

"Must have been."

"And that other scum. That white dude fightin' for Charlie! Man this is a weird war. Just don't know who's who."

"There it is," said Duke. "Got a cigarette? I'm dying." He took one from the lieutenant, lit up, and drew deeply. What the hell, he thought, all that's left now is to *get out*. His new wound meant Purple Heart number three: ticket home.

CHAPTER FORTY-FOUR

The paratroopers secured an LZ and a helicopter touched down in the cemetery across the Street of Peace from the alley. The men loaded the four American bodies in. Duke and Jungle Jim followed the bodies aboard. The helicopter rose up over ground that looked as if it had been plowed up by a berserk farmer. All of the bodies looked bad and Duke tried not to see them.

"Better dump the speed," he said, fishing ampules, mostly broken, from his pockets. He felt his finger in one and decided to leave it for now.

"So the man's a hero." Jungle Jim kicked Warren Buckle's body.

"That's as good a story as any," said Duke. "At least he's a dead one."

The helicopter swerved and dipped and rose. They were taking ground fire. Duke tightened his sphincter muscle along with the rest of him, naturally. He eyed Jungle Jim. "Pucker motherfucker," he said. It was about all they could do. The doorgunners let it rip.

The ship climbed high and careened away to the big Second Field Force complex at Long Binh. The landing strip was a busy one. Choppers dropping down loaded with casualties and popping up to gather more. Ambulances and trucks and jeeps drove constantly shuttling the wounded and the dead. The guys from Graves Registration were bagging and tagging as fast as they could unzip and zip body bags.

Duke and Jungle Jim got on a deuce-and-a-half with other walking wounded. The truck rattled to a medical unit where the two men were separated, Duke's wound being of low priority.

The place was packed to the walls with activity, rush hour in the emergency room. And these medical people were in the second day of it. Duke had never seen such a concentration of living victims: military and civilian, of all ages and every conceivable injury. Burned bodies and broken limbs, missing limbs and torn bodies, bloodsoaked bandages covering major portions of bodies, and heads without recognizable faces. And there was a lot of crying, loud and soft; and blank silent shock. And so many doctors and nurses and medics and anyone with stomach enough to help, up to their shoulders in blood.

Duke was herded with others into a wide empty room and told to make himself comfortable and wait. The room had just been cleared of the last wave of low priorities. A doctor and medics would see to them ASAP. The place smelled of antiseptic and rot. Nobody said much; they all sat smelling the swamp of their own rank flesh. Duke, for one, was damn glad he could. And being out of the rain was a plus.

Christ! he thought, Charlie is working hard, sinking the entire area into the Deep Serious. A hell of a way to bring in his new year, his new lease on time, his new beginning. This must be a signal, an omen of his single-minded attitude: The mindless Yellow Peril, an inexhaustible sea of gooks that would never stop killing and burning and looting. It didn't matter who was there, after everything else Luke the Gook would turn on his own to purge. And satisfied that he had been burned clean from the violence, he'd seek someone else to convince, to kill. This Tet raging was a sign all right, it signified time to get the fuck out.

His hand had begun to pain him, a hot throb. That hand was his ticket to the World, his way out. The Three-Heart

Rule demanded that any soldier wounded three times on one tour of duty be removed from the combat zone. This was his third bloodletting and he was still on his first tour, albeit extended.

The occasion for his first Purple Heart occurred after his first three months in-country. He was acting as RTO for a mock recon patrol outside Camp F-J. A badass captain was explaining the ropes to a general and two bird colonels in an area secured by an infantry company. A group of helicopters buzzed overhead after a combat assault. The gunners kicked out ammo boxes of 7.62 brass casings and M-60 belt clips. Brass and belt clips and boxes rained over the position for a minute or two. Duke and the captain and the general and the colonels all got nicked on the shoulders and back by the brass and clips. The general even caught an ammo box, bouncing it off his steel helmet. He was knocked down. Duke called for the general's chopper, and the bullshit recon patrol (he, the captain and the general and the colonels) were evacuated. It had been a rough one: Purple Hearts for everybody. Duke and the captain had laughed like loons when they heard they had been put in for the medals, even harder when they got them. "A brass nick on the Brass," Duke had said, "is evidently just as rough on a corporal."

"And don't forget the helmet dent," the captain added. "No telling what that merits."

His second Heart resulted from his leg wound on the day the rest of the patrol died. The third was directly related to the second in a way, the same man responsible for it.

A doctor entered the room along with several medics and carts of tools and medicine. He was a young man in a bloody blue jacket. He looked as fierce and sad and beat as any grunt Duke had seen, maybe more. He examined the low priority wounded and gave orders to the medics who worked on the wounds, cleaning and suturing mostly, administering drugs. When he got to Duke, to Harry Pitts, he unwrapped the compress and said the finger was gone. Duke took it from his pocket and asked if it might fit back on. The doctor fingered it and said no, there wasn't enough left and nowhere to put it.

They were near the doorway to a hall and heard the uncontrolled babylike sobbing before the kid stood in the frame. The sobs converged and the sound was hollow and compelling. A little Vietnamese that might have been male or female just stood, slightly bowlegged, arms hanging away from a mottled torso. Most of the child's hair had been burned off along with clothes and skin. Some filthy gauze hung raggedly from what appeared to be hands. The kid just stood there and flipped tiny wrists and screamed from some deep place within that charred body.

Duke took his finger from the doctor and, when the man glanced at him, said: "See you later, Doc."

The doctor knelt and gathered the child gently and the screaming at least subsided to great sobs. Then they were gone.

Duke sat on a bench and a medic stood over him. Duke raised his hand. "Sew it up. And don't forget to numb it, or give me morphine, or something."

The medic went to work and soon the hand lost all feeling. Dead babies, Duke thought and saw them. Dead and torn-up children were the worst. Anybody else was just as dead or gutted, but there was some immense universal failure about the violence done to children. Nonetheless it was done, and done again. People produce children to sort of shake their fists at the face of death. They know they can't beat it, but they can prolong the line, cheat the old deep six another tiny chunk of time. But don't let the little fuckers get in the way of the games; they're easy to crush. He knew there was a corner of his mind that would never sleep again.

He looked at his hand and didn't like what he saw. "Don't forget to wrap it, Doc."

CHAPTER FORTY-FIVE

Duke's arm was set in a sling that wrapped his hand over his heart. He had his pain pill prescription filled at the pharmacy. The druggist had eyes like golf balls. Then a clerk processed him in and out of the medical station at the same time, transferring him back to the CRIP which, in fact, no longer existed. The clerk informed him that the medical group at Camp F-J would handle him. The clerk was evidently unaware that all hell had broken loose; maybe he was a new guy and thought this was business as usual. A cool sort if that were the case. Duke left him filling out forms, stamping them, filling out more. He found Jungle Jim in a crowded ward, his upper arm and shoulder all wire and plaster cast, his eyes tranquilizer glazed.

"It's Japan for me," Jim said. "Shoulder's all fucked up. Probably have to find a new line of work in the World, climbing's most likely out. Hope I'll be able to swim all right though. I like to swim."

"I'll get in touch with Mother Brigade, advise that we're alive, that we 'escaped and evaded.' The word is this whole country is one big fire fight. From the DMZ to the Delta, Victor Charlie is killing and being killed." Duke pointed to his own slung arm. "It's the World for me, three Hearts."

"Luck . . ." Jungle Jim faded out. He had been given additional drugs and was far away.

"Be good."

Duke left the ward. On his way out of the hospital he passed a large, steamy kitchen full of cooking and boiling medical tools. He went in. A few tired attendants milled around. Nobody paid much attention, although he looked as if he'd recently crawled out of a dung heap. He snatched up a scalpel from a table covered with them and found a metal bowl. He placed them on a metal stool in a corner and dropped his finger in the bowl. He went to work with the knife, skinning the bones as clean as he could with only one hand. The sharpness of the blade helped. He trashed the flesh in one of those containers with a step-knob for popping the lid. He tossed the scalpel into a boiling vat, filled the bowl with water and placed it on a cooker: a flat hot grill like short-order cooks fry on. He dropped his bones in the water and waited. He wasn't thinking as much as simply moving and doing. The drugs in him were winding down toward crashing depression. It just seemed like a good idea. He had lost more of him than he knew and he wanted to salvage all he could from what remained. He used tongs and took the scalding bowl and dumped the water and clean bones into a sink. He turned on the cold and steam rose, adding to the rest in the room. He put his finger bones in his jacket pocket: the one between his bad hand and his heart. He went to recover his weapons.

The M-16s were stacked in unguarded racks and Duke imagined insurgent gooks wiping out the wounded and dying with their own weapons. He found his and slung it. He hadn't given up his .45 or remaining bandoleers. He dropped all the bandoleers but one and felt for his dagger and pistol. Satisfied, he ducked out among incoming casualties.

He was in the rain again and hoped it wouldn't bother his hand which he still could not feel. Night was pressing full darkness around. Mortars began dropping somewhere near the outer perimeter. He slogged to a communications complex of wide buildings, Quonset huts and big bunkers. The roads around it were back-in-the-World paved. It had only been a matter of weeks since he left this Long Binh base, mostly bad days and flaky nights; these days of Tet the longest. He began to feel it; he needed to crash and burn. And what would hold him together now? He knew it had to be survival again, getting out, going home.

He found an officer and explained who he was, where he'd come from, and that the Brigade should be notified. He was led to a cot. It was obvious he was walking and talking in his sleep. His unit would be contacted, but now he could sleep. His exhaustion cut through any residue of the speed and catapulted him crashing through a mercifully brief hallucinatory dream so ugly it was only dark figures in darkness, vast and dimensionless. He couldn't move for a monkey crouched on his chest, an enormous ape with foul breath and dripping fangs and red eyes. He crashed through and bottomed out, falling under a sweet catastrophe of dreamless sleep.

CHAPTER FORTY-SIX

Like a turd that survived the flush, he had lived another day. The thought amused Harry Pitts, the Duke. But he neglected to grin. He was able to take a cold shower in the morning. It felt better than the rain and he brushed his teeth until his gums bled. He got into a clean set of fatigues, altering slightly his wild and stony appearance. His attitude measurably improved from the previous day's murderous one.

A Brigade Intelligence officer came to the communication complex accompanied by a major in aviator shades representing some special investigatory outfit. They came to debrief. They debriefed for hours. The intelligence man Duke knew to be one of the officers who had questioned him about his final mission with the LRRP; one of the men who understood how confusing events must have been then, a man who wouldn't divulge Warren Buckle's name. The other officer was unfamiliar, as was his unit and function. The intelligence man did most of the talking, never openly acknowledging their last discussion some several weeks past. He assured him that all the CRIP bodies would be recovered because this seemed to bother Sergeant Pitts. The intelligence man had a report filed by the lieutenant who found Sergeants Pitts and Grogan. He pointed out the officer's description of the apparent heroic rescue attempt by the helicopter pilot, one Warrant Office Warren Buckle. He looked levelly, directly at Duke's eyes. And Duke looked blankly back.

"Oh, yeah," said Duke, "I almost forgot. But he never got a chance to do what he came to do. Got shot down on the roof."

"Too bad," said the officer. "The Army will most assuredly swing medals for everybody. Of course you and Sergeant Grogan will be the only ones to receive them alive." He emphasized *alive*, then looked away.

"Of course." Duke did not look away. "I'm only interested in the Heart; it's number three."

The officer nodded, saying that a soldier *should* be hospitalized forty-eight hours to qualify for the Purple Heart, but not to worry. Orders were being cut to ship Sergeant Pitts stateside, ASAP. "Calculating time left in the service and accrued leave, the sergeant may qualify for an early-out. Unless the sergeant plans to reenlist." He stopped speaking and a smirk cracked his mask.

Duke knew there were no reenlistments in his future. But he wasn't sure about slapping the shit out of this wimpy pogue. He didn't like the man's tone.

Then the other officer, who wore no insignia save his major's leaf, stepped forward. He took a manila envelope from his breast pocket. "Exactly who eliminated the Caucasian guerrilla, Ralph Judd?" He asked, turning the envelope over in his hands.

"Why?"

"All units such as yours should have known the man had a price on his head." The major looked at Duke, but he did it from behind those aviator shades.

"I do remember hearing that, recently as a matter of fact."

"Who gets paid?"

"Me and Grogan."

"Fine." The major handed over the envelope. "That's what we expected. We'll see to Sergeant Grogan."

Duke looked inside the envelope and saw Uncle Sam's

own green. "Who pays?"

"The donor will remain anonymous. We are authorized to distribute the funds. Call it a bonus, a gift from the people of the Republic: a secret one. This Ralph Judd had infected other American military personnel and now the less said about the situation the better. The bad guy is dead and the U.S. Army men at the scene died heroes, all of them. That about right, Sergeant?"

"About," said Sergeant Pitts. "Right enough, sir."

The officers returned to their offices. Sergeant Pitts transferred to an area populated with soldiers waiting to rotate out of country: Rotation Station. You're gonna wake up soon. The fires at Tan Son Nhut Airbase were being extinguished and the seven hundred or so sappers who invaded were being killed or driven out by the Twenty-fifth Infantry Tropic Lightning Forces. Duke knew them to be effective gook greasers, so his wait promised to be a short one. He checked back at the hospital and learned that Jungle Jim had been flown to Japan, to a superior facility.

The reward money had surprised him. Wanted, Dead or Alive: Ralph Judd, Outlaw. But the surprise didn't last long. Bounty Hunter, add it to the list of accomplishments compiled here in No-Man's Nam. Then the bucks bothered him some. Bought off. Bloody hush money. But that idea didn't last long either. Duke absorbed it as icing on an otherwise bitter cake. His own honor had been served and it had nothing to do with official histories. Wrongs had been righted in his reality. And besides, it was quite a roll.

CHAPTER FORTY-SEVEN

Tet attacks and American counterattacks raged and the atmosphere at the Rotation Station stung with the smell of fear. The men had been relieved of their weapons, their guns at any rate. Duke had stashed his .45 in his AWOL bag, along with the Montagnard dagger, and his finger bones which were already his luck, his charm. There were three pieces—he liked that. Three was a magic number but it could be an unlucky one; you could crap out with it. So the thing could never become more than it was: a curious charm, a reminder that luck had two sides, and part of himself. He had bound the fragments together with a rawhide bootlace he'd purchased along with the AWOL bag.

He sat alone, dry and smoking cigarettes; and if he didn't feel good he at least felt calm. His center had to hold. He knew it and locked out the terror and uncertainty that packed the space about him. Designedly, he was as nervous as a rock.

He scrawled a note to Ann in the World. It succinctly stated that he would be in California in a matter of days. He'd meet her at the place where they had originally planned to see each other, before his extension. If she could make it. He signed it. He was an unnatural lefty and it was a bitch and the scrawl showed it. He posted the note and tried hard to recall exactly what she looked like. He could not.

His number came up and he was transferred to the air base

241

proper. Transportation was by one of those OD school buses with barred windows. He didn't like it one bit but guessed it beat walking, faster anyhow. The bus rumbled past some shell-shattered Quonset huts and one of them was where Jungle Jim's buddy, Lieutenant Rizzo, worked. The dude had seemed a decent enough sort. Harry Pitts hoped Rizzo hadn't been unlucky enough to have been sleeping on his desk when the rockets landed.

The terminal at Tan Son Nhut Air Base was crowded with soldiers and gear. A frazzled green milling mass, mumbling and smoldering. A cigarette smoke cloud bank grew continuously above all those heads that formed the top of that mass. It brought Pitts's mind back to a swamp, down in the delta, bubbling, seething just beneath the moss and slime surface, hissing and leaking a dense silver swamp gas, letting off steam.

He checked in and found his way to the appropriate boarding line. He thought that once out of the Army he would attempt never to stand in line again. He smoked cigarettes, grit his teeth, and listened and didn't listen to the commotion about him. A familiar deep chant and rhythm rose to his front.

"Gooks gonna get us! Rockets gonna grease our asses while we boardin' the bird! Blow our balls all to hell!" Cpl. Red Green glanced around sucking a Kool that was mostly ash. "Gooks gonna mash us, mix us with monsoon and use us for fence paint in the Great Dink Hell!"

Harry Pitts was flushed with gratitude for the man's presence. He walked right up to him. "Red," he said, "don't touch shit, even with gloves on."

Red Green turned and his face told the story of his gladness. "Well if it ain't Mr. Pitts," he said through his smile.

"Getting there."

"We heard Ho Nai got lit up and all you dudes got zapped, man."

"All but me and Jungle Jim. He caught some shit in his shoulder. They sent him to Japan."

Red Green had already noticed Harry Pitts's wounded hand because he had to pound the top of the left fist in greeting. "Hurt much?"

"Got some dope for it."

"How much?"

"Enough." He fished out the big plastic jug and laid a fistful of Darvons on Red.

"Thanks, maybe this shit'll mellow me some. How'd it go for Peters?"

"He went down helping me. He was one solid dude and I wasted the geek responsible." Harry Pitts decided to leave it at that. There was enough truth in the statement and more might make matters worse. "He's getting some fucking medals," he added.

"Cold comfort."

"Maybe it's something for his folks."

"Bullshit."

"Yeah."

They fell quiet for a time. Outside their transport was visible. In the shadowy stretches beneath it wisecracking cargo crews loaded coffins and body bags.

A bright symmetrical sign loomed large near their exit: HUNGER, STARVATION, MURDER: ALL OVER THE WORLD. A grim proclamation, not totally out of place. None of the soldiers Pitts questioned about it had a clue to the reasons for its posting. They just leered and said "Wow" or "Far out" or "What sign?" A skull-faced soldier sat beneath it, his gear underfoot, his eyes hollow dead smudges. There *was* scuttlebutt about him: He had been there for days—weeks maybe—missing plane after plane. Some great weight anchored his ass. He wouldn't budge, risk the rockets to make his flight. So the sap sat, continuously risking total destruction. It occurred to Harry Pitts that perhaps the man was already destroyed and afraid to risk going home.

They shuffled out of the terminal building toward their plane, but were near the end of the line. So when they heard the whistle and screech and felt the boom, they hugged the black tar runway. Harry Pitts, the Duke again, tried to tunnel into it. The stuff was hot and slick and blacker than a jungle midnight.

Incoming! A frantic bummer of a moment. Red Green had been right. Rockets ripped the sky and crunched the runway. Duke understood this to be the lamest of ends: get blown to atoms and blotted up by black tar. Have jets taking off and landing on his dispersed particles and molecules, pieces of him adhering to the tires and touching down on all manner of shabby terrain. Plainly an unfitting way to go.

The blasts and tremors did not grow more distant. He looked at Red Green who pointed at the plane.

"Let's *didi mau*, Pitts," he said. "Beat feet fucker," he went on. "Assholes and elbows, Harry my man." He picked himself up and ran, his face and hands like hunks of licorice leaping from a sheet of it.

Harry Pitts scrambled to his feet and followed. Race, he told himself. Your time can't get shorter. Miss this and you'll lapse, become as redundant as the time and space you'll inhabit. Join the ranks of the random: unnecessary, unplanned for, uncontrollable.

They bolted and drove through any unanimated troopers who didn't know what to do, whether to shit or go blind. And as Harry Pitts boarded the plane, he considered the condition of the first human to utter that line about bowels and eyes. He concluded that the man must have been quite frightened.

The men within were uneasy, edgy. They demanded the pilot take off. They muttered and threatened. Pitts told him there was nobody behind him. And it was true there wasn't a soul in his immediate wake.

"Those dudes on the ground must be dead," a soldier said and the rest agreed, loudly. But the pilot needed little motivation. He looked down at the men on the ground and then up with an expression that said he concurred. He had the hatch shut. He was gray and beaded with perspiration, a pasty face full of farts that kept escaping. Reminded Pitts of an empty potato sack: this his guide, the man in charge of his hasty exit. He was glad to see him slink to the cockpit and gladder still to feel the plane taxi. He was *ready*. At that point he'd have split in a wagonload of lepers pulled by a team of paddy rats. And he'd have whipped those rats.

He looked out a window at some soldiers dodging back to sandbagged bunkers near the terminal. He felt their hesitancy demonstrated an imbecilic lack of timing. Terror was understandable but that was masochism. To come that far and punk out indicated the actions of your basic dumb fucking dipstick. Or of the Totally Spooked Fool. Doc Ratchit might have diagnosed them as simply freaked out. Perhaps they'd find spots beneath the HUNGER-MURDER sign. He could understand staying in-country, but not that way, not there. Hanging out on the brink, the asshole of the universe, afraid to commit. Scared to stick, scared to split. Never knowing what would come down next, or when. Life in a pisstube. Poor bastards didn't know whether to shit or go blind.

CHAPTER FORTY-EIGHT

There was rock 'n' roll turbulence all around as the 707 taxied. Dusk didn't happen. Darkness dropped like a lead curtain. Rockets landed and lit up the terrain and shrapnel slapped the plane. Flares zoomed and popped and fired the sky. But the flarelight sputtered and faded, hissing, hissing. Doused by monsoon that exploded like a flash of vomit and sustained itself. The runway rumbled and sparked as if an avalanche of flint rock rolled just behind the big jet plane, hungry to scorch and crush it.

The jet climbed and in its belly the men were a diminishing, then invisible target. The lights of Tan Son Nhut and Saigon were a failing blur. Then gone forever. Harry Pitts looked down at the deep, impenetrable dark, the Vietnamese jungle. He tried to feel secure and apart from it. But the attempt failed. Like trying to keep your ass dry while sloshing through a rice paddy. Like trying to cop Zs during a fire fight.

Some of the soldiers cheered loudly. They overdid it trying to convince themselves they were finished with the war.

Harry Pitts didn't know quite what to do. He was fidgety. He felt like talking but Red had settled into staring out a window in seeming deep contemplation, his black face nearly blank. He went to the cockpit.

"Hey, where are the stewardesses?" he asked the pilot. "I heard there were stewardesses with miniskirts and big

American thighs."

The pilot looked at the copilot dully and rolled his eyes. He turned his gray sag of a face to Pitts and blew Chesterfield smoke from it. He took a magazine from the copilot and tossed it to Pitts. It was an old issue of Playboy that looked more used up than his dead face. "Your stewardess couldn't make it, Sarge," he said. "She's blowing some airline captain at the Hawaiian Hilton."

"Thanks sport."

"Don't mention it, Sarge, think nothing of it. My pleasure." The pilot rolled his eyes again and showed the back of his head: a dandruff farm, a blanket of white scabs itching to be scratched.

Harry Pitts dropped the magazine in the aisle and sank in a seat behind Red and surveyed the dark. It was nice to have a window seat. But then the cabin wasn't crowded. That amazed him. The jumbo jet that brought him in-country had been packed with cargo: men and guns. Even had some stewardesses. Going home he expected standing room only.

He liked the window seat; didn't want to miss anything. He remembered from some past millennium, that someone had written about how so many GIs slept while traveling through historic moments during World War II. Like sailing on a transport, away, past the Statue of Liberty, the last time for so many of them. Yeah, the man's name was John Steinbeck, he had even been to the 'Nam. Duke had seen his picture in the *Stars and Stripes*: a great old man decked out in khaki bush duds, walking a dike. Yeah, John Steinbeck. Once There Was A War, he wrote. Well, here was another, and Sgt. Harry Pitts was leaving it. Christ! It had been forever since he'd read a book. He didn't want to miss winging away from that jungle stinkhole, gliding above the terror, across the white beaches and out over the South China Sea. About as historic as the way those five scouts went out, or the men of the CRIP. A bitch for them, but they weren't the first. Centuries of history held heaps of dead

247

soldiers. And sure as dead meat rots, they wouldn't be the last. Still it was quite something for each of them: the ends of their histories, their final anything. Leaving the war the way he did amounted to history as well, for him anyhow. A shot at a new everything. He hadn't the first notion of how to confront this. He felt that he should, however. Later.

So far above and without sound, the eruptions of light in the jungle below seemed nothing more than a Fourth of July shindig in the woods. Distant firecrackers and clustered starbursts harmlessly waxing and waning, silently. Isolated tiny celebrations, a lunar new year. A summertime picnic instead of the flare-lit bloodfeast that it was. An irregularly choreographed death dance that drenched the killing ground with itself.

He knew he was relieved to watch it become horizon. Couldn't help hoping they wouldn't end up bobbing and weaving in the ocean though. Chum for the sharks due to some technical malfunction. Or pilot error. But he was armed. He was glad to have his .45, as if it would come in handy. Shoot the sharks maybe. Still a .45 was nice, easier to carry than an M-16, or a cannon. But a cannon would be a sweet machine back in the World. His own self-propelled one-seven-five, eighty-pound rounds. He'd be one secure citizen. Have to float it back on a boat though, and unloading it might be sticky. No, a .45 should do, along with the dagger and his finger bones.

"I'm going to kiss California," Red Green said it. He still stared out the window, down at the sea. He said once more, louder. "I'm going to kiss California!"

Some of the men within earshot chanted "Amen"s and "right on"s. Then a whiskey-whacked voice blurted, "Fuck California!" He barked it again. "That's what I'm gonna do. Drill me a hole and hump the U.S. dirt. Be better than any dink pussy. Might be as good as burning gook babies. Nipping commies in the bud is tough to beat though."

Some men laughed. They would do that: laugh. Harry

Pitts had heard it before. Most of them wouldn't burn babies, but they would chuckle at the line. Especially those who had been grunts. Those who had been neck-deep in death had to joke. They might be forever sadder for the immersion, but could not always be solemn about it.

Still the son-of-a-bitch who was going to fuck the earth didn't look like any grunt. The fat man looked like one of those ass-wipe colonels Warren Buckle had entertained. Pitts wanted something to bite his cock off when he fucked California. Something dark and foul from the muck of America's underbelly.

He was going back to the World away from the war. So was the baby burner, the earth fucker.

He thought again about being armed and knew he would be most uneasy if he weren't. He wondered if the feeling—the anxiety about being unarmed—would leave him like he was leaving the war. But everything stays stored in your eyes and the war probably wouldn't depart. It would stick like . . . like what? Not like some gem to be treasured and polished and kept and passed on. Not like stirring bugle calls in your ears trumpeting images of solitary valor. No bugles, no drums. A brand in your face wouldn't burn bright to the world, *warrior*. A gargoyle wouldn't grow from your neck to be borne forever as a consequence of your going. No, it would probably lodge deep within him where he could remember and laugh and cry without changing expression, without cracking his mask. Deep where he might feel it forever. Deep beyond expulsion, beyond acceptance. Deep and always and unexplained. It would simply be a part of him. And his hand. For how many years would he see the ghosts everytime he shook hands? But that was all right. He considered those men who were maimed mercilessly, the amputees who must always and each moment be reminded of their going: How they must howl.

Red Green peeked over his seat, his face a grin, ear to ear. "Want some acid?" he asked. "Got it in the mail last week.

249

Saved it till I got on the plane. Got two hits left."

"No thanks, Red. I'll pass." Acid, LSD: Harry Pitts didn't quite understand it. He decided Red was a little nutty. Not that he had anything against him or his ways. The man had saved his ass on occasion, when they had been scouts. But he was a little nutty.

Red opened the pink palm of his hand. He smiled at the tabs. Perhaps digging the design: a bright swirl of blue and white confusion. He ate them. "Blue cheer," said Red. He gave the two-fingered V sign which meant peace. Then gazed out the window.

Harry Pitts assumed the man felt good. He believed he did himself. He was actually alive and headed for Hawaii, the refueling stop. He decided to nap until arrival because he wanted to experience waking with the knowledge that there would be no fire fight that day. And he knew no mortars would smash him while sleeping. So he settled in feeling snug. He didn't sleep though. Stared mostly, his thoughts drifting in strands, shifting and unfocused. He hoped he might eat in Hawaii, he was empty enough to snatch a dog's dinner.

Somewhere over the Pacific the jet crossed the International Date Line. He couldn't pinpoint exactly when, but he knew it happened. He was really skying out, heading away from where he had been to truly another dimension. A survivor in the womb of a great metal bird that split the sky, shooting him into another time zone, another day. He was crossing the Pond coming back to the World. He flew from Sunday to Saturday.

The jet careened in descent. Bouncing, it touched down smoothly. His stomach reminded him of helicopters and hot LZs, of Cobras and Chinooks.

The men disembarked and were instructed to remain in a roped-off area near their gate. Red Green and Harry Pitts left the area and went into a less crowded rest room. The ones near their gate were jammed. Red got into washing his face and looking in a mirror; he was zonked.

Harry Pitts walked out to the terminal. The place appeared spacious and incredibly clean. It was crowded with well-dressed people. He found a bar and considered having a drink. He had enjoyed drinking in the World. He approached the open doors and heard a loud drunken argument between a black soldier in class As and the Hawaiian bartender. They sounded sad and mad and shrill. They shouted about free lunches for little niggers and slopehead sisterfuckers and bluegum bastards and dink motherfuckers, burrheads and zipperheads. The men probably didn't even remember what they were screaming about, what had started the tiff. Harry Pitts decided he wasn't really dressed for it, and skipped the drink. He walked away. He was getting closer to home.

He sat down and watched women walk about. Ann, who might meet him, was at once enticing and unsettling. They had known each other always. They had become close and relentless; their flesh had been burning and young. He had left and now didn't know exactly what or who was coming home. And she could no more be the Ann he left than she could have remained the girl she was prior to her first coupling. If he were worth anything positive at all, he thought she had something to do with it. She tried damn hard to mold what decency he possessed into part of his manhood. She may have been successful to a degree, he thought, but he was young and the amount of decency she had to work with severely limited the prospects. He sat there in Hawaii dreaming of her, the closest he had been to her in a long time. But the closer he came to her the more apprehension he felt.

The flight was announced to be departing and it was blessed with a new captain and crew. Stewardesses greeted the men, all smiles and sensuality. Harry Pitts didn't care that the smiles were plastic and the sensuality beyond his reach. They looked fantastic. He wondered if one could forget how to fuck—it had been awhile. He decided it was one of those never-forget-how-to's, like swimming. He found his seat and Red.

The 707 soared east for the Western World.

Red Green stood addressing the troops, his voice brittle and loud. He fell into a mad bebop rap in a language beyond English. Then he broke back into English, talking shit, literally. "All shit stinks, my fellow grunts, but there are ranks." He pointed his finger upward, a beacon. "And if you don't know that, you don't know shit." He bowed and returned to his seat.

The people on the plane were relieved. Some applauded. Harry Pitts sat next to Red. "Be good, buddy," he told him. "We're almost home."

Red gazed at him, full-face and in the eye. Red's eyes were wild, and if there were any logic behind his speech, it was obscure, apparent only to Red. "Right," he said. And he didn't speak again until they were on the ground.

The stewardesses served filet mignon and spuds and salad. The men ate like orphans.

Then inertia set in and Harry Pitts existed in a twilight, now half awake, now half asleep, his thoughts dull. The final descent approach and landing time he found sweet, tinged with a receding emptiness, a retreating void that might become the space where what he had been would dwell. Perhaps one day he would attempt to sort it all out, see clearly who was responsible for what. That kind of investigation could be endless. Who would accept his own share? How much of the murder and mayhem could be laid on Harry Pitts himself? Where would the old buck stop? He trusted he'd be able to remain satisfied that stopping Warren Buckle in Bien Hoa was the right attitude—in his own scheme of things at least. Of course that hunt and kill set in motion another chain of events shot with violence and ruin. Just who was who, and who was responsible for what? How far up the ladder could he take the question? Why are we doing what we're doing? If we weren't there, this and that wouldn't have happened. The chain of command led to the President and the President was elected, they say, by the people. That grim horror show back in the jungle was acted out by, of, and for the people? Maybe so. The war was an old song that had a sad and hollow ring to it. A looney tune. Figure it. Well, maybe someday . . .

Now a warmth penetrated most of him. Sitting in that plane on a runway in his own country: a good place to be, then. A few whoops and cheers went up, but mostly it was a quiet time.

Fat Colonel Baby Burner annihilated the mood. "I made it back by Christ!" He didn't speak to anyone in particular, but he did it loudly. "I dodged them bullets better than any of those suckers who came back in a box. War is hell I heard. Well, those poor bastards got burned. Fuck them! Better them than me!"

Sergeant Pitts watched the man waddle and vacate the cabin. While it was true that losing a buddy in a fire fight was tough, dragging your own ass out made it a lot easier to take; but he doubted the colonel truly knew it. If the blockhead were ever stranded in the desert, dying of thirst, he could count on Harry Pitts for a canteen of sand. Hot sand.

Pitts nudged Red Green and led him off, down the ramp to American tar. It was a dark time: huge floodlights illuminated the air base. They made for a bus and Pitts saw that the colonel had dropped his drawers and a small group milled to watch him fuck California, evidently a man of his word. They boarded a bus and sat again. The night air was cool and they lit cigarettes. The bus groaned off and Harry Pitts didn't look back at the big metal bird. Shadowy crews unloaded coffins from the plane's cargo holds.

CHAPTER FORTY-NINE

Harry Pitts was in a dull daze, the taste of tobacco about the only sign of his senses. He and Red left the bus and passed through another light flood which receded abruptly when a metal gate clanged behind them.

The hall was dim and cold and echoed coughs and dragging feet. They stopped at the larger-than-life-size, one-dimensional cardboard soldier that greeted them. Big smile on his phony face, flanked by the stars and stripes, bunting, and a banner that proclaimed Welcome Home Soldier. Your Country Is Proud of You!

"Some parade," said Pitts. "But they forgot the ticker tape."

Red shot the sign a bird and said that he was so whacked he could barely walk. He dragged his duffle bag.

They emerged to a terminal, a resounding din, glaring fluorescent light. It was a processing plant, turning out civilians and soldiers on leave. If you were slated for leave you were out in a few hours. If you were leaving the service, it might take ten. His accumulated leave subtracted from time left in his hitch qualified Sergeant Pitts for an early out.

"You want it, Sarge?"

"Does the Pope's shit stink." He didn't argue. He fell into the ten-hour slot. So did Red. They began the process of hurry-up-and-wait, the confusion usual. The grand design, the big picture of this final pattern was as sensible as wrestling in a minefield.

Pitts nearly passed out several times. But he was determined to survive, to get out. He would not permit himself to lose consciousness even for a moment. A doctor examined his hand, which wasn't feeling great and instructed him to visit a VA hospital during the next few days. Or right away if the thing didn't look or feel right. Pitts wondered how a four-fingered hand with stitches down one side to the wrist should look and feel.

Red stuck with him and they took hot showers and were issued clean greens: class As. They were almost home, waiting for separation papers and travel pay, when Red went down.

He stared at Harry Pitts, eyes bulging and rimmed red, foam bubbling from his mouth. He put both hands to his throat and keeled over. His big body started to spasm, convulse. Pitts whipped off his belt and managed to shove it between Red's teeth without losing another finger. Red never took his malaria pills—a lot of guys didn't—but he swallowed that acid on the other side of the planet. Pitts was frightened for him. Medics arrived with a stretcher and a doctor. Red calmed and appeared lucid as they tightened the last strap over his chest, trapping his arms. "What's this?" he asked.

The doctor put a hand to Red's forehead and said, "It's been a long trip, hasn't it son? You'll be fine now; we'll see to it." Doc was a sallow sort, a buffalo breath with all the demeanor of that gaseous pilot who flew them away from the war.

"But Doc, I'm getting out of the Army in an hour, maybe less. I gotta go home. My time is done." Red's eyes glassed.

They lifted the stretcher and he jerked for a moment against the bonds. The doctor placed a hand on his head again and told him to be at ease. Red looked at Harry Pitts, his eyes imploring, his nostrils flared from rapid breathing. Then his face softened, his attitude became resigned. "Shit,"

255

he said. He shut his eyes, moisture trickled from them. They took him away down a hall into a labyrinth: a maze of additional hallways and doors, doctors and medics in green and white.

A chilly antiseptic sting hung in his nostrils and Harry Pitts knew he should make some pitch for Red. Intervene on the man's behalf. Help him out of a shitty spot. Explain that Red was fine, just a little tired from all that fighting for the Flag. "He's in the same shape as I," he might say. "Just beat. Hell, if you take him you might as well take me!" Yeah, he should stick with him. But he just stood there determined *not* to be taken. He refused to consider faltering that late in the game, for any reason. He had to *get out*. So much for camaraderie, loyalty, the old fraternity of fellow combatants, a man who had saved his life. He had never known a black man well before Red Green. For a time they had been tight and close, brothers. They had wept and fucked and killed and laughed together. But that was there.

And things were different there: basic and tight. The people close to you were the only ones you could usually count on. You grew very close very quickly. Reference points were needed in the general insanity that swirled about. He recalled grunts at the rotation station exchanging addresses and promises with each other prior to leaving country. They were all going to get together and celebrate stateside. Raise hell and stay in touch. He imagined that a few might, but he was sure most of them knew it was bullshit. The reality of that bullshit had just smacked him in the brain and he had already taken giant steps—whether consciously or unconsciously he wasn't sure, but he had taken them: giant strides away from what he had been. And like most movements of any consequence, he knew this to be a good thing, and bad.

Instructions blared from loudspeakers; an erratic, dazed babble ebbed and flowed. The place rang like a gymnasium, smelled like a locker room. The air was electric with desperation. He moved his eyes watching the lines of men meander. From guarded eyecorners he caught the hollow eyes of returning grunts: cornucopias devoid of fruit, horns of empty.

He fell in with them and managed to obtain papers and pay and become a civilian. Nobody noticed that he was nearly batty. But then everybody seemed about the same: exhausted and indifferent. He assumed he simply fit in.

That cardboard soldier standing sentinel in the hall had a pecker drawn neatly across his smile and FUCK THE ARMY scrawled over his forehead. A puddle of yellow urine reeked at his spit-shined boots. Grunt work surely. Mr. Harry Pitts didn't imagine anyone attempted to stop it. He was happy to be getting away from it.

Outside was dark, a light rain hung suspended, clinging to everything. He checked his AWOL bag: .45, dagger, finger bones, and money: security, protection, luck, and bounty. He walked. Seemed like it had been dark for days, wet forever. It was drizzling and he was humping. At least the famliar ache from the weight of a pack was absent. He wore a uniform and didn't feel much of anything except out of place. The lights were so numerous and bright on the military compound that walking at night made him feel like glancing to the rear; something felt wrong. Like tooling around a prison. He moved on, checking the ground.

A bus-stop sign loomed ahead, light glinting from its slick metal, piercing the rain. He threw his bag down next to it, and leaned on the post. He popped some pain pills and smoked damp cigarettes for over an hour until a bus arrived. He climbed aboard and smoked, looking out the streaked windows. He rode for a long humid while. He got off at the end of the line: somewhere in Oakland.

He found a hotel, a shitbag of a place. He climbed the stairs to his room. He locked himself in and switched on the lamp; shafts of bright shot through tears in the shade. There was no TV.

He smoked more cigarettes and took in the city through the window. Prick Peters was from Oakland. He had not been permitted to return and sit among his people and tell war stories. Even though Harry Pitts knew that combat spared more grunts than it totally wasted, it seemed that one hell of a load of meat was being shipped back dead.

He caught himself whistling "Taps." Damnit no! he thought, and he was furious. I gotta get that dreary fucking tune out of my head! But he couldn't. Taps was the worst of all blues, not moaning about money or pussy or love or dreams in general, but death. It was the final sound after all the fuck-ups and wrong thinking that got the poor SOBs to the battle line. Taps was always blowing somewhere in Vietnam. But during the days of Tet, which were likely still raging, he was sure the tune blew all over the country. Along with Victor Charlie's version.

The sun started to rise. He couldn't see it for the smog but the sky brightened and the rain began to burn off. He speculated on the probable relationship of this rain to the monsoon. Products of the same single sea known by a catalog of names. And there was a strong warm current that flowed from the Orient to the American northwest coast, the Chinook: warm wind and spring rains. And the Chinook were a people: slant-eyed Indians, hunters and fishers of that North American coast. And the Chinook was forty feet of double-rotored helicopter. Chinook. Wind and rain. Flesh and blood. Green metal flying machines. Chinook. Could be life or death. Now he hoped to get away from the death. This place offered escape from the hunger and the starvation and the murder. Here one might avoid it. Here he had a much better chance. It was better here. He knew it. He had to know it. He focused on individual drops and wanted to see only water, no longer an ally, an enemy, a ruler.

He had an appointment to keep. Ann. That round-eyed lady was probably waiting at a place in San Francisco, Berkeley actually: a friend's apartment. He didn't know the friend but the apartment would probably be plush so he would be uncomfortable. And what the fuck would he talk about?

He told himself not to worry. Take your time getting there. No sense to rush things. She may not even be there yet. Likely she's not. Give it a day or two. Or three. It won't be long before the liquor stores open. You might procure some booze. Haven't been tanked in some long time. That's something you'll remember how to accomplish. And you can sleep. Yeah, it would be nice to sleep. Been quite some time since you've done that. Honest, deep sleep would be tremendous. You could practice up. It'll take some practice.

He listened to his thoughts, the sound distant and tinny, off Western key like Oriental music.

Date line crossed, time zones traversed, the Western dimension attained: today became yesterday. And yesterday today was already dead. All of those increments, that time, amounted to the day he departed the war. A winter Sunday that spanned three days, being and going and coming. A circle in time to complete the circle in space: circles of confusion. Those dimensions of place and distance collided to bring him to the country he had left over a year ago. He knew a year to be a short time or a long time, depending upon one's age and circumstances. He had been a long time from home. It was not possible that he was where he was now, so quickly and so easily, after being where he had been. However it was obvious that the transfer had occurred.

What had he done? What had he defended? Himself mostly. Himself and what the shifting situations told him he was. Now he was here, in the World. Where supposedly sanity reigned. He didn't feel a part of it, or anything for that matter. He truly did not know when he might see those clean, jagged stone mountains of Maine that had been his home.

Well, he was free and he thought about it. Free from what? Free from the Army, that's all. What the hell was freedom other than varying degrees of permissible behavior. No more shootin' and salutin' dickheads, listening to the most inane of commands. Free from that particular test he supposed the war put him through. Free from that quest for some honor. Free to what? To do nothing and have nobody doing you, would be perhaps peaceful, and he might enjoy it for a time. He didn't know what courage was, but he had witnessed it; he wondered if he would again, just as he wondered about that undefinable notion, honor. Some saw the thing as highfalutin' bullshit, a figment of lunatic imagination. He knew a different idea. He understood his conception of the thing and questioned where its expression lay now that his Mission was accomplished. He hoped to discover another right and honorable direction for himself. Perhaps hope was the wrong word. He understood hope to be a final attempt, beyond reality: What you've got when you've got nothing else.

He fired up yet another smoke. The world outside was clearing, becoming a little brighter but not much: shades of gray gradually sharpening, taking shape. He hadn't been in-country long and figured the joy would come in time.

CHAPTER FIFTY

It was three days before he arrived at the meeting place in Berkeley. Three days drunk in the Haight-Asbury district of San Francisco. Drunk and wandering about watching the love generation dance barefoot and mind-blown on the winter streets.

In Oakland he had purchased some boots and jeans, a heavy shirt and a denim jacket; and dumped his uniform into a Goodwill bin. He traded his AWOL bag for a Boy Scout day pack into which he stuffed extra clothes and his .45 and finger bones. Everything fit and the pack fit comfortably over his shoulder. His arm was still slung high, hand over heart. He caught a bus and rode over the Bay Bridge and the fog on the bay reminded him of monsoon.

The city of San Francisco looked good to him even though the weather colored the sky slate gray and the wind buffeted him unceasingly. He walked the streets and enjoyed the walking. He ducked into bars and drank beer and ducked out to walk the streets some more. That first night he bought a half pint of Wild Turkey and nipped it intermittently between beers. He had not drunk like that for a long time and it felt as good as walking the streets. In the morning however he felt like someone had beaten him for years with sacks of twenty penny nails, both inside and out, from his brain to his soles. He found himself in a cheap hotel and didn't remember renting the room. When he hit the streets, it was afternoon.

He spent the next two days in much the same manner, except he used full pints of Turkey. He hung around the park, drank there and in bars, slept late in the cheap hotels, popping pain pills all the while. The park was green and damp and clouds of dopesmoke, people fucking on the ground, in trees. The people in the park and on the streets were thin and had the thousand-yard stare. (That fixed blank look grunts took after being too long in the shit.) There were no rockets and mortars booming, no automatic weapons cracking, no artillery thumping. But the pounding sound of electrifying rock music blared and blasted everywhere. Eruptions of harsh sound and screaming haunted singers. It was The End, time to rip it all down and rise anew from the ashes, they had the numbers. The devil was due sympathy and they were street-fighting men, low-down and nasty. What was a poor boy to do? And love was tough, a ball and chain. The sound was violence and gristle and sinew, sexually undefined, dark erotic power: compelling. Harry Pitts saw it as a confused array hemorrhaging and craving more confusion. He knew of a place that could squash the desire, the delusion of violence and destruction as positive forces. A place so confused the dead hung out above the ground.

He smoked some grass but had apparently lost his taste; it only made him uncomfortable. He drank the feeling away.

Her face toward the wide window, the winter sky. Her eyes closed. "Come back, Harry." Her eyes open, face to his face. "Please come home."

How many times had he seen it? Heard the words. How many moments deep in his sleep and how many snatches of time, walking awake?

And before those last words she had spoken to him, there had been a night. Eating alone together in her sister's house.

"Suppose," Ann said, "suppose I were pregnant?"

"What are you saying?" Pitts put his drink down. Looked at her.

"I said suppose I were pregnant?"

"Suppose you were."

"What would you do?"

"I guess there would be another life to consider, worry about."

"There are abortions."

Pitts picked up his drink, drank. "That would be up to you, I believe. Old Ethan might know a doctor."

"Why would it be up to me?" She kept looking at him, directly.

"Who else would it be up to?"

"You wouldn't have an opinion?"

"Are you pregnant, Ann?"

"No. Not that I know of."

"Then why all this?"

"Answer me, Harry. Would you have an opinion, or not?"

"Sure. Of course."

"Well?"

"Ann, you said you are not in the old family way, so how can I have an opinion? I don't believe I can speculate at this particular time."

She looked away, and back, away.

Pitts watched her.

"You wouldn't stay, would you?" She said to him. "You wouldn't stay here and run off with me, would you?"

"Run where?"

"Canada."

"No."

"I read a book once, about a soldier who did that. His lover became pregnant and he left the war he was in and they ran off."

"I read that myself. You remember the end?"

"She died. The woman died."

263

"Ann, let's talk about something else."

She began to clear dishes from the table. They went into the kitchen and began to wash the dishes. Pitts took his drink.

Ann said: "Are you going to get drunk tonight?"

"I don't plan to."

"Well, just in case your plan changes later on. Let's stop wasting time here on these dishes. Let's go for a record. See if we can make love another time or two today. Think you're up to it?"

"I am."

After a time, lying together on the bed in the dimly lit room, Pitts watched shadows move on her as she moved. Light changed with the rise and fall of her body.

"How do you think it will be for us when you come back?" Small glints of light flicked on her eyes.

The fog of it all gripped his most spectacular visions of the far future: smooth success, endless fine time with her, himself secure. "I'll have to think about that. Not that I haven't already, but I don't have an answer. I know it will be different. We'll have this behind us and everything to move toward."

"I'll be finished with school when you get back. I'll be able to work for halfway decent money. What do you think you'll do?"

"Maybe I'll start again."

"What do you want, Harry?"

"You know, I'm not sure. That's one reason I'm in the Army. You might want me to say, 'It's you, Ann, it's you I want.' Which is true, but there has to be more. I've got to be somebody I can respect, like a little better anyway. Make any sense?"

"I suppose. I don't like what's happening but I suppose I understand. I'll say so, at least. But I don't like it, Harry.

264

Sometimes I hardly believe it's happening."

"You're certain you want to wait for me to come back? It's a rough commitment. I think I'd understand if you didn't want to make it."

"What?"

He felt her body tense. He saw the frown around her eyes. She shifted herself on the bed to look directly at him.

"I'm not saying I'd like it, Ann. But I could understand, I believe."

"There is no question in my mind," she said, coming closer.

They made love again. Ann cried softly and Pitts tried to understand. They held on to each other tightly. The moment was one to believe in.

In his sleep a corpse danced on him. A rhythmless shuffle, like a marionette. A loose-jointed thing without feet or hands. A head without eyes, a mouth that was wrong. It danced on Pitts's chest and on the bed and on the floor, up the walls, across the ceiling. The dancer left dark tracks. Down again on Pitts's chest, the dancer sang a muffled chant:

"WHERE ARE MY FEET?
WHERE ARE MY HANDS?
WHERE ARE MY EYES?
WHERE ARE MY BALLS?"

Then down on the bed next to Pitts's face. "Everything hurts. Where am I?"

Pitts woke himself and heard his heart thump. He lay still, looking ever so slowly about for the dancing corpse. He felt relieved and sat up. The hotel room looked the same: cheap. He guessed he was still in Oakland. He suppressed an urge to check under the bed.

Where am I? was a good question. He thought it was about time to find out. He looked out the window. Dark. He sat back on the bed.

"How do you think it will be for us when you get back?" He heard her ask it from across time.

He didn't think he was in such grand condition.

But he thought, he knew that in a way, the bad times he'd done in Vietnam were only half the story. One side of all the wrong. Her side, Ann's bad times and broken dreams were in reality unknowable to him. He wondered if he might ever realize the pit of loneliness, the banal horror of her life alone. What decisions was she faced with? Just how had she dealt with this impossible situation? He could not truly know how she had come through it all, or what she thought of herself for doing what she did.

He didn't want to go to sleep again. He was not interested in a repeat performance from the footless hoofer. He lay back on the bed, sweating.

"How do you think it will be for us?" He heard her say it.

Then he saw her face toward a wide window, a winter sky, her eyes closed. "Come back, Harry." Then her eyes opened, her face to his face. "Please come home."

CHAPTER FIFTY-ONE

Harry Pitts cleaned up and shaved and made it back over the bridge and on to Berkeley. Bundles of skinny, longhaired kids were clumped about, carrying signs and chanting about the war. He saw veterans joining the protests by simply offering their maimed presence. He was glad for his clothes. From a bar he dialed the number he had committed to memory and heard Ann's voice; she had come. He asked for the address and hung up. He hailed a cab outside and rode to the apartment which was in an old, renovated Victorian house. He took a full swig from his pint and paid the cabby. He stood looking at the house, breathing hard.

She emerged from the place, Ann, moving tentatively at first, then running toward him, a full athletic stride. She appeared so different, but then he had lost an accurate image of her. Her hair seemed so much longer and a deeper brown. Her face was thinner, almost drawn, but its open beauty undiminished. Those—such dark—blue eyes were brimming with tears and she blotted them against his shoulder. She kissed first his hand, his wound. Then she pulled his head to her and found his mouth. If she tasted the booze, she didn't say.

She led him into the house, to the apartment. The owner, the friend, had gone visiting. She spoke quietly in that husky tone he had not heard in so long a time. She told him that she had missed his presence in unexpressible terms. He said that, at the moment, he thought he was himself something unexpressible.

She felt the tenseness of his face with her hands, her warm hands. She led him to the bedroom

He was oddly embarrassed as she undressed him, and when he got on the bed he covered himself to the waist with a sheet. He was astounded by the beauty of her form.

The brownness and hardness and severe angles of his body, knotted so harshly with muscle and sinew and bone beneath the scarred flesh, was in deep contrast to the winter white and taut smooth roundness of her. He hadn't seen anything like her in a long time. She came to him and he lay watching her move over and down to him. The clear cold dullness of his hollow self refused to melt under the onslaught of her simple radiance, her glow. His ears were full of blood roar. He pushed her away. It was inconceivable to him that he had done it. Just as impossible as the flash zoom quickness of his journey away from the war to the World. And just as obviously true.

Her face fell and filled with a blank horror at the rejection and all the ramifications it might hold, held. She sat at his side and regained her composure, but not all of it. He saw a piece of herself shredded for eternity in the gesture of a moment. He saw himself alone, with nothing left behind. He was small and frightened and in that vast dark place. He damned himself for being there because it dragged her there too.

He did manage to kiss her eyes before dressing. The last time he had tasted that salt was when he had left her for the war. She dressed as quietly as a leaf falling from a tree. He was confident there was poetry in him, but he was incapable of expressing it. He watched her and knew he was a dog from hell. But the knowing didn't change matters.

He walked outside and sat on the wooden stoop and the gray day felt okay, better than some, worse than others. Maybe he should take a hike in some western mountains.

Walk it off. Sleep under the stars. A camping trip. Maybe do some fishing. Fish with flies instead of grenades. Maybe after his hand healed. Maybe after the snow melts. Maybe he should have remained a soldier. That astonished him, not remaining a soldier, but that he had thought it. The camping trip fit better in his brain. A good hard hike on high ground. The day should be hot. Not a jungle scorch, but a high and snappy warmth. The trees should be tall and strong and straight: green-topped pines. The solid green and brown forest would feel familiar and good. He would set himself up on the bank of a fine, clear river. Yes, he thought, and his heart beat. A river would be righteous. He would camp under the pines; set his tent but he didn't think he'd sleep in it. He'd like to see the stars in familiar spots. He'd drive big nails into a tree to hang his gear on. He could pack onion sandwiches and smoke cigarettes in the crisp air and take a nip of Wild Turkey now and then. He might just sit and survey things from his camp in the woods, the river showing through the trees. Maybe he would fish it. He would have the time. Yes, he thought: he had survived and sometimes that was enough.

Other men had survived to return to what had been home. Others had experienced as savage circumstances, many even more horrific and for longer stretches of time. His own father had done the Second Big War for the duration plus. His grandfather had returned from France and the War to End Wars. This was of little solace, however; for Harry Pitts had only his own time and circumstance to truly know and deal with. He didn't have anything with which to compare it. Still, others had survived, and still others would. Men had returned to live and work without cracking their masks. Some did crack of course, and some broke utterly. The berserk did the big deed on wives or strangers, and always on themselves. And there were war stories galore on all the skid rows, in all the madhouses. But most men returned with some grace. Survived. Bit the bullet. Camping, functioning out of human bounds, understanding some of the more natural things of the earth, perhaps his father had something there. Fishing, moving, looking, doing. Hell, some poor bastards couldn't even do that, being limited by the stumps of their former bodies. Yes, he had survived like his fathers before him and maybe certain details and angles of perspective would take new significance. Maybe.

Again he considered his short time in-country. And again Harry Pitts figured the joy would come in time. He had not yet begun to hope for it. Hope. That would come next.

TOP-FLIGHT AERIAL ADVENTURE
FROM ZEBRA BOOKS!

WINGMAN (2015, $3.95)
by Mack Maloney

From the radioactive ruins of a nuclear-devastated U.S. emerges a hero for the ages. A brilliant ace fighter pilot, he takes to the skies to help free his once-great homeland from the brutal heel of the evil Soviet warlords. He is the last hope of a ravaged land. He is Hawk Hunter . . . Wingman!

WINGMAN #2: THE CIRCLE WAR (2120, $3.95)
by Mack Maloney

A second explosive showdown with the Russian overlords and their armies of destruction is in the wind. Only the deadly aerial ace Hawk Hunter can rally the forces of freedom and strike one last blow for a forgotten dream called "America"!

WINGMAN #3: THE LUCIFER CRUSADE (2232, $3.95)
by Mack Maloney

Viktor, the depraved international terrorist who orchestrated the bloody war for America's West, has escaped. Ace pilot Hawk Hunter takes off for a deadly confrontation in the skies above the Middle East, determined to bring the maniac to justice or die in the attempt!

GHOST PILOT (2207, $3.95)
by Anton Emmerton

Flyer Ian Lamont is driven by bizarre unseen forces to relive the last days in the life of his late father, an RAF pilot killed during World War II. But history is about to repeat itself as a sinister secret from beyond the grave transforms Lamont's worst nightmares of fiery aerial death into terrifying reality!

ROLLING THUNDER (2235, $3.95)
by John Smith

Was the mysterious crash of NATO's awesome computerized attack aircraft BLACKHAWK ONE the result of pilot error or Soviet treachery? The deadly search for the truth traps RAF flight lieutenant Erica Macken in a sinister international power-play that will be determined in the merciless skies — where only the most skilled can survive!

Available wherever paperbacks are sold, or order direct from the Publisher. Send cover price plus 50¢ per copy for mailing and handling to Zebra Books, Dept. 2723, 475 Park Avenue South, New York, N.Y. 10016. Residents of New York, New Jersey and Pennsylvania must include sales tax. DO NOT SEND CASH.

THE SURVIVALIST SERIES
by Jerry Ahern

#1: TOTAL WAR	(2445, $2.95)
#2: THE NIGHTMARE BEGINS	(2476, $2.95)
#3: THE QUEST	(2670, $2.95)
#4: THE DOOMSAYER	(0893, $2.50)
#5: THE WEB	(2672, $2.95)
#6: THE SAVAGE HORDE	(1232, $2.50)
#7: THE PROPHET	(1339, $2.50)
#8: THE END IS COMING	(2590, $2.95)
#9: EARTH FIRE	(1405, $2.50)
#10: THE AWAKENING	(1478, $2.50)
#11: THE REPRISAL	(2393, $2.95)
#12: THE REBELLION	(2777, $2.95)
#13: PURSUIT	(2477, $2.95)
#14: THE TERROR	(2775, $2.95)
#15: OVERLORD	(2070, $2.50)

Available wherever paperbacks are sold, or order direct from the Publisher. Send cover price plus 50¢ per copy for mailing and handling to Zebra Books, Dept. 2723, 475 Park Avenue South, New York, N.Y. 10016. Residents of New York, New Jersey and Pennsylvania must include sales tax. DO NOT SEND CASH.